Red Eyes

A Deirdra Halley Tale

Audra Ann

PAGE PUBLISHING
Conneaut Lake, PA

First originally published by Page Publishing 2023

ISBN 979-8-88793-132-6 (pbk)
ISBN 979-8-88793-140-1 (digital)

Printed in the United States of America

Acknowledgment

To Anthony, thank you.

Prologue

Billy didn't notice the warm, wet sensation between his legs or the cold sweat. He was only aware of the scratching. Not of his heavy breathing, the tears streaking his face, or even the pounding of his seven-year-old heart. Just the scratching. His body was safely hidden under his Star Wars sheet, but he trembled fiercely while grasping Teddy. Billy was about to make the most important decision of his young life—stay hidden as silently as possible or brave a glance at the window.

(The scratching)

He thought about his big brother, Tom. He was ten and very brave.

(Scratch, scratch)

He would look. Something deep inside (that little voice that tells you right from wrong) tells him to stay hidden. That it'll...

(Scratch, scratch)

Go away. Billy squeezed his eyes shut and tried to will away the noise, the source of the noise, away. He tried to remember prayers from Sunday school.

(Scratch, scratch)

And promises God that he'll be good. He lays in bed, willing it away, before the scratching stops. Billy's eyes are wide, his ears are alert, his body aches with readiness. He stays this way until morning, until he hears the scream. The horrified shriek of a mother. The sound that can only be assigned to the danger of her children.

Billy was right about Tom. He was brave. In his bedroom, two doors down from Billy's, the Johnson family saw where Tom's courage took him.

Tom's bedroom window was open, the screen tossed to the ground. On the carpet beneath his window lay Tom's lifeless body.

His eyes were opened wide, his mouth agape. Billy thought he looked startled and was not sure why Tom wasn't blinking. Their mother scooped Tom into her arms as she fell beside him. She rocked him back and forth, sobbing as tears and snot ran down her face. She pleaded with any god that would listen.

"Not my baby, please. Not *my* baby!" was all she could say.

*****

Ally Snyder was peacefully dreaming of pony rides across rainbows when something…

(Scratching)

Woke her from her slumber. Her big blue eyes focused on a red pair in her window. They seemed to float in the center of her window. A strange curiosity took over her eight-year-old mind. Ally was a good girl. She always listened to her parents and teachers. She respected adults and knew they were here to protect her. Protect her from strangers, bad things—evil things—and monsters. The ones that lived in her closet, under her bed, and the ones that drove vans and offered (good girls) candy. When Ally heard a (familiar) adult voice in her head telling her to go to the window, she went without hesitation. She walked toward the hungry red eyes and felt no fear. Ally could hear her daddy's voice telling her that everything was fine, to walk faster. She walked in a trance toward the red eyes and did not feel the terror until it was too late. She looked the monster in the eye, face-to-face, and barely had time to feel betrayed by her father's voice. Ally tried to scream, to run, to…anything.

Mandy awoke to soft beams of sunlight on her face. She stretched and looked toward her sister's bed. Empty. She jumped out of bed and tripped over something hard on the ground. Mandy laid facedown on the floor and looked back to see the cause. Mandy's scream echoed throughout the house, the neighborhood, the town for years. Pretty little girls weren't killed in the night. Horrors like this didn't happen, not in quiet towns full of good-hearted church-going folk. Not to picture perfect families. Not to innocent people. Horrors like that didn't exist, couldn't exist.

*****

"Chris? Did you hear that?"

"Hear what?" he asked sleepily.

"That noise...outside...scratching." Alex was breathing fast and starting to tremble.

"You're such a baby. Go back to sleep," Chris said through a yawn. He looked at his alarm clock, 2:45 a.m. "It's late, I'm—" Chris stopped. Something

(Red)

Had caught his eye. In the window, were those red...lights? No, something else. Red.

Alex focused his attention on the window, the direction his brother was looking. He knew what was in the window. Those eyes locked with his. He felt his bladder go and began screaming. Chris joined in. Their parents' room was down the hall, and their dad was in the room within seconds of the first scream.

His boys were staring out the bedroom window. They didn't notice his arrival. As he asked what was wrong, Jim thought he saw something

(Red)

Move quickly in the window. He went to the window but found nothing. He thought he must have imagined it.

(them)

He wasn't eight anymore. Adults do not imagine things like that. They don't see

(Red eyes)

Things that are not there. He dismissed the thought and went to his boys. They spoke of a monster, and Jim gave reassurance. But somewhere deep in his mind, Jim was remembering. And that little part of his mind wouldn't—couldn't—let him dismiss those eyes.

*****

As the creature scurried away, it thought to itself that it must be quicker. It was hungry; it needed to feed.

Chapter 1

A beam of sunlight reflected off the sheriff's freshly polished badge, giving her an almost glowing effect as she walked down Main Street. The sheriff had a tough career. She worked in a man's field, and she took pride in her position. She was the first female sheriff in the county's history, and that weighed heavy. In her career, she's never tried to prove that women belonged, only that *she* belonged. She was fit for duty, and her male subordinates respected her. She had not heard "That woman sheriff" in a while and was not keen on hearing it again.

Her first term was accidental. Most of the county thought they were voting for a man. She learned early on that her last name would take her places, hopefully not the drunk tank. People both respected and pitied her family. Her life in law enforcement wasn't charmed, but her reflexes were good, and her instincts were better. She had earned her place in this town, this community, this life.

She glanced at her watch, 10:15 a.m., right on schedule as she reached the café. Jack's Hole was a small place, with six tables and nine stools around the horseshoe counter. It suited the town. She was greeted immediately by Tug and Bob, always at the counter, always together. The two lived (separately) outside of town for most of their years. It was rare to see one without the other. The sheriff could not remember if she ever had.

"Mornin', Sheriff," a cheerful voice with a sincere smile came from Susie. "The usual?"

"That'd be great, Suze," she said as she took her seat at the counter. "Busy morning?"

"Yeah, you're lucky to get a seat," Susie joked while handing her a mug of coffee. "It's been packed since six." Susie went back to busying herself with the tasks of being a waitress—stocking sugars and creamers, filling salt and pepper shakers, and marrying the ketchups. Usually, Susie would talk with the sheriff about her seventeen-year-old life—boys, school, but mostly about getting out of this town. Susie knew she was destined for something big. Big career, big life, and big money. The sheriff rarely saw Susie work, especially during the slowest time of the day. She knew instantly why Susie was busying herself.

"Is Jack in the back?"

"Hmm?" Susie asked, looking up. "Oh, yeah. He's in the office."

Jack Murphy was the owner of the small café. He was in his midthirties, never married, and outside of this café, his life was dedicated to fishing.

"Ask him if he wants to have a cup of coffee with me. My treat."

Susie gave a knowing smile and told the sheriff she would go get him.

"Is this official business, Sheriff?"

"Could be, Tug. Could be." The sheriff smiled at Tug and sipped her coffee. "You could be next." This got the old men laughing and talking about simpler times.

Jack walked through the kitchen doors on Susie's heels. He was wearing faded jeans and a white T-shirt, his typical uniform. He looked a little hungover, but he was happy to see the sheriff. She stood and hugged her old friend when he reached her. It was a little longer and a little tighter than a casual hug. When they let go, she noticed he was grinning slightly.

"The fish aren't biting today?" the sheriff asked sarcastically as they took their seats at the counter.

"Nah. I just thought I'd get a little work done. Make sure Suze earns her wages." Susie, who had been eavesdropping, blushed and moved to the other end of the counter. "How's the job?"

"You know, slow, quiet, boring. How's the café?"

"Slow. Quiet. Boring." He smiled coyly. She gave him a friendly smile and finished her coffee. Susie's interruption with more coffee was not unwelcomed by them both.

A familiar voice beckoned her from her walkie-talkie.

"What's up, Dawn?"

"You'd better get here right away, Sheriff. The station's a madhouse." Dawn, who was never exactly calm, sounded excited and nervous.

The sheriff stood, hugged her friend, and gave quick goodbyes. She was almost out the door when Jack stopped her.

"Dinner tonight? You know, after you handle the crisis," he asked with a cocky smile and hopeful eyes.

"Um… I'll call you later. Listen, I really have to—"

"Yeah, go. I'll see you tonight."

*****

Upon arrival at the station, the sheriff found Dawn on the phone with all three lines lit up. Dawn, her daytime dispatcher, was in her mid-twenties and had a certain disposition that suggested she would never be taken seriously. She had blond hair and large breasts, which she accentuated. Despite her insecurities and fear that the sheriff did not like her, the sheriff was quite fond of Dawn. She found her competent and (pretty) smart, despite popular consensus. Dawn's light-hearted spirit and silly sense of humor brought a welcomed light to a sometimes dark and ugly profession. Two of her on-duty deputies looked confused and lost. Not a new sight for the sheriff. Of her five deputies, one was worthy of the badge. The rest were barely capable, and the sheriff worried one may accidentally shoot himself in the foot. Most days, she felt more like a babysitter and less like a sheriff. But she had to make do. There were not many applications for rural county deputies who would not see much action.

The sheriff was sure it was a typical morning, no need for alarm. Multiple service calls for the elderly, vandalism from the weekend just discovered by local business owners, and of course, the speeder on Mulberry Street. Her deputies, having zero motivational skills between them, were awaiting orders. She sent them on their first calls and had dispatch take it from there. It was amazing how once they were out in the field, they could actually function. They just needed that first push.

She spent the rest of the morning and early afternoon dealing with endless paperwork. The police radio was always on in her office, and she half listened. Her deputies were handling calls as expected. Deputy Collins was handling a vandalism call at the McAllister Warehouse that sounded not quite interesting but different. Normal vandalism calls involved *S+R 4-EVER* or *Patty is a slut*. This new vandalism seemed to be a warning. The sheriff thought about taking a drive over to have a look.

"Sheriff?" Dawn called to her over the intercom.

"Yes?"

"Mr. Dobbins is on the line. He's asking for you again."

Ray Dobbins was a constant issue in Eggers Cove. As the wealthiest man in town, he thought that earned him certain privileges. Retired in his early thirties after wise investments, Ray moved to what he called "the Sticks" to live out his life in peace. Growing up in Brooklyn, he didn't experience much quiet in childhood and even less on Wall Street after college. He always wondered what small town life would be like and thought maybe there he could find a bride. His house sat on a hill and looked down at the town (and the people). It was a fitting a place for him to call home. Ray never found a bride, and his bitterness showed in his sixties.

*****

Eggers Cove was settled in 1812 by Franklin Eggers, his wife, and two small children. Franklin was a determined man. He came to America just ten years before from Germany. He met Greta on the ship, and the two became inseparable. They tried life in New York but found little work and almost no money. Franklin knew to become successful, they had to leave. They had to find somewhere that hadn't been found, somewhere without bigotry, without bias, without Americans.

Franklin read an article about the Great Frontier. He was sold. This was where they would set up roots, start their family, become something. In Germany, he was nothing—poor, destitute, alone. Here, in the Great Frontier, he would be something.

They arrived on land without a name, without a known history, without a memory. On this land, Franklin saw promise—the promise of today, tomorrow, and times he could not envision. Franklin found his home. Greta followed Franklin. She loved him, believed in him, and somewhere deep, knew he would provide. Greta was alone in this world, parents both deceased and no siblings. Greta was brave. She sailed to the Americas on her own. She knew her future was there. When she met Franklin, she knew. Sailing was right, leaving was right, and this was right.

They built an empire in nowhere America. They were successful and created generational wealth. Franklin had a vision, and Greta had heart. Together, they were unstoppable. They raised their children, their farm, their mill, their town. And people came. They came to find prosperity, a home, anything. Franklin and Greta gave hope, gave meaning, gave everything to those who were looking. When the townsfolk started talking about a name, the only thing mentioned was Eggers. He was a respected man, eventual mayor, and a lasting presence. He added the cove as tribute to the river that ran through his property. Near his home, there was a bend in the river, and it created not only a swimming hole but also a place of solace, of thought, of peace. It was a cove, and it had to be remembered.

*****

She resisted a sigh. "Put him through."

"Line two."

The sheriff pushed the button and asked how Mr. Dobbins was today. Most of the townspeople liked to be referred to by their first name, but not Ray Dobbins. He was to be addressed as Sir or Mr. or His Excellence (that title was only in his head, but one could hope).

"Well, Dee—"

"Sheriff Halley," she interrupted. She could demand respect. She knew *she* had earned it.

"Sheriff Halley," Ray Dobbins said with obvious contempt. "There are several issues that need to be addressed, again. First, those teenagers are trespassing and leaving their trash all over my property. Second, the pothole on fourth is only growing. Third, I am not going to tolerate…"

Deirdra Halley, Dee to her friends, listened to the bitter old man drone on and stared out her window. A handful of kids, two of whom she recognized as Alex and Chris Stevens, were mulling around a park bench. There were six of them, some with baseball mitts or bats and the occasional skateboard. She longed for those days, early teens, no responsibilities, no appeasing angry old men or babysitting staff. Things seemed easier then, quieter, better.

*****

Strawberry blond curls were flying as twelve-year-old Deirdra Halley sprinted down the street, two boys on her heels. The fire hydrant was the goal, the finish line. This time, she would win. She had come close before but had always been bested by Jack. Dee felt Jack and Jimmy close behind. She had to kick it up a gear, thirty feet. She crossed the finish line a fraction of a second before Jack, a full second before Jimmy. Both protested she cheated, as children do when they lose.

"Suck it!" Dee laughed. "I was miles ahead." The three friends laughed, and a rematch was promised.

"Hey, Dee, there's your dad." Jack pointed up the street to a tall athletic man in jeans and boots. And the unmistakable shine of his badge. He cast a long shadow, and with his hat, he resembled more a cowboy than a small-town sheriff. Conor Halley had been sheriff for three years. His father had been sheriff, and his father had been a beat cop in the city. Liam Halley had moved his family to Eggers Cove when he found his career halted. An honest cop in his days was hard to find, and when they were found, they were usually punished.

Dee waved at her dad and ushered her friends the other direction. Seeing her dad in the middle of the day usually turned out bad for her. He would find more chores or something she should be studying, anything to get her away from those boys. Conor did not have any specific issues with Jack or Jimmy. He just thought Dee should be spending more time with some *girl* friends. He knew it was his fault she liked playing more with the boys. Between her older brothers and him and no mother, it was inevitable. Today, Dee was lucky as her dad only waved and did not call for her.

Margot Kelly was the most beautiful girl Conor had ever seen. Her family moved to Eggers Cove when she was fourteen, and Conor was in love. Self-assured and confident, he was the first to approach her. He often thought that was how he won her, being there first. Her family was from the city and looking for a slower paced life, a safer place to raise their family. She hated her parents for making her leave the city and friends, but after meeting Conor, she loved them. He was cute, a little overconfident, funny, and she fell in love immediately.

They married after college and quickly started their family. Her parents were less than pleased with the union, but *they* had wanted the slower life. Margot reminded them of that every chance she got. When they first objected to her suitor, tried to ground their adult child, Margot made it clear. This was her choice. She would not be pushed around. She had always been strong-willed and stubborn. Her parents could not control her as a child. She didn't know why they were trying now. Conor was from a respectable family. His father was sheriff, but they didn't have a lot of money. She never cared about that. She just wanted a home full of love and respect.

Margot taught at the elementary school, and Conor became a deputy. They had three children. Deirdra was their last. Their family was happy and thriving for several years. Then the unthinkable. Cancer. It was stage 4 before they caught it, and there was not much hope. Margot died in the summer of Deirdra's eighth year, devastating her family and the town. She was loved by her students, their parents, and the local groups where she volunteered.

Family life was an adjustment after Margot. Conor did not know how to raise a daughter. He only knew how to make boys men. He leaned heavily on his sister, but Deirdra had always been a daddy's girl. She didn't care for dresses or silly shoes that slowed her down. Being the youngest, she had to be quick, tough, and smart.

Dee and her friends were headed to the river when they heard a familiar voice calling to them. Charlie Wilks was furiously peddling his bike, trying to catch the trio.

"Wait up!" Charlie was ten but big for his age. He didn't have any friends in his class, and the trio had adopted him. He was clever enough to keep up with Jack's wit, smart enough to keep up with Dee (or ask questions without shame), and brave enough to impress them all, especially Jimmy.

The group spent the afternoon dunking each other in the river and seeing who could do the best flip off the rock. Most of their summers had been spent that way—avoiding adults, racing, swimming—but this summer felt different. Next year started junior high for the trio. Charlie would be left behind at the elementary school, and he feared he would be forgotten.

*****

"Sheriff Hailey?" Ray Dobbins sounded more annoyed than usual. "Are you listening to me?"

"It's Halley, Mr. Dobbins. As you well know, as I've corrected you before." Dee emphasized the *alley* in her name. She often told people it was pronounced like alley with an H.

"Sheriff Halley, excuse me." Dee could hear the distain in his voice. "As I was saying—"

"Yes, teenagers, potholes. I can send someone out to patrol a couple of times during the night, if it's slow. But as I've told you before, I have no control over the road conditions. I recommend you contact the mayor's office." Dee smiled at this thought. She felt a little bad siccing him on Charlie, but it does come with the office.

"And the other matter?"

Ray Dobbins had been feuding with almost everyone in town, but none more than his immediate neighbor, Jane Russel. First there was an issue with the fence, then some dispute about a tree. He did not approve of her book club meetings on Wednesday nights. The list went on. The further down the list, the more childish it became. Dee did not have the time or the patience to deal with this squabble.

"Did you try discussing the matter with Jane?" Dee knew the answer before she asked.

"There is no talking to that woman!" Ray Dobbins was noticeably agitated.

"Sheriff?" It was Dawn with impeccable timing, calling over the intercom.

"Please hold, Mr. Dobbins." Then to Dawn, "Thank you! Is there something you need?"

"Deputy Collins is requesting you at the warehouse. Says it's weird."

"*Weird?* Any details on that?"

"Nope, that's all he said. He asked that you hurry." Dawn sounded concerned.

"Tell him I'll be right there." She clicked back over to Ray Dobbins. "Sorry, I have to go. I'll try to swing by and talk to Jane later today." Dee hung up the phone without waiting for a response. She said goodbye to Dawn as she passed her desk and headed for her truck.

The warehouse was on the other side of town, which took five minutes without lights and sirens. Dee had barely parked her truck, and Deputy Collins was at her door.

"Hey, Sheriff. Sorry to call you out here. This is just…"

"Weird?" Dee finished for him.

"Yeah, weird." Deputy Collins looked bemused, Dee thought. Maybe a little scared? She was not sure if it was fear she was seeing or just confusion.

"Let's see what you have, Matt." The two walked to the side of the building where a few workers were milling about.

On the side of the building were two large eyes outlined in black with blood red centers.

9

The ominous words below: Death Follows

Dee studied the words, the eyes. It did not look like local work. And there was the obvious threat, but to whom?

"Weird," Dee said. "You photograph it? Get some measurements? Statements?"

"I got some good shots and measured it. The whole piece and the individual parts." Deputy Collins had the digital camera out and was showing off his shots. Dee nodded in approval, noting to herself the initiative even if it was not necessary in this case. "I asked the workers, and no one saw anything. But I do have the names and phone numbers of the night crew, and I'm going to follow up with them."

"Good work, Matt. Did you see anything else around the building? Anything suspicious or out of the ordinary?" She was already walking, doing her own canvas around the building. There was trash, overgrown bushes or weeds or both, a random sneaker, the usual suspects near a large building. The only thing of note was the dumpster. It looked off-center. Too off-center. Dee knew it wasn't garbage day and went to take a closer look. "Give me a hand" she called to Deputy Collins as she put on gloves. They pushed the dumpster away from the wall, and on the back was another set of eyes and three symbols:

"Weird."

"Let's find a new word, shall we?" Dee had a strange feeling in her gut. It was familiar. Something was wrong. Dee had good— excellent—instincts, and she trusted them. This was the beginning. Of what, she had no idea. "Get shots of this, too, and dust it. I doubt it'll result in anything, but we should try."

"Sure thing. Sorry I missed it, Sheriff."

While Deputy Collins took pictures and dusted for prints, Dee questioned the workers again. She did not think she would hear anything new, but she might notice behavior that Deputy Collins would have missed. The interviews went as expected with no new insights, except an eyebrow raise or twitch. Or…she could not put her finger on it and dismissed it. Rather, she filed it away for future reference.

As Dee gave final instruction to Deputy Collins, her phone buzzed. It was Jack, and she could not help but smile. "Hey, what's up?"

"Just confirming dinner. My place, seven?"

Dee looked at her watch. It was almost five. "That should work. See you then." She had enough time to swing by Jane Russel's and try to sort out that mess. She radioed Dawn to let her know where she would be.

Jane Russel was widowed, and her two children had moved out of Eggers Cove years ago. They rarely visited. She spent her days gardening. She was proud of her many compliments on the best yard in town. Jane relished her insert in a well-known gardening magazine. She was the central piece of that issue. She hosted a book club once a week for several other lonely women and women trying to get a few hours of "me time" away from their families. She was well-liked by everyone in town, everyone except Ray Dobbins.

When Dee pulled up at her house, she admired new rose bushes along the walk. Before Dee reached the steps to the porch, Jane greeted her from the door. One of Jane's pastimes was watching the neighborhood, the town, everything. She was quite the gossip, but it was harmless. People knew she was lonely.

"Good afternoon, Sheriff. Would you like some lemonade?"

"No thanks, Mrs. Russel. I'll only be here a few minutes." Dee did not enjoy this part of her job—settling meaningless squabbles between people with nothing better to do—but it was a part of *this* job. "I'm sure you know why I'm here."

"It's Jane, Sheriff. That Dobbins, he's a menace. A menace. He was just here yesterday, yelling about my book club. What on earth could be wrong with a women's book club?" Jane was obviously upset. Dee understood the toll living next to Ray Dobbins must take.

"I know it's frustrating. I was thinking maybe a few of the ladies could carpool. Less cars on the street?" Dee knew that would not solve anything. Ray Dobbins was unhappy and would not quit until the whole town was as miserable as him. The women chatted for a few minutes, and an invitation was extended, again, to Dee to join the book club. Dee declined as always but thanked her for her thoughtfulness.

"Well, I have to be headed back to the station. I'll let Ray know we talked. Maybe he'll quiet down for a while."

"You take care, Sheriff. With any luck, that grouch will move away."

Dee thought, *Your lips to God's ear.* "Thanks, Jane. Have a nice evening."

*****

Dee arrived at Jack's just before seven and let herself in as she always has. "Jack?"

"Kitchen!"

Dee made her way through Jack's living room and into the kitchen. He kept a tidy home, and it was tastefully decorated. She found Jack in his kitchen, opening a bottle of wine. His grill was on his back porch just off the kitchen, and Dee could smell the steaks through the open door. She hugged her friend and grabbed a glass of wine.

"I thought we'd eat outside. It's a nice evening." It was late fall, and nice evenings would be disappearing soon.

"Sounds good. Where's Ralph?" Ralph was Jack's eight-year-old Belgian Malinois, and he usually greeted company.

"He's out back. I think the squirrel has returned." The two made their way out to the porch and found Ralph running back and forth along the fence. That squirrel was his archnemesis, and Ralph would dispatch the menace accordingly. He came running over, tail wagging, tongue hanging out, when he noticed Dee. Jack joked often that Ralph loved her more. Dee knew he did. She scratched his head and then his belly when he rolled over.

Dee joined Jack at the table after Ralph was satisfied. "How was your day? Any excitement at the diner?"

"There was the lunch rush. Four people at noon." Jack did not buy the diner to get rich. It was more of a project, something to keep him busy now that he was retired. Until a few years ago, he had been a detective in the city, well respected and decorated. One night, a bad situation turned worse, and three surgeries later, Jack found himself medically retired. He didn't talk much about that night. Dee knew the story, but no one else in town did.

"Maybe you should think about expansion. Move to a larger location. Maybe buy the empty place next door and knock down the walls? You know, get ahead of the obvious popularity coming your way." Dee had been giving Jack a hard time since they were kids. Jack gave it right back. They had been best friends for as long as either could remember. They laughed, ate their dinner, and finished the bottle. Conversation was always easy, the food was always good, and there was nowhere either of them would rather be.

After Dee helped Jack clean up the dinner mess, they opened another bottle, sat on the porch, and looked at the stars. Dee told him about the vandalism and showed him a picture of the symbols on her phone.

"What do think those are? Native American? They seem familiar. Send it to me and I'll do some digging." The cop in him could not resist. Solving puzzles had always appealed to him. Dee had anticipated this and welcomed it. She bounced ideas off him when cases were not going well. It was nice to be able to brainstorm with a seasoned officer.

"Already sent." Dee was stroking Ralph's head, which had found itself in her lap. She missed having a dog, but with work, she did not have the time a dog deserved.

"How bad did Collins botch the scene?" Jack knew the struggles Dee faced with a subpar team.

"He was fine. Maybe a little overzealous for a vandalism scene, but at least he's trying." Dee thought with some more mentoring, Matt Collins could be a good cop. "Enough shoptalk. What should we do with the rest of our evening?"

"I don't know. It *is* a school night."

"It's *always* a school night. I'm the sheriff, and you own the only diner in town."

"You wanna watch a movie? Or we could light a fire?"

They settled on a fire in his firepit, and their conversation was light. Both were thinking about the symbols, trying to remember why they were familiar.

Chapter 2

Chris and Alex Stevens found themselves downtown after school as they usually did. Their friends would soon join them, and trouble would follow. There was a bench they met at. It was across from the sheriff's station and close to the candy store. Tom Johnson owned the Olde Time Ice Cream and Candy Shoppe. He had designed it based on his childhood hangout. His ice cream selection put Baskin Robbins to shame. He had every type of candy he could find available for distribution. Tom hired mostly kids in high school, and he typically covered the first shift. It was after three now, and that meant a surge of children, some looking for ice cream, some for candy, and some just looking. He had a lot of collectibles in his store, like old candy tins, vintage lunch boxes, and various figurines.

"Hey, guys!" Abigail was the first of their friends to arrive at the bench. Their bench.

"Hey, Abs. What took you so long?" Chris had been friends with Abigail since she first arrived in town five years ago. She was cute—important—but she was also clever and not afraid to hang with the boys. She had proven herself over the years as capable, strong, and funny. He is still grateful that he reached out to her when she first arrived. She lived two doors down, and his mom said it was the neighborly thing to do. Go introduce yourself, be a good neighbor. Nine-year-old Chris had no idea of the friendship waiting behind that door.

Abigail's father was an accountant, really boring as far as she was concerned, and he was successful. After making his fortune, he and his wife longed for the simpler life. A quiet life away from the bustle of the city. They found Eggers Cove during a road trip and knew it was the life they wanted. George Thomas bought a storefront in town and opened the Thomas CPA Services. He did not need the money, but he did enjoy working.

"Stupid Fraser, again." Don Fraser was the Social Studies teacher at the junior high. He demanded his students respect the clock, although he rarely did. He often kept students late yammering on about nonsense. That's how the students felt. Abigail had absolute distain for the man. She tried to transfer out of his class but was unsuccessful. "Where're the other guys?"

"I see Brian just up the block. Steve and Billy should be here." Chris had not been friends with Billy until around five years ago, after Billy lost his brother, Tom. Billy was two years younger than Chris, but in a small town like this, you look after those that seem lost. Chris took care of everyone in their group. He thought it was what big brothers were supposed to do. "When they get here, let's hit the candy store then head over to the river."

Billy found himself walking toward Maple Street, the street his family used to live on. Shortly after his brother died, they moved across town. His mother said she could not live in that house, that she would go insane. He was not sure why he was headed in that direction. He was supposed to meet his friends downtown. Something was pulling him, tugging at him.

Billy stood in front of his old house. No one lived there. No one had lived there since his family moved out. He looked at his brother's bedroom window and shivered. The hairs on the back of his neck were at full attention. He did not notice the tear rolling down his cheek. He did not hear Steve approaching, calling his name.

"Billy? Billy!" Steve noticed Billy walking the opposite direction he should have been and decided to follow. They did not go to the same school. Billy was still in elementary, but the schools were close enough together to run into students from both, no matter which direction you were headed. Billy looked pale and zoned out. Steve was worried. He finally caught up to him at Billy's old house and could not imagine why the kid would come back here. "Billy!" Steve shook his shoulders.

Billy turned his head, blinked a few times, and finally recognized his friend. "Hey. What are we doing here?"

"No idea, man. No idea. Let's roll." Steve turned Billy back toward town and gave him a little push. The two walked without speaking to meet their friends. As they approached the bench, Steve called out to the group waiting for them, "What's up, losers? Let's blow this place. We got shit to do!"

Chris started to open his mouth, and Steve shook his head and gave him a "don't ask" look. Chris and Steve were best friends since before kindergarten. He would speak with him later about Billy, but not in front of the group. Maybe he would include Abby. There was no reason to embarrass Billy. The kid had been through enough.

The group of friends went to the candy store as planned, each getting candy except for Billy. He just walked around the store, not really looking at anything. Chris bought him something for later, in case. Then they headed toward the river, toward their fort. It seemed silly to call it a fort at their age. They had begun calling it their spot until the right descriptor could be found. They had all pitched in over the years, and it was a pretty cool spot. So far, none of the older kids had found it—or cared about it.

They spent the afternoon laughing, daring each other to do extreme feats, and making jokes at one another's expense. Just regular kid stuff, the same as they did most days. There was a heaviness today. No one mentioned it, but everyone felt it. As the sun started to set, they knew they had to hustle home. Everyone had a streetlights rule.

They walked down Eggers Lane, named after the Eggers family, and it also served as the driveway to their family home. Each took their exit toward their homes. Chris, Alex, Abigail, and Steve all lived on the same street and always walked home together.

When the four were alone, Abigail was the first to speak. "Weird day, huh? What's up with, Billy?"

Chris and Steve exchanged a look. Abigail was familiar with this look. The two had an unspoken language. She was still learning it. This was the "should I say it in front of them?" look. Chris nodded.

"He was at his house today. His *old* house." There was silence for several minutes as they thought about what that might mean. Billy had not gone to that house in years, not alone.

"He seemed fine yesterday. I haven't noticed him being weird in forever." Abigail was the first to speak.

"I know. Let's just keep an eye out, make sure he's okay. Alex and I'll go to his house in the morning and walk him to school." As the leader of the group, everyone agreed with Chris and volunteered to go along. "Not this time."

Abigail's house was first. She said her byes and told Chris she would call him later. Steve crossed the street to his own house, and the Stevens boys went to theirs. Chris knew Alex would want to talk about Billy, talk about that week five years ago. Chris knew he would have to talk to his brother, no matter how painful it was.

*****

The Stevens boys rushed out of their house early with Mary Stevens on their heels, urging them to eat more breakfast. They each took an apple and trotted off toward Billy's house a few streets over.

The door opened, and Chris asked for Billy. Gabrielle Johnson was still in her bathrobe. She was pale and skinny. Very little of her beauty remained. Losing a child affected parents differently. Her husband had thrown himself into his work. She stopped living. In any way that mattered. She still cleaned the house and prepared the meals, but she was no longer present. Chris's heart broke for Billy every time he saw her. He could not imagine losing his brother *and* his mother.

"He's sick. Staying home." With that, she shut the door. Chris and Alex looked at each other then started walking toward their schools.

Two blocks later, Alex spoke. "What do you think is wrong with him?"

"I don't know. I'm sure it's nothing." Chris was not sure. Chris was worried. Billy had come so far. He was almost a normal kid again. Silence filled the rest of their short walk to school.

Steve and Abigail were waiting for them when they reached the junior high. Chris told them Billy was sick and reassured his friends that everything was fine. Abigail knew better. She saw the worry in Chris's eyes. The first period warning bell rang, and they all went to their classes, promising to meet at lunch.

Chris had a hard time paying attention to his classes. His mind kept going back to that week five years ago. He had only been nine and was sure some of the details were imagined. He knew that three kids had died, at night, in their bedrooms. The adults all claimed it was the work of one man, someone just passing through town. It was easy for adults to pass blame on a transient or some nobody. *They* had not heard the scratching. For months, Jim and Mary had told their boys they had imagined the scratching, the red eyes in their window. Billy remembered the scratching. He had told Chris about it not long after the two had become friends. Alex remembered the scratching. He still talked to Chris about it.

Chris made his way to their usual lunch spot and found his friends already there. With Brian there, no one spoke of Billy or the events of yesterday. The afternoon classes passed just as the morning classes for Chris. He prepared for the after-school events, the show he would have to put on. He did not want his friends, especially not his brother, to know how worried (scared) he was. He felt a darkness had fallen on his town, and he did not know what to do about it.

*****

Chris and Alex showed up at Billy's door the next morning to walk him to school. Gabrielle Johnson informed the boys he was still sick. He would call when he was feeling better. Again, the boys walked to school in silence. They were worried about their friend, worried about their friends, worried about their town. Chris thought about talking with his father after dinner. He just had to figure the right words.

Abigail was waiting for the brothers a block away from school. She asked after Billy and Chris let her know he was still sick. Abigail had moved to Eggers Cove after Tom and the other children were

19

killed. She could not fully understand the weight Chris felt, but she could feel his energy. She had helped Chris and the others bring Billy back from darkness all those years ago. She hoped they could do it again. The trio walked the block to school and found Steve and Brian waiting on the front lawn. The group did not speak of Billy. Steve read their faces. For most of the group, the day passed as usual. Chris spent it working on the words to tell his father.

After the Stevens boys cleaned up the dinner dishes and put the food away, Chris found his father on their back porch.

"Dad? You got a sec?"

Jim looked up from his laptop and nodded to his oldest son. Chris looked tired, worried, much older than his fourteen years. Jim had seen this look before five years ago. He closed his laptop. "What's going on?"

"There's something wrong." Chris met his dad's eyes. He wanted to be taken seriously, wanted understanding from his dad. Mostly, he wanted help.

"Is it you? Your brother? What?"

"It's all of us." Chris told his dad about Billy, how Steve found him at his old house, that he had been home sick for two days. Chris told his dad that he was scared. He was not sure why, but he knew something bad was coming. Or worse, it was already here.

Jim told his son he would call the Johnson house and check on Billy, although it would be a waste of time, Jim thought. The Johnsons were different people now. He found Gabrielle to be indifferent at best, and Ben was absent. He tried not to judge them. He was not sure how he would handle the loss of a child, but he would be present for the surviving son. He knew that much.

Jim called the Johnson house and received no new information. Billy was sick, and he would call when he felt better. Jim thought about his conversation with his son, about how scared he looked, about that face he showed tonight, the same face he had five years ago. Jim texted his friends and asked if they could meet up sometime tomorrow. He said it was important. Dee had been here five years ago. She knew what had happened as well as anyone else in town—probably better. Jack had not been here. He would take convincing.

Before Chris went to sleep that night, he texted his friends (including Billy). He told them to close their windows, close their blinds, and not to look outside until morning. It sounded crazy. He thought his friends may make fun of him, but he was not taking chances.

*****

Friday morning around ten, Dee was walking toward the café to see Jack. It was her usual routine, coffee at the café then off to the station. Jack's Hole was missing Jack this morning, but Tug and Bob were in their usual spots at the counter.

"Mornin', Sherifif," Tug greeted Dee, and Bob raised his mug in her direction.

"Gentlemen." Dee smiled at them and asked Susie for coffee. She drank her coffee in silence, lost in thought. She was not sure what Jim wanted, why the urgency. She hoped it was nothing.

A couple in their midtwenties walked in. Dee did not recognize them. Susie said they could sit anywhere. The two were laughing, obviously not from around Eggers Cove, probably just passing through. They asked what there was to do in town, and Susie laughed. Dee finished her coffee as the two were ordering the daily special. Dee giggled to herself. The daily special never changed. She dropped a five on the counter and headed toward the station.

Dawn was on the phone when Dee walked in. Deputy Collins was at his desk, and Ray Dobbins was seated in what passed for a lobby. She thought about turning around and walking out the door, but she had already been spotted.

"Sheriff, I've been waiting." Ray Dobbins rose and started to say more.

"Good morning. Mr. Dobbins. As you can see, I'm just arriving. You're going to have to wait a few more minutes." Dee gave Dawn a look of utter annoyance and walked back to her office. She motioned Deputy Collins to follow. Once in her office, she asked him to close the door.

"Sheriff?" Deputy Collins was nervous, a common state for him. "Something wrong?"

Dee smiled at him. "No, Matt. I was just looking for an excuse. I'm not ready to deal with him." The two sat and chatted for a few minutes about his family. Then on to business. "Anymore vandalism? Like the other day?"

"No, nothing like Monday. I'm keeping an eye out."

"Okay, thanks, Matt. You're doing a good job." Dee dismissed him and busied herself for a few more minutes before asking Dawn to send Ray Dobbins in. He entered her office, red-faced, agitated, and ready to spar. "Thank you for waiting, Mr. Dobbins. How can I help?"

"You said you were going to speak to that Jane Russel. There were twice as many cars this week." Ray Dobbins continued his rant. Dee nodded and pretended to pay attention. Some days, she wished she had gone to the city, been an officer there. Police work anywhere had its downfalls, she thought. Maybe the city would have less Ray Dobbins and more actual police work.

At an appropriate pause, Dee cut in. "Mr. Dobbins, I'm aware that you and Mrs. Russel have some issues. I've spoken with her. Have you noticed the patrol car after dark? We've been out every night this week. Did the mayor help with the pothole?"

"Sheriff?" Dawn called from the intercom. Dee picked up the phone and asked what was needed. Dawn, wise beyond her years, was only offering the sheriff some relief.

"Thank you, Dawn. Tell them I'm on my way." Then to Ray Dobbins, "Sorry, I've gotta cut this short. I'm needed. You know you way out."

Ray Dobbins rose. "We are not finished, Sheriff. I will be expecting your call." With that, he huffed his way out of the office, out of the station, to everyone's relief.

Dee was on her way to thank Dawn when her phone buzzed. It was a text from Jack. He was at the café and hoped she could pop over. Dee checked the street and saw Ray Dobbins's Mercedes pulling away. She told Jack she could be there in a few minutes. She let Dawn know where she was headed and walked the two blocks.

Susie was gone for the day. She had afternoon classes at the high school. Ben was behind the counter. He worked noon until close on most days. Tug and Bob had already moved on to the hardware store where they spent afternoons. Dee said hello to Ben and asked after Jack.

"He's in back. Said you could head on in. You want something from the kitchen?" Ben was twenty-four. He did not excel in school, did not have any real dreams. He knew he would spend his whole life in Eggers Cove. He would work where he could, when he could, maybe have a family. He had a few good buddies, and that was enough for him.

"Not right now, Ben. Thanks." Dee went to Jack's office and found him sitting at his desk. He had not yet showered after the morning fishing trip. She wrinkled her nose and commented on his new cologne.

"Trout for lunch? I caught a couple nice ones." He smiled at her. It was his signature smile. He had used it often over the years when they were kids, when they were teenagers, and when he returned after too many years away. He knew this smile always worked on Dee. She couldn't resist.

Dee rolled her eyes. "Just a sandwich." Jack called to the kitchen to make them a couple of turkey sandwiches and asked that they be brought to his office. "What do you think Jim wants?"

"I dunno. His text was pretty vague."

"You think Mary will join?" Dee knew the answer before she asked. It was no secret the Stevens' marriage was rocky at best. Sometimes getting married when you are both twenty and pregnant works. Most times, it does not. In high school, Jim was a football star. Mary saw him as her ticket out. Out of Eggers Cove, maybe even out of the state. He won a football scholarship, full ride at State. A knee injury late in the season junior year of college sealed their fate. She was already pregnant and thought seriously about not keeping it.

Jack gave her a knowing look. "Doubt it. I'll ask though. I'm making dinner." Jack pulled out his phone and sent a quick text to Jim. An almost instant response confirmed Mary would not be in attendance.

Dee was grateful. She found it difficult to talk to Mary. They had little in common, and Dee found her bitter and no fun. She felt bad for her lifelong friend, but there was not much she could do for him. He did have some pretty great kids, a respectable career, a nice home. Most of the boxes were checked. Maybe when the kids were grown, he could find happiness in a relationship.

"I'll bring the beer."

"How long has it been, the three of us, together?"

Dee thought back. Last year? The year before? She could not remember. "Wow, I'm not sure. It'll be fun to get the band back together." Dee paused for a second. "Should we call Charlie?"

"I think Jim would have included him if he wanted him there."

Dee shrugged her shoulders. With Charlie came Jill. The two were inseparable, and the trio were not close with her. They agreed to leave it as is for now, and the two enjoyed their lunch. Dee heard some chatter on the police radio, but nothing her boys could not handle. She was about to leave then remembered to ask, "You find anything on those symbols? The ones from the warehouse?"

"No match yet." Jack opened his laptop and navigated to an open webpage. "These are close, but not quite right." The page was for local tribal history. It was full of imagery and short on text. Dee was not impressed. "I know, I know, it's lacking. But the imagery is close. There's some better sites, more scientific, but none had these." He pointed to a handful of symbols. Dee admitted they were close.

"Well, keep digging, I guess. Thanks." Dee gathered her things and started out of Jack's office. "See ya tonight, around seven."

Jack stood and hugged her. "Yep, see ya then."

Dee had no desire to go back to the station. Her truck was there though. She must either go back or walk around town. She made a quick call to Dawn just to check in. With nothing emergent, Dee opted to walk. It was a nice afternoon. She wanted to take advantage. Cold days were coming, bitter cold days. She would enjoy the sunshine, soak as much of it in as possible. She walked around the downtown park, checked on some empty storefronts, and said hello to the hardware store regulars, Tug, Bob, and Ernie. They were there most afternoons, sitting out front, talking about the old days and how the world was going to hell. Dee thought every generation must think that about the subsequent generations that they were the worst. They would destroy everything.

"Sheriff?" It was Dawn calling on the radio. So much for a quiet afternoon.

"Go ahead."

"Deputy Collins is asking for you. He's out at the Dobbins' place."

"Let him know I'll be there shortly." Dee wondered why he had not radioed himself. She made her way quickly back to the station to grab her truck. Dee arrived at the Dobbins' residence and found no street parking. She pulled into his driveway. An anxious Deputy Collins was jogging toward her, an angry Ray Dobbins on his heels. Dee took a deep breath.

"Hey, Sheriff. Sorry to call you out here," Deputy Collins started. And of course, Ray Dobbins interrupted.

"Sheriff, glad you could join us."

"Mr. Dobbins, if you would just stand over there," Dee motioned toward his yard. "And I'll be with you shortly." Ray Dobbins reluctantly went to his porch, not his yard. Childish defiance. Dee shook her head. Then to Deputy Collins, "What's going on, Matt?"

"I guess Mrs. Russel doubled up on book club this week. All these cars." He pointed to the jam-packed street. "All book club goers. I told him it's a public street, that she can have people over. She isn't breaking any laws. They aren't even being loud." Deputy Collins was frustrated. Dee did not blame him. This was not police work. This was a neighbor dispute among adult children.

"Okay, I'm gonna pop in next door and chat with Mrs. Russel. I'll be right back. Keep him as calm as you can." Dee did not get a chance to knock. Jane Russel was opening the door when she hit the first step to the porch. "Good afternoon, Mrs. Russel."

"Oh, dear, you call me Jane. I've told you a million times."

"I didn't realize book club was on Fridays now."

Jane gave a noticeable smirk. "Oh, yes, we need to meet twice weekly. There's a lot to cover."

"And it doubled in size?" Dee pointed at the cars parked along the street.

"Word got around town. This is the place to be."

"Glad it's going so well. Just make sure no loud noise after eleven. I don't want to have to send someone out here." Jane agreed to continue to keep the noise level down and extended another invite to Dee. She declined and walked back to speak with Ray Dobbins.

"Mr. Dobbins, I'm sorry for the inconvenience of the cars parked on your street. I've spoken with Mrs. Russel, and she assures me that they will continue to keep the noise level down. Beyond that, there is nothing we can do. If the noise level rises after eleven, you can give us a call." She motioned for Deputy Collins to head toward his cruiser. "You have a nice evening, sir." Dee joined Deputy Collins before Ray Dobbins could argue. She told her deputy to meet her around the corner so they could chat.

Deputy Collins apologized again. He said he wasn't sure what to do. Dee let him know that if he stated the law and explained the situation, much like she had, she would support him and defend him. He was young and fairly new to the job. She saw potential and did not want to lose him over this nonsense. "Why don't you go patrol around the tracks and head back to the station after?" Deputy Collins agreed and drove south toward the railroad tracks.

Dee radioed into Dawn, asked if she was needed anywhere else. Dawn said no, and Dee headed back to the station. She still had several hours before she had to meet the guys. She might as well tackle some paperwork.

*****

Dee arrived at Jack's just before seven. She saw Jim was already there. Ralph greeted her at the door with a ball, whole body wagging, ready to play. She loved on him then found the guys on the back porch. They both stood to hug her, and she handed Jack a twelve-pack.

"Someone's thirsty," Jack joked as he unpacked the beer into his outdoor refrigerator then handed one to each of his friends.

"Please, it's only four a piece. That's just a start. Remember high school?" Dee teased. "What are we eating?"

"Ribs."

Dee threw the ball a few times for Ralph, took a few sips of her beer, then, "Why are we here, Jim? It's nice to see you. We should definitely hang out more often, but the text. It was..." She drifted off. She could not think of the right word. No word would have to do.

"Yeah, it's great to see you guys," Jim started. He took a deep breath. "My kids, Dee. Chris's face last night. Same face from five years ago."

Dee sat down. Jack looked a little a puzzled. Dee had filled him in a little on what had happened. If Jim was right, they would have to fill him in all the way. Or at least as much as they could remember. A shiver ran through her as she went back to that week. She thought it had been a week. It felt like years.

"Are you sure, Jim? What did he say?"

Jim went through his conversation with his son. He described Chris's tone, body language, face. Jim knew. He said they needed to prepare, plan. They needed to keep the kids safe. Jack just listened. He let Dee ask the questions. He was out of his league here. He was at least two steps behind. Dee had told him that some children died in an extraordinary way, but she had not elaborated.

"I want to talk to him, his friends, Billy. I don't think Gabrielle or Ben are equipped to handle this." Dee was in what she called "cop mode," working the problem, asking questions, developing a plan. She needed Jack. She needed his experience, his instincts, his brain. He was better at puzzles than anyone she had ever met, and he was great with interviews. Both suspect and witness, people just opened up to him. They wanted him to like them. "Jack, you'll help?"

Jack took a big swig, swallowed, and looked at his friends. "I'll do what I can, Dee. You know I will. I'm not exactly sure what I'm helping with." On cue, Ralph came over and placed his head in his dad's lap. Jack stroked his head, told him he was a good boy, then looked to Dee.

Dee met his eyes then looked to Jim. "You want to start, or should I?"

Jim told Jack about that night five years ago, when he awoke to his boys screaming, speaking of monsters, something red (eyes) in the window. Jim told him that he saw them too. It was the first time he admitted it to anyone, including himself. He spoke of the days to follow, the panic, the fear. He told Jack that Billy had survived. His brother had not. As he got deeper into the story, he knew how crazy he must sound. He counted on his lifelong friends to understand, to believe.

Jack was quiet. He had known Jim their entire life. They had been friends since before kindergarten. He knew him to be an honest man. A prankster, sure, but not a liar. He looked at Dee. He had known her just as long. They were closer. She looked scared. Dee never looked scared. She would be his first pick in a fight, as backup, in life. "Should we eat?"

Dee and Jim both laughed and said yes. The trio ate. After, they took turns throwing the ball for Ralph. "Does this story have anything to do with the vandalism you showed me?" Jack asked.

"What vandalism?"

Dee quickly brought Jim up to speed and showed him pictures from her phone. "I don't see how it couldn't be related." Jack went inside and returned with printouts from various websites, research on the symbols, the eyes. They went over the documents, some far less believable than others. Then Dee asked, "When do we loop Charlie in?"

Jack and Jim exchanged a look. Dee knew what they were thinking. She was thinking it too.

"We'll meet him without Jill. Make up an excuse to exclude her." Her friends looked doubtful. "I'm the first to say that I don't like the bitch, but I...we...love Charlie. One of you can come up with some reason to get him to meet without her."

The trio talked for another hour, made no real progress, and decided to call it a night. Jim was tasked with getting Charlie alone. As he left, Dee hugged him. "Your kids are going to be fine. We got this." She stayed behind to talk more with Jack. Not about the events of tonight or of those five years ago. Just talk about nothing. She needed her friend, her best friend, to distract her. The problem with living alone was that you were alone when you got home. There was no "How was your day?", "Did you get the promotion?", "Think it'll rain?", and no "Good night. I love you." Dee was not lonely. She was happy living alone, but sometimes, times like these, she longed for the conversation, the companionship.

"You staying over?" This was not an unusual question. Dee did spend some nights at Jack's. Neither of them knew what it meant. Neither of them was ready to define it. They tried dating in high school. It was uncomfortable, awkward. They decided they were better as friends. Best friends. Dee thought they had missed their chance when Jack moved to the city to be a cop. Then he came back. Feelings came back.

"I could use some Ralph snuggles." Dee smiled at Jack. He was in love with her. He had not found the moment to tell her. He knew she loved him. He hoped it was not just friendship. If he were honest with himself, he had always loved her. He hated leaving her for his career. He had hoped she would go with him. She never offered. Jack thought she couldn't offer. Her family had always been sheriff here. He knew her obligation.

*****

A noise woke Chris from a deep sleep. It took him several moments to fully wake. It was a noise he had heard before

(Scratch, scratch)

He leaped from his bed and ran to his brother's room, careful not to look at the window. Alex was still asleep, blinds closed. Chris was grateful his brother listened to him. He sat on the floor, facing his brother. He would stay here all night, this night, and every night. He willed himself to stay awake, but he started to drift. Then…

(Scratch, scratch)

He heard a familiar noise. He did not look at the window. He focused all his attention on his brother. He did not sleep any more that night. He had to protect Alex. He had to. He remembered his friends. They were alone. He hoped they had closed their blinds. He hoped they had listened. He hoped.

Chapter 3

Saturday in Eggers Cove was much like a Saturday in any small town. Men did yard work. Women went to the city for shopping. Children could be found playing in their streets, at the park, or down by the river. Teenagers would be skulking about, loitering, or trying to score beer. Ray Dobbins did have one valid complaint—teenagers drinking on his property. It started years ago and was passed down to incoming high school students. Not only was it satisfying to mess with "Tubby" Dobbins, but it was also a good place to drink. It was secluded, police rarely patrolled, and you could make quite the bonfire. It was cool this morning. The last signs of summer were fading.

Dee woke to the smell of bacon cooking, another perk of staying at Jack's. He loved to cook. She felt a wet nose on her hand. Ralph knew she was awake. She gave him a few scratches then went to the kitchen for much-needed coffee. Jack met her with a cup and asked how she slept.

"Great. What's the ETA on that bacon?"

"A few minutes. You going to the office today?"

"For a bit. You?"

"Yep. Meet for lunch?"

"Sure."

Jack plated their breakfast, and the two ate in mostly silence. Neither knew what to say about last night. They both knew they needed more information. Dee helped clean up breakfast then headed out. She had to stop by her place for her uniform, then to the station. Saturdays were usually quiet. She hoped today was. She had a lot on her mind. She wanted to talk to the kids today. A busy workday would be less than ideal.

Dee found the station quiet, thankfully, and there was minimal chatter on the police radio. Saturday nights were busy. Three deputies were on, and Dee made herself available. She spent a few hours doing paperwork and returning calls. The police radio was still quiet. Dee headed to the café.

Ben was behind the counter; Susie was absently wiping tables. There was a table of three sitting in a corner booth. Dee did not recognize any of them. Ben told her Jack was in back, expecting her. Jack had lunch waiting for her.

"Thanks. I'm starved." As the two ate, Dee told Jack she planned to meet with the kids today. At the very least, Chris and Alex, but she hoped to see Billy too. She invited him to come along, and he agreed. He needed to finish a few things, and Dee needed to change. She did not want to show up in uniform. It seemed too official. Jack said he would pop over to her place when he was finished, and Dee went home.

She was unlocking her door when her phone buzzed. It was Jim. He wanted to meet. She texted him back, explaining that her and Jack wanted to meet with the kids anyways. Jim suggested they meet in the park, not at his house. He would try to bring Billy too.

Dee and Jack drove the six blocks together in Jack's truck. The drive was quiet. They were busy with their own thoughts. Jim and his boys were not hard to spot, and they had a couple of strays. Dee had seen the other kids on many occasions hanging out with the Stevens boys, but she could not remember their names. Jim introduced Abigail and Steve to Jack and Dee, while Dee got hugs from Chris and Alex. Small talk commenced, and Dee had to hear how terrible school was, that awful Mr. Fraser, and they all wished it was still summer. Jim offered to throw the football for "Three Flies Up," and Dee and Jack stole Chris away for a private conversation.

Chris and Alex knew Jack, but not like they knew Auntie Dee. Chris was hesitant at first. Dee encouraged him along. Chris started with the night five years ago. He thought it was best to start there because Jack had not been around.

When he finished, he said, "I know I was just a little kid, but that's how it happened. I know what I saw. Alex saw it too, and maybe Dad."

"We believe you." Dee took his hand in hers. "Now tell us about the last few days."

"The other day, Steve and Billy were late meeting us after school. We always meet at that bench." Chris pointed to their bench. "When they finally showed up, Billy was off. He was quiet and looked sick." Chris continued with his account of the last few days. He told them how scared he was for Billy, for all of them.

"Then last night…" Chris trailed off.

"Last night what?" Jack asked.

"I heard it, the scratching. First on my window, then on Alex's. I stayed awake all night in his room, on the floor. I didn't know what else to do. He's my brother, my responsibility." His eyes were watery, but he held back tears. Dee thought she had never seen an older-looking fourteen-year-old.

"Did you tell your dad?" Dee's turn to ask a question.

"Yeah, this morning. He said I should have gotten him. I was too scared to leave Alex." Chris looked at his feet. He felt small.

"You did the right thing, Chris." Jack patted him on the shoulder. "You notice anything else lately? Or even last week? Something that was just different. Maybe in one of your friends, or?"

"No, Mr. Murphy."

"Jack. Call me Jack."

"Okay, Jack. You guys should talk to Steve since he found Billy."

"He's next. Thanks, Chris." Dee sent him off and asked him to have Steve come over. She looked at Jack, could not get a good read on him. She knew he believed Chris was scared, but he was probably having a hard time with the reason why. Dee herself was having a hard time believing it, and she had lived through that week five years ago.

"Hey, guys! We gonna talk about monsters, ghosts, goblins, maybe vampires?" Steve definitely could make an entrance. Dee and Jack both laughed.

"I think Chris should have warned us about this guy," Jack said to Dee. She rolled her eyes at both of them.

"All kidding aside, can you tell us about the other day? When you found Billy?" Dee asked.

"Yeah, I saw Billy walking the wrong way. We always meet at the bench. He looked out of it, you know? Like, totally lost. So I followed him." Steve told them where Billy ended up, how it took him shaking him to get him to respond. He continued with how he told Chris and Abby and Alex, and that Billy had not been back to school. "I'm worried about the kid. Five years ago, Chris told me we had to look out for him, after Tom. I promised. *Promised.*" Both Dee and Jack could see the sincerity in his eyes. They knew he meant it.

"Okay, Steve, have you noticed anything else lately? Not just Billy or anyone else at school?" Jack asked.

"No, nothing except…" He looked at Jack then Dee. "Chris texted us all on our group chat the other night. He said to close to our blinds. Not to look out the window. I thought he was pulling a prank, but I closed my blinds. Have every night."

"What about five years ago?" Dee asked, and Jack gave her a puzzled look.

"What, those kids? Tom?"

"Yep. You notice anything then? I know you were young, but do you remember anything?"

"Nah, just the kids and Chris telling me we had to look out for Billy. And that's when Abby moved here."

"Okay, thanks, Steve. If you think of anything, you can tell me, Jack, or Jim, if you're more comfortable."

"Yeah, sure. You gonna interrogate the other two next?"

Dee liked this kid. She could tell Jack did too. "Not interrogate, just ask some questions. Can you send Abigail over?" Steve walked toward the group and told Abigail she was being summoned.

"Chris says you guys are okay. I'm sure this is about Billy. I haven't seen him like this in forever. That's what I told Chris. He's been good, really good for a long time. Not like before." Abigail seemed to want to get all her facts out immediately.

"That's what we've heard." Dee needed to wrangle this girl in. "We're more curious about what you've seen. Anything unusual? With your friends or classmates?"

"Just Billy. And Chris. And Alex. And Steve. They've all been strange. It's like when I first moved here. Billy is a mess. Chris wants to fix and protect everybody. I just want to help."

"Have you heard anything at night?" Jack led.

Abigail looked at him sideways. "You know about Chris's text. To close our windows, blinds, curtains. I thought it was weird, but I trust Chris. He's my best friend. He never lies."

"Have you heard or noticed anything at night?" Dee followed up.

"No, but I sleep with earbuds. I like going to sleep to music, and it usually plays all night." Abigail looked at Dee and very seriously said, "Should I stop? Is there something I should be listening for?"

Dee thought, of course the girl in the group asks if she *should* be listening for something. Dee liked her too. Her "nephews" had a good group of friends. "No, I think you can continue to listen to your music." Dee thought it might actually be safer for her to listen to music. "Thanks, Abigail. If you see anything, let me, Jack, or Jim know."

Abigail agreed and walked back toward her friends. Jack asked if they should talk to Alex. Dee said not now. Chris probably knew the most, next to Billy. They were going to have to talk to Billy. Jim came over to talk with his friends.

"So did you find out anything new?" Jim was anxious, scared for his family.

"Pretty much same story you told. Various degrees of detail," Dee started.

"They're scared, Jim. I don't know how much of it is imagination, how much is real." Jack was skeptical. Dee needed him to be. She and Jim were ready to buy silver bullets or crosses or whatever you used against whatever kind of creature was terrorizing their town.

"I hear ya, Jack. I know my boys. They aren't this imaginative. I wish they were." Jim looked west. The sun was going down. "I better get all these kids home before dark. Talk soon." Jim hugged them both then herded the kids to the car.

Dee and Jack went to Jack's. Ralph was probably desperate for attention. They ate leftover ribs and drank the few beers remaining from the night before. They spoke a little about the conversations from the afternoon, mostly about how much they liked the kids.

Chapter 4

Silly Sally Simpson was dreaming early Sunday morning. This time, she was hunting dragons. At six years old, she loved fairy tales, but she always related more to the prince or hero or in this case, dragon slayer. Silly Sally, as her mom called her, thought the boys in the stories had all the fun and the girls were boring. Some nights, she dreamed that she was a knight fighting for the honor of her kingdom. In dreams, girls could be the heroes.

Victoria had started calling her daughter Silly Sally when she was just a few months old. Her precious little baby had always made silly faces and noises. Silly Sally was born. Victoria knew she was not going to be able to call her Silly Sally much longer, at least not around other kids. Sadly, Silly Sally was growing up. She would soon just be Sally.

Silly Sally was tracking the dragon to his lair when a noise invaded her dream. She looked around her dream riverbank and into the dream forest. She did not see anything, but she heard it again.

(Scratch, scratch)

Often in dreams, a real-world sound can creep in, usually causing the dreamer to wake. Sometimes, it takes several noises—or the same noise repeated several times—to wake the dreamer.

(Scratch, scratch)

Silly Sally opened her eyes, disappointed that she did not get to slay the dragon. She was disoriented and rubbed at her sleepy eyes.

(Scratch, scratch)

Her head whipped left toward the noise, toward the window. Silly Sally thought this was her chance to be brave, really brave. She got out of bed and slowly walked toward her window. It was closed, locked, and the blinds were down. She lifted the bottom corner of the blinds to take a peek. Her eyes locked with another set, a red set.

Silly Sally wanted to scream, wanted to look away, wanted to run. She could not do any of these things. She was frozen. She felt those eyes burning deep in her head. She tried to close her eyes. Her lids would not budge. She felt the eyes pulling at her, sucking her in. Her six-year-old vocabulary could not describe what was happening, but she knew she was dying. She knew the creature was stealing her soul. She wanted her mother. In her mind, she begged the creature to let her go.

Victoria woke around six Sunday morning and went to the kitchen for coffee. She stopped by her daughter's room, as she always did, to check on her little girl. She was a young mother, only twenty-three, and Silly Sally was her whole world. Her parents wanted her to give up the baby. The father claimed—still claims—she is not his. Victoria would not listen. That little baby growing inside her was her miracle. It was her future, and she would do anything for it.

She pushed the bedroom door open. She always kept it cracked, and she saw Silly Sally on the ground near the window. Her first thought was that her daughter had been up late playing and fell asleep on the floor. It would not have been the first time Silly Sally had been up after bedtime, playing quietly so as not to get into trouble.

Victoria crossed the room to pick up her little girl, but it felt wrong. There was an emptiness in the room, a lack of life. Silly Sally's room was always full of energy, even when she was sleeping. She reached out to touch her daughter's shoulder. It was cold, and her body was motionless. She turned her daughter over and screamed. Her daughter's face was contorted into a silent scream. Her eyes were huge, haunted. There was no life left in that precious little body.

Neighbors heard the screams and called the sheriff's office. Five minutes later, Deputy Adams pulled up and forced his way into Victoria's home. He found her holding her daughter, rocking back and forth, screaming. He tried to comfort the young mother, tried to check on the child. It was lifeless. He radioed into the station and asked Nick, the night dispatcher, to send the sheriff. He put his arm around Victoria and let her scream. He wanted to scream.

*****

Dee woke to her phone buzzing. It was the station. "This is the sheriff."

"Sheriff, can you get over to Victoria Simpson's? Deputy Adams is there. He asked me to call you."

"What is it? Domestic?"

"No. Something happened to her daughter. Sheriff, Dylan says she's dead."

Dee said she would head right over and asked Nick to call the coroner. She gave Jack a quick goodbye as she dressed and prepared herself for another dead child.

Upon arrival, she found the door to the Simpson house damaged, open. She entered cautiously and called for Deputy Adams.

"Back here, Sheriff," Deputy Adams called. Dee went toward the sound of his voice. In what Dee presumed to be the daughter's room, Victoria was rocking her lifeless daughter, sobbing. Deputy Adams had his arm around her shoulder. Dee motioned for the deputy to move away as she leaned down to look at the child.

"Ms. Simpson, I'm Sheriff Halley. I need to look at your daughter." Victoria did not notice the sheriff. She did not respond. Dee looked at Deputy Adams. "Can you go outside and wait for the coroner? Let me know when he gets here?" He nodded and followed orders.

Dee put her hand on Victoria's shoulder and shook her slightly. "Victoria?" She shook her again. "Victoria? Victoria, I need you to let go. I have to look at your daughter. At Sally." The mention of her daughter's name seemed to snap her back into reality. New tears formed.

"Sheriff, please help her." It broke Dee's heart to hear this young mother pleading. Victoria gently handed her daughter over. Dee took her as gently as she could and laid her on the ground. She was so small. Dee brushed Sally's hair out of her face. She immediately wished she hadn't.

Deputy Adams walked in with the coroner and two paramedics. Dee focused her attention back on Victoria. "We need to get out of the way. Let them work." Victoria rose to her feet with Dee's help, and Dee escorted her out of the room. The pair sat on the couch. Dee tried to question her and failed. Victoria was in no condition to answer questions. It would have to wait.

The paramedics placed Sally's lifeless body in a body bag and rolled her out of the house. When Victoria saw the tiny bag containing her baby, the screams returned. Dee knew she would not be able to calm the mother, so she held her. She tried comforting words, but in the end, she just held the grieving woman.

Dee met with the paramedics and coroner outside for a few minutes while Deputy Adams sat with Victoria. The coroner left with the body, and the paramedics went back inside to evaluate Victoria. A few minutes later, they emerged with Victoria and took her to the hospital. The initial thought was shock, but a full workup should be done.

After thanking the paramedics, Dee radioed in for more deputies. Then to Deputy Adams, "Let's process the house. Focus on the child's room, back door, and windows." She looked at her watch. "Shit, you were off at least an hour ago. You can go home if you want, after you finish your report."

"No, I need to see this through."

Dee went back inside and looked at every entry point. The only thing amiss seemed to be the front door. Deputy Adams said he had to kick it in. It had been locked as well. The other deputies arrived, and Dee sent them to talk to the neighbors.

"Ask about overnight, the past few days to a week. Did anyone see anything out of the ordinary? Did they hear anything? Let's get an idea of what a typical day or week looks like in this neighborhood." The deputies did as they were told, and Dee walked the exterior of the house.

Dee did not find any evidence of disturbance around the house. She focused most of her attention around the child's room. She found what appeared to be animal tracks near the window. She could not identify them. She photographed them and would look them up later. She went back inside to help Deputy Adams finish up.

"Anything of note?"

"Nothing, Sheriff. Windows and doors all locked from the inside. I dusted the front door even though it was locked when I arrived. The house is clean. Nothing looks disturbed. I guess we could ask Ms. Simpson when she's feeling better."

"Okay, let's seal it up and head back to the station."

*****

On her way back from the house, Dee texted Jack. She wanted to see if he was free later. She needed her best friend. Jack was at the café. He would be available when she was. As she drove up to the station, she saw Ray Dobbins's Mercedes parked nearby.

"Not today," Dee said to herself. Then she called in and asked if he was in there waiting for her. Nick said Ray Dobbins was, that he had already been there an hour. "Tell him you just spoke with me. I'm three hours out, dealing with a case." Dee watched from around the corner as an agitated Ray Dobbins went to his car and drove off. Dee let out a sigh of relief. She waited a few minutes before going in, in case he doubled back.

She said hello to Nick and asked if she was needed anywhere. He told her that other than the Simpson call, the phones had been quiet. "Good. Thanks, Nick."

Dee went to Deputy Adams's desk and asked him to join her in her office. After they settled in their seats, Dee said, "That was a tough one. Kids always are, but that one was worse." She tried to read the deputy's face. He was trying to hold it together. It was part of the job. "Let's just go through what you did and saw before I arrived."

Deputy Adams walked her through everything he did and saw. When he described Sally, his voice cracked. Dee understood. She wanted to cry. She was waiting until later for that release.

"Thanks, Dylan. You did good. Comforting Ms. Simpson was the right thing to do." Dee paused for a moment, thought about how that young mother's life had and would change. "Do you need a couple of days? We can cover."

"Nah. I'm off tomorrow anyways. Honestly, I'd rather be here than home alone." Dee dismissed him and told him to get some sleep. She knew sleep would be hard for all of them.

Dee finished her report and sent a quick text to Jack. He could meet her at his place in ten. Perfect. On her way out, she told Nick not to bother her unless absolutely necessary. Have the deputies out canvasing leave their reports on her desk. She hoped it would be a typical Sunday evening and night, not a lot going on.

At Jack's, she put on his old sweats and snuggled up with Ralph. This was just what she needed, both of her best friends. She told Jack about little Sally. Her mom had called her Silly Sally. Dee did not know how or why she knew that, but she did. She cried a little, more when she said the child's nickname. She was not worried about judgment here. Jack never judged her.

Jack made dinner, and Dee ate, but only because she knew she had to. She did not feel like eating. She just wanted this day to be over.

*****

Dee must have drifted off because the buzzing of her phone woke her. It was the station, and it was Monday morning. "This is the sheriff."

"Deputy Collins is asking for you. He says it's more vandalism, like last week." It was Dawn. She sounded a little flustered.

"Where?"

"A couple of buildings downtown."

Dee let Dawn know she was on her way. She looked at Jack, somehow still sleeping soundly. She wished she could stay. Ralph licked her hand. He probably needed to go out. Vandalism could wait. She let Ralph outside so he could do his business. When he was done, they came back into the house, and Dee grabbed his dish. Jack had woken and said he would finish up. Dee kissed him and left for work. As she drove away, she wished she had Jack and Ralph with her. The three of them could just keep driving.

That was a different life than the one she chose. She chose to stay in this town, to protect these people. This was her life, and her deputy was waiting.

Chapter 5

Dee parked at the station and walked across the park to meet with Deputy Collins. She found him in front of one of the empty storefronts with several people, one of which was the property owner.

"Morning, gentlemen."

"Sheriff," Ronald Blackwell greeted Dee and shook her hand.

"Mind if I steal my deputy, get a quick rundown?" Dee and Deputy Collins walked around to the back of the building where a door was ajar. There was damage to the frame and lock, not unusual for an empty building. Deputy Collins pointed at some graffiti on the exterior walls. It was of the usual variety.

"It's inside, Sheriff. I saw the broken lock and investigated." He led the sheriff inside and used his flashlight to show the large menacing red eyes on the wall. Dee used her own flashlight to look around and found a light switch. She switched it on. The overhead lights came on, and several roaches and rats scurried away to new hiding places out of the brightness. "Sorry, Sheriff."

"Don't be. A lot of these buildings don't have power running to them anymore. I just got lucky." The pair continued to look around the mostly empty building for any other unusual graffiti. Dee found a cluster of symbols like the ones from the warehouse and had Deputy Collins photograph them. In what used to be an office, they found more symbols etched into the desk. The deputy photographed them as well.

"What do you think, Sheriff? I don't think this is kids just goofing."

"I don't know, Matt. It's similar to last week. I don't know what it means yet." They finished looking around and went out to talk with the owner. Dee suggested Mr. Blackwell get the door fixed sooner rather than later, and a couple of cameras couldn't hurt. He was not excited about either suggestion. He complained he was losing money on these buildings every day.

"Cameras are a good deterrent. Could keep repair costs down." She shook his hand and asked the deputy to show her what else he had found. He led her to another shop a few doors down. There was no break-in, and the eyes were right on the door. Black outline, blood red centers, exactly the same.

"I'm assuming you photographed these too?" Deputy Collins said he did.

"I spent time looking all around this area. I didn't find anything else. The other shops are clear."

"Good work. I'll just take a quick look for myself. Another set of eyes can't hurt." They both looked at each other. "Poor choice of words." Dee looked at the exterior of the remaining shops, and nothing looked out of place. She concluded her deputy had in fact done a good job and told him so. "I'm going to head to the station. I'll see you there when you're finished."

At the station, Dee looked over the reports from the neighborhood canvas from the day before. It appeared to be a quiet neighborhood, mostly families with normal routines. Nothing jumped out. She would have to speak to her deputies and see if they noticed anything *not* in the reports. Luckily, Collins was one of them and would be back soon.

While she waited, she texted Jack to see what he was up to and a quick text to Jim to see how the kids were. Jim said his kids were doing about the same. They were looking out for each other, and they were keeping their blinds and windows closed. The boys had started sleeping in the same room. They moved Alex's bed into Chris's room. Jack was at the diner and wanted to bring Dee lunch. She asked for a burger and onion rings.

Deputy Collins returned, and Dee asked that he join her in her office. "Get everything wrapped up across the way?"

"Yes, Sheriff. It's all good. Just need to write it up."

"Great." Dee took a drink of water. "Yesterday, I read over the reports. Did you notice anything *not* in the reports? Maybe something subtle, a twitch or a look? Just something off?"

The deputy thought about it for a few moments. "Yeah, maybe. I'm not sure. The neighbor, I think she's the gossip of the street. In everyone's business, peeking through the blinds. You know the type."

"Yeah. Seems every street has one. What stood out with this one? What's her name?"

"Gloria. Gloria Miller. She was very helpful. Too helpful. Gave a lot of details until I asked about the night before. She said she didn't see anything. I think she was holding back now. At the time, I heard so many people say they hadn't seen or heard anything, I didn't think anything of it." The deputy looked at her. "Did I miss something, Sheriff? Something that could help?"

"I'm not sure, Matt. It's good you remembered it at all. I'll go back and interview her again. You want to come along?" He said he would, and Dee said they would go after lunch.

As Deputy Collins left her office, Jack walked in with lunch. "Hey, Matt. I left yours on your desk. Hope you don't mind cheeseburger and fries."

"Thanks, Jack. I'm starving."

"You trying to score points with my staff?"

"It's never bad to have cops and deputies in your corner." He winked at her and thought back to his time on the job. Eating a meal was rare. Typically, you inhaled whatever was in front of you and went back out. In retirement, he tried to help as he could, and bringing food was one way. Jack set their lunch down on Dee's desk. As they ate, Dee described the new instances of vandalism and showed him digital pictures that Deputy Collins had taken.

"Similar to the others, but doesn't feel like kids. It's not gang. I'm not sure what to make of it." She paused then, "I have something else to show. I took these outside the girl's room." She showed him the pictures of the "animal" tracks. "Do you recognize them? I'm pretty good with tracks. I can't place these."

Jack studied the pictures. The tracks showed four toes with long claws spread wide. "Were these the only ones? Did you see a trail?"

"Just those two. I'm headed back there after lunch. I'll look around some more." Dee gave Jack another moment to look at the pictures. "So? Any ideas?"

"No. It's familiar, but I don't know what it is."

"Guess we could google image it." She immediately did. "Found a cool identify animal tracks site. Rat or mouse looks close, but not large enough."

"I doubt we're looking for a six-foot-tall rat. We'll have to keep searching."

Dee rolled her eyes at him. "Okay, pack it up. Time to go. Some of us have work to do."

"Yeah, yeah. I'm going," Jack played along. "See you tonight? What do you want for dinner?"

"Surprise me." This was Dee's typical response, but Jack did not mind. He enjoyed cooking. He enjoyed surprising her. He enjoyed her.

"Let me know when you have an idea of what time you'll be over." With that, Jack left. No hugs or kisses. Not here. Dee smiled at him as he left. Then she called for Deputy Collins to come in.

"You ready? To interview that witness?"

"Yeah, Sheriff. Let's go."

"Great. I'll meet you there." On the way out, Dee stopped by dispatch and asked Dawn if she needed anything. She did not. She asked if she was coming back after. Dee said she would let her know, but she was always available on her cell.

Gloria Miller met them on her front steps. She saw them drive up. She was already talking. "Good afternoon, Sheriff, Deputy. Are you back about that Simpson girl? Such a tragedy." She only paused to take a drag off her cigarette.

Dee grabbed the opportunity. "Yes, in fact, we have a few more questions. If you don't mind."

"Sure, sure. Whatever you need. I know this neighborhood, just like I told your deputy yesterday. Come on over and have a seat." She gestured toward her front porch chairs.

"Mrs. Miller," Dee started.

"Dear, you call me Gloria. I ain't never been a missus."

"Okay, Gloria. We're trying to establish a timeline. Anything you can tell us will be useful. Do you know what time the Simpsons went to bed?"

"Sally's light went off around nine, but there were other lights on in that house until well after eleven. I only know this because I go to bed early, and if there's even one light shining in my room, I can't sleep."

"That's very helpful. Thank you. At any time last night, did you look out your window? Toward their house?"

"Well, yes. The light was on. It was shining in my room. I wanted to see what light."

"Good. What did you see? When you looked for the light?"

Gloria Miller paused and took a quick read of the sheriff's face. "Nothing. Just the light."

"Have you noticed any animals, wild or stray, lately? I found some tracks outside Sally's window." Dee was hoping this questioning would lead to Gloria elaborating and sharing what she saw. Dee knew she had seen something.

"I thought I saw a coyote, maybe. But it was standing on its back legs. Just outside Sally's window." Gloria looked at the sheriff again, then the deputy. "But that can't be. My eyes ain't what they used to be. It was probably a shadow."

"I'm going to take another look. See if I can find some coyote tracks. Gloria, have you noticed anything out of the ordinary during the past few days?"

"No, and I would know. I'm retired. I'm always here. It's just so sad. That little girl was so cute. Sheriff, nothing like this has ever happened on this street. And I don't want to speak out of turn, but, have you looked at the mother? She has men over, different men. Not a good environment for a little girl."

"Thank you, Gloria. We are looking at every piece of evidence, following every lead. I'm sure we'll resolve this timely," Dee lied. She knew something like this could take months, years even. "Here's my card. You call if you think of anything else." Dee shook her hand, and she and Deputy Collins left.

As Dee and Deputy Collins walked toward their cars, Dee asked him to follow her. They went to the Simpson house. "There was no forced entry. Doors and windows were all locked from the inside, but I still want to have a thorough look at the exterior. Look for anything that doesn't belong."

The pair walked around the house, stepping carefully, looking closely. They found nothing. The tracks from the prior day were gone. It did not look like even a branch of a tree had been disturbed.

"Weird," Dee said, not realizing she had spoken.

"What?"

"Nothing. I just thought we would see something. I think we're done here. You can head on back to the station."

"You told Ms. Miller you found animal tracks. I don't see any signs of an animal. What was that about?"

"I was just giving her an option. Something to claim she had seen. We both knew she was holding back. I was giving her a way to tell us what she was holding."

"Oh, good thinking. I have a lot to learn. See ya tomorrow, Sheriff."

"Bye, Matt." Dee gave the exterior another walk and still came up empty. She texted Jack she was done for the day. He said that he and Ralph were waiting. She went by her house and grabbed some clothes. She planned on staying for at least a few days. Dee did not want to be alone. Jack's house felt more like home.

*****

Dee walked into Jack's, bag in hand, and greeted Ralph, who was wagging his whole body and spinning. She set her bag down to give Ralph the attention he required. Jack heard her come in and came to greet her.

"Moving in?" Jack asked, pointing at her bag.

"I thought it would be easier, having some things here. I'm here all the time anyway. Ralph says it's okay."

"Well, if Ralph says it's okay, it's okay." He picked up her bag and took it to his room, hoping it would become their room. "We still have about thirty till dinner," he called.

"Sounds good. I'm gonna take this guy out back. Throw the ball or something." At the word *ball*, Ralph started spinning again. Ball it was. She took him out back and threw the ball several times before Jack joined them.

"Find anything new? At the house?"

"Nope." Dee looked away. She had started to think she imagined the tracks. The pictures proved they were there, but where were they now? Dee let out an audible sigh. "I don't know, Jack. I don't know what's going on. I know Victoria didn't kill her daughter. But there was no signs of forced entry, or any entry. And how did she die? What was the cause? I hope we know more after the autopsy."

"You know what I know?"

Dee looked up at him. "What?"

"I know you'll figure it out. I know that if it were my kid, I would want you on the case. I know you're the best police I've ever met. I know that you are the smartest person I've ever met." Jack put her hands in his. "I know you're the best person I've ever known. You've got this, and I can help. Whatever you need."

Dee knew she loved this man. She had loved him her whole life. He was definitely the best at giving pep talks. "Thanks, Jack. That all means the world coming from you."

The two ate dinner, some clever pasta creation, quietly. Ralph lay nearby, in case there were treats to be had. After dinner was cleaned up, they sat around the firepit outside.

"No marshmallows?" Dee joked.

"Not tonight." As they sat around the fire, Dee realized she was not afraid of the night. Not like the kids. She only felt fear for those kids.

"Jack?"

"Yes?"

"We have to talk to Charlie. He's one of us. He needs to be included. I know we said Jim would set it up, but I think you should. Tomorrow."

"What happened today, Dee? You're different. You brought the bag. Not that I'm complaining. I just want to be looped in. I need to know what's happening."

"The tracks were gone, Jack. Like they were never there. I don't know how that happened. The area was taped off. I can't imagine a person would erase, for lack of a better term, them. And Gloria Miller said she saw a coyote standing on its hind legs outside the girl's window. I'm not sure what it means. I just think the four of us can make sense of it. We've done it before."

"I'll text him now, set up a time. Then we'll tell Jim." With arrangements made, the two spent most of the night in silence. The air felt different, heavier. Dee used the time to prepare herself for the days to come. She knew they would be hard. Five years ago, she was not the sheriff. She had less responsibility with those cases. This time, it was all on her. The weight on her shoulders was substantial. She did not want to let anyone down. She did not want one more dead kid on her watch.

Chapter 6

Dee woke early after a mostly sleepless night and checked her phone. Nothing emergent. She decided to go for a run and clear her head. Jack was getting ready to go to the café. She opted for Ralph to be her running partner. When she grabbed his leash, Ralph started spinning and jumping. He loved going places, for a walk, a run, a car ride. It was all exciting for him.

They ran through town and down by the river, Ralph wanted to go in. Dee told him another time. Without realizing it, Dee had steered them toward Jim's street. She saw the Stevens boys and waved at them. They were waiting in front of their house, Dee presumed, for friends. She stopped to say good morning, and the boys loved on the dog. He rolled around in the grass and showed off his tummy. The boys were delighted. Ralph was always the star of the show. Abigail and Steve came over and made Ralph's day. The four of them took turns petting and praising Ralph.

Dee chatted with the kids for a few minutes then told them to have a good day at school and shooed them off. She looked at the Stevens house and saw Mary watching from the kitchen window. Perfect. Dee and Mary did not get along. She thought she might have to be polite and talk to her. As she raised her hand to wave, Mary closed the curtain. Dee waited a few moments to see if the front door would open. It did not. Relieved, Dee continued her run.

They ran through a few neighborhoods then downtown to the café. Dee popped her head in and asked Susie for a bagel and some water for her and the dog. She said she would be sitting outside with Ralph.

"Oh, and let Jack know I'm here, please."

Susie said she would, and Dee sat at one of the outside tables. Susie emerged moments later with a bowl of water for Ralph and a bottle for Dee.

"Your bagel will be right out."

"Thanks, Suze. Busy morning?"

"No, just the regulars. Tug and Bob have been here since we opened, and we had a few people get some coffee to go." Susie turned to walk back in. "Jack said he'd be out in a few minutes."

Dee thanked her again and drank some water. Ralph was already ahead of her, slopping his water all over the ground. He would need another bowl before they left. Jack came out with a bagel, two cups of coffee, and more water for Ralph. "I figured he'd make a mess out the first bowl."

They both laughed, and Ralph greeted his dad by rubbing his body on Jack's leg. "You guys have a good run?"

"Yeah. We ended up at the Stevens house, saw the kids. They made Ralph's day." Dee took a sip of her coffee. "Saw Mary. She closed the curtain when she noticed I saw her. What a bitch."

"It's a shame. Jim deserves better."

Dee ate her bagel and confirmed their one o'clock meeting with the guys. Then she and Ralph headed home. To Ralph's home. Deputy Collins drove by while they were walking and offered them a ride. Dee passed. The cool air was doing her some good. She let him know she would be at the station within the hour.

*****

Chris was happy to see Dee this morning outside of his house. He liked her checking in on them. To him, it meant that she either believed his story, or she cared enough to pretend like she did. He hoped she believed at least part of it. He was sure she did. The rest of the group expressed their delight in seeing her as well.

"She's cool, for an old chick." High praise coming from Steve.

"She's cool, for any chick," Abigail retorted. She looked ahead as the group walked to school. "Is that Billy?" She pointed at what looked like Billy, his head was down, shoulders slumped.

"Yeah, I think so," Chris agreed. "Billy!" he yelled while picking up the pace. He was at a jog before catching him. "Billy?" He grabbed his arm and turned him around. The others had caught up. Billy had dark circles under his vacant eyes, and he was more pale than usual.

"Shit, kid. You look awful." Steve was always ready to make people feel their best.

Abigail hugged him. "Billy, what's wrong?"

Billy looked up but did not meet her eyes. "Nothing." Billy continued walking.

"We should walk with him. Maybe tell the nurse at his school," Chris suggested, and the others agreed. They walked the remaining three blocks in silence. When they arrived at Billy's school, Chris walked him to the nurse. After answering questions about who he was and why he brought Billy in, the nurse said she would look after him and call his parents if needed. Chris thanked her and said good-bye to Billy.

He returned to his friends and did not offer any hope. They all knew Billy's parents were not capable of caring for the boy. He texted his dad and then Dee. He hoped they could help. The four walked to their school and found Brian waiting for them. Chris let him know that Billy was back at school but did not elaborate. Brian was their friend, but they were not close. Not like the rest of the group.

The group finished their school day and met at their bench. Billy did not show. They split up in pairs to look for him. Chris and Abigail went toward Billy's old house. Steve and Alex went toward his current house. Text messages confirmed no sign of Billy anywhere.

Chris suggested to Abigail that they go inside the house and have a look around. After a little persuasion, she agreed. The doors were locked, but they found a broken window and climbed through it. There was no electricity, and some of the house was dark. The air was heavy. It smelled like mildew and rotting flesh. The only signs of life were dusty cobwebs. Abigail suggested they look around quickly and get the hell out. Chris agreed. It was the worst place he had ever been. They went to Billy's old room, then to Tom's.

"Do you hear that?" Chris asked. There was a quiet low voice.

"No, what? Is someone coming?"

"No, I guess it's nothing." Chris looked around at the empty house. "Let's get outta here. There's nothing to find. Billy isn't here." Relieved, Abigail agreed. She had not heard a noise. She had felt something pulling at her, deep in her head. It was so strange. She could not describe it.

"Should we meet up with the guys?"

"Yeah, I'll text them to go to my house. No one should be home yet." Chris texted the guys while he and Abigail started toward his house.

"Did you hear back from Dee or your dad? About Billy?"

"Dee thanked me. She said she would follow up with the school. Dad said he'd call Billy's mom again."

"I'm sure his mom rushed right over to check on her precious son." Abigail's sarcasm and anger were warranted. Chris agreed with her.

Alex and Steve beat Chris and Abigail to the house. They were waiting on the back porch. Chris and Abigail recounted their experience in Billy's old house, and Steve made a joke about the pair on those two.

"Bigger than yours," Abigail joked. They all laughed. They needed it. They spent the afternoon speculating about Billy, where he was, what was wrong with him, and most importantly, how they could help him. Mary arrived home around five and sent Abigail and Steve home. Everyone agreed to text or call later. They all shared a look before the two left. They were preparing for another night. Another night that may end their mornings.

*****

On her way to the station, Dee received a disturbing text from Chris about Billy. She let him know she would help and changed direction toward the school. She called Dawn and let her know she was headed to the elementary school, but she was available on her cell. Dee did not think she would get far at the school, but maybe she could get a look at Billy.

Dee stopped by the administration office to let them know she was on their grounds. She assured everyone there was no need for alarm. She was there on more personal reasons. She explained she was a friend of the family and was asked to check in. That was mostly true. She never specified which family. She went to the nurse's office and saw what she assumed was Billy sitting in a chair. His head was down, shoulders slumped, and although she could not see his face clearly, he looked pale to her. Dee introduced herself to the nurse and asked if his parents had been called. Before the nurse could answer, Gabrielle Johnson walked in.

"Mrs. Johnson, I'm glad you're here." Dee put her hand out. Gabrielle focused her attention on the nurse.

"What seems to be the issue? He was fine for school this morning."

The nurse tried to explain that Billy was mostly unresponsive and thought he should be seen by a doctor. Gabrielle barely listened, told the nurse she knew what was best for her child, grabbed Billy, and left. Dee followed her out and called after her a few times.

Gabrielle stopped, turned, and gave Dee a hard look. Dee had seen this look before. Angry parent who thinks they are being accused of bad parenting. "As I told that nurse, I will handle my child." She turned, grabbed Billy's arm, and started walking.

"I just want to help. Take my card. Call if you need anything." Dee put her card out, and Gabrielle snatched it from her hand then continued walking. Dee doubted she would ever hear from that woman. Her phone buzzed. It was the station. "This is the sheriff."

"Hey, Sheriff. Ray Dobbins is here again. I wasn't sure how long you were going to be gone." Another reason Dee liked Dawn. She was really good at giving a heads-up.

"Let him know I'm going to be awhile, probably hours. And, Dawn, has the hospital called back? About Ms. Simpson? I asked them to call when she was more responsive, able to answer questions."

"No, Sheriff. Do you want me to call them?"

"No, thanks. I'll just give them a call. It could keep me away from the office for a bit." Dee hung up to giggles from Dawn. The hospital informed Dee that Ms. Simpson was on a psych hold, seventy-two hours. The doctor did not think she would or even could be helpful at this point. She thanked the doctor for his help. She sat in her truck in the school parking lot and tried to think of her next move. She thought about texting Chris to let him know about Billy, but she did not have any helpful information for him.

The station it was. She could hope for a call en route. She drove slowly the few blocks and scoped out the streets for Ray Dobbins's Mercedes. With it nowhere in sight, she parked on a side street next to the station. She greeted Dawn and saw Deputy Collins and Deputy Adams talking near Adams's desk.

"What's up, guys? Something I need to know?" Dee asked as she approached them.

The men exchanged a glance, then Deputy Adams spoke. "We were comparing notes. Matt was telling me about the vandalism. Strange stuff. I was thinking maybe it was related to the Simpson case somehow." He waited for a response from Dee. She gave him the continue nod. "I was thinking it's odd we get these weird vandalism calls, and the Simpson girl. That was strange too. What do you think, Sheriff?"

"I think it's a little early to connect the two," Dee lied. She had connected them immediately. "We have more investigating to do. We did not see any of the symbols at the Simpson house, but if you two want to go back and look, I'm okay with it. Ms. Simpson is still on a hold at the hospital. I doubt she'll go back to that house when she's released. I probably wouldn't."

The deputies exchanged another look. Then Matt spoke. "We could go right now. Really look the place over." Dee loved his enthusiasm. She wished them luck, and the two left. She did not think they would return with anything, but if it made them feel useful, that was at least something.

She went to her office, looked at her messages and her paperwork, and decided not to deal with those. Instead, she went on her computer to look up the images from the two vandalism scenes. A website for a local tribe seemed very promising. She started clicking on links and found herself down a rabbit hole. Luckily, her phone buzzed before she got too lost. The internet is a funny place. Often you find more information than you need, much of which is not related to your original search.

It was Jack asking about lunch before they met up with the guys. She looked at the time. Almost noon. She replied she would be there in a few minutes. She let Dawn know she was headed out for a few hours. Then she walked to the café.

Jack was waiting at an outside table for her. "I thought we could eat out here."

"Sure. It's unseasonably warm today. We have to take advantage." Dee hugged him when he stood. Then they both sat. "What's on the menu today?"

"Pastrami? It sounded good to me." Dee agreed. He asked about her morning. She explained about Billy, her call to the hospital, and the wild-goose chase she sent her deputies on. "Feeling useful is helpful when dealing with a case like this. I bet they're happy to be doing something."

"Agreed. I was glad they went." She paused for a moment. "I lied to them Jack. Lied. I told them there wasn't a link between the two, but I know there is. My gut knows. There's no evidence."

"You didn't lie. You just encouraged them to investigate more. We both know gut instinct isn't admissible." Jack was right. She just did not like misleading her deputies in any way. She also knew it was the right thing to do.

Ben brought out their lunch. Dee had a bag of Cheetos on her plate. She smiled at Jack. He knew her comfort foods. He smirked back at her, and the two ate their lunch. "Ralph seemed to enjoy his morning with you."

"You know he loves me. And he loves going anywhere." She looked at Jack and smiled. "I enjoyed it too. It's been too long since I've had a decent running buddy."

"I'm sure he would be agreeable to making it a more frequent occurrence."

"I'm sure he would." Dee looked at her watch. "It's a quarter till. Want to start meandering over?"

"Sure. I'm going to let Ben know I'm leaving. Be right back." He took their plates and trash with him. He returned moments later, and the pair walked across the street to the park. They went to the spot where they met with Jim and the kids and waited for their friends.

"I forgot to ask. What did you tell Charlie to get him to come here alone?"

"I told him I wanted to talk about you. I knew he wouldn't bring Jill to talk about you. Although he doesn't say it out loud, he knows Jill hates you."

Dee was a little embarrassed to be used as the excuse. "Smart thinking. It's sad how bad our friends did at picking spouses." She thought for a second then joked, "Do you think Mary and Jill are best friends? Their personalities are similar."

Jack chuckled. "That's not nice. We should probably stop talking about them. We don't want them to overhear." Dee agreed. She felt a little bad, but only a little.

"Speaking of, there's Jim." Dee pointed across the park. Jim spotted them and waved. He hugged Dee when he arrived and shook Jack's hand.

The three kept their conversation light while they waited for Charlie. Jack noticed Charlie first, arriving from the other end of the park, from the direction of the mayor's office. "An ambush, I see," Charlie half joked.

"Nah. Just wanted to get the band back together," Jack retorted. He shook his friend's hand, then Jim shook it. Dee waited for last to hug her friend.

"We miss you, Charlie. It's been too long." Dee meant it. After the obligatory questions and answers of "how's the family? The job?" and, of course, comments about the weather, Charlie dug in.

"Why am I here? It's obviously not to discuss Dee with Jack."

Dee joked that she could hire Charlie as a detective then asked Jim to start. Jim carefully went over his part of the story, about his boys and their friends, and about what he saw five years ago. Then Dee filled in with her story, the vandalism, the deceased child, and Billy this morning. Jack offered only a little about the research he had conducted so far.

Charlie listened, at times looked skeptical, and at many times looked like he was the butt of the joke. Charlie loved these guys.

They had been close since he moved here as a child. He trusted them, but he was also a logical man. "We've eliminated six-foot-tall rats. That's basically all we know?"

Dee sighed audibly, Jack shook his head, and Jim looked like he was getting angry.

"Charlie, I know this all sounds crazy or far-fetched," Dee tried to reason with him. "But we can't ignore it. There is something terrible happening. We need to figure it out. We need to stop it."

"Are your boys really sleeping in the same room, at their ages?"

"Yes. And I've thought of moving in there too. To keep them safe." Jim was serious. Dee thought the only thing holding him back was Mary. She would never understand this.

"Okay, so what do we do? Where do we start? How can I help?" This was the Charlie they loved. He always dives in headfirst, ready to conquer the world, to help his friends. Fierce loyalty. They all had it in common.

"Jack has been researching the symbols. Jim is, well, keeping the kids safe. I've got my deputies trying to link the cases. They think it's their idea," Dee started. "I'm also looking through old case files, looking for patterns."

"What if we meet when we have more information, lay it all out, and see where the pieces fit?" Jack was the puzzle solver of the group. The group agreed. Charlie had to get back to his office and said goodbye to them.

Jim said he needed to go as well. Dee stopped him. "Can you tell Chris that I tried with Billy this morning? I didn't want to text him about it because I don't think I did anything. Except piss Gabrielle off." Jim said he would explain it to his boys then left. To Jack, Dee asked, "So what do you think? Think he believes? Or wants to?"

"I think you and Jim are all in. You two probably think it's supernatural. I think Charlie wants to help. It's what he does." The part about her stung a bit, but she understood. "As for me, I just want to solve it. And I want to help you."

"I don't need you to be all in. I need your skepticism, especially with Jim. Just keep an open mind, and I will too." Dee meant it. She needed Jack to keep her grounded and to avoid tunnel vision.

Jack walked Dee across the street to the station and said he would see her later at home. Dee said she couldn't wait and hugged Jack before he left.

Chapter 7

A familiar noise woke Steve from a deep sleep. It took him a moment to adjust his eyes to the darkness of his room and to fully wake. He looked around his room. His door was still closed. Nothing looked amiss. He looked toward the window, closed, blinds down, just as Chris had told him. He looked toward his closet and immediately dismissed closet monsters. That was little kid stuff.

(Scratch, scratch)

His head whipped back to the window. The noise. He tried to swallow and found his mouth and throat dry.

(Scratch, scratch)

The hairs on the back of his neck were at full attention. He felt goose bumps on his arms. He tried holding his breath, like somehow that would deter whatever was at his window.

(Scratch, scratch)

No luck. He thought momentarily about hiding under his covers. Again, that was kid stuff. Little kid stuff. His next thought was to find a weapon. He was not sure what would work against the thing at the window.

(Tap, tap)

"Shit, that thing must know I'm awake," Steve thought. Or may have even said out loud. He was not sure. He looked toward the window. There was a red glow. He immediately looked away. He thought about where he could go in the house, somewhere without windows.

(Scratch, scratch, tap, tap)

Hallway bathroom! He grabbed his phone and the baseball bat next to his door then flew down the hallway to the bathroom. The whole time, eyes focused on the ground. His heart was racing. He did not dare look up. Looking up meant…he did not know what it meant, but he sure as shit was not going to find out. He made it to the bathroom and shut and locked the door behind him. Steve was not taking any chances.

He flipped the light on and sat on the floor. He was shivering, wishing he had brought a blanket, or at least a sweatshirt. He was not going back, not until morning. He looked at his phone. It was just after one in the morning. He thought he had around five hours until sunup. Guess that's why they invented apps for phones. Games to kill time.

A tapping at the door woke him. He must have drifted off. He looked at his phone. Dead. He had no way of knowing what time it was. "Yeah?"

"Steve, it's Mom. Are you okay?"

Steve let out an audible sigh of relief. "Yeah. What time is it?"

"Quarter after six. Are you feeling all right? Do I need to call the doctor? Maybe you need the day off?"

"No, Mom, I'm fine. I'll be right out." Steve stood and looked at himself in the mirror. He could not be sure, but he thought he looked older somehow. He exited the bathroom, pushing his mom away. He needed his phone charger. He needed his friends.

Steve returned to his room. He immediately made plans to improve it. He was going to need wood, nails, and whatever that foam was they used in recording studios. He was going to need a lot for him, his friends, and any kid that would listen. He plugged his phone in and waited for it to be useable. His first text was to Chris. "We need a shitload of wood, nails, and that foam they use in music studios. We need it yesterday." For the first time, Steve thought he was being proactive. For the first time, Steve believed Chris. "And duct tape. A lot of duct tape."

*****

Wednesday morning started out busy for many in Eggers Cove. A few teenagers woke to a call-to-arms text messages from a friend. Parents of those teenagers woke to their kids with a newfound rush to get to school. A morning dispatcher found herself overwhelmed with calls. Several buildings had been vandalized overnight, and there was a major traffic collision just outside town.

Some self-proclaimed morning people were uncharacteristically slow and behind, incapable of finding their normal spunk. The pot of coffee to wake a crowd needed a pot and a half. Many children were lethargic from disrupted sleep.

Dee was tying her running shoes when her phone buzzed. It was Jim. Steve had been "visited" early this morning. He was at Jim's house, and the kids were planning. Before she could respond, her phone was ringing. It was the station.

"This is the sheriff."

"Sorry to bother you, Sheriff, but it's crazy here. There's a TC. Several buildings were vandalized. Can you come in early?" Dawn was more frazzled than usual.

"Be right there." Dee told Jack about the text from Jim and asked if he could run over there. He said he would and texted Jim. "Maybe take Ralph? The kids really love him." Dee kissed him and ran out the door, grateful it was not another dead child.

Police radio chatter indicated Adams was at the TC, and Hagen had an ETA of three minutes. Collins was at vandalism one. Dee knew Adams could handle the TC, and Hagen might learn something. Collins would ask if he needed help. With no need for her in the field, she headed to the station to help Dawn.

Jack pulled up to Jim's house as Mary was leaving. He waved, and she pretended not to notice. He shook his head, sighed, and got out of his truck. Jim met him at the door and led him to four excited teenagers. They were excited about their plan, excited to see Ralph, excited to be missing a day of school. Jim told his boys they could take today off. He did not check with the other parents. Jack thought the idea of boarding up bedroom windows and using soundproofing foam seemed a little extreme, but he also knew the power of taking control of a situation, one where you feel powerless.

When Dee walked into the station, Dawn was taking a call for a suspected break-in at a store just two doors down from the station. Dee thought that was brazen, told Dawn she would take it. Before

Dee could think, "What else?", all three phone lines lit up. Guess that break-in would have to wait.

Ray Dobbins was sitting on his porch and documenting the cars on his street. He had been keeping records of the cars that parked on his street, where their passengers went, how long they stayed. He never thought this was how he would spend retirement, but somebody had to take control of this street. Statistics showed that more traffic could lead to more crime. He ignored the local statistics that did not support the nationals.

Jane Russel watched Ray Dobbins from her living room window, as she did most days. She was having a few of her friends over later for a midweek brunch, a new tradition. She had many new traditions. She knew it was childish, but she could not help herself. Ray Dobbins was an ass, worse than an ass. And if she could disrupt his day in any way, she was happy to do it.

Tug and Bob spent their morning in the café as usual but did not speak much. Susie was glad for the quiet. Normally, those two wouldn't shut the fuck up. She was having a hard day. She slept through her alarm and was late for work. She opened the café thirty minutes late, and she still had to tell Jack. She did not know why she was so tired today. Normally, she had a ton of energy in the morning.

Jill Wilks kissed Charlie goodbye and wondered what to do with herself today. She was lonely here and did not have any friends and did not work. Charlie had introduced her to his friends, but they did not mesh. He introduced her to colleagues' wives. Again, no luck. She had never had problems making friends as a child, but no one seemed to like her here. She missed her friends in the city, long lunches, brunches on Sundays, shopping. She looked out her front window and sighed. She was not cut out for small-town life.

Mary Stevens arrived at work late again. She was still angry with her husband for letting the boys stay home for no reason, inviting Jack over, and probably missing work himself. This was not the life she was promised. She should be a lady that lunches. She heard that on a television show once and thought it sounded fabulous. Instead, she was a lousy receptionist at a lousy doctor's office. She would never travel the world. She would never be wealthy. Her dreams would never come true. She was trapped in this life, trapped.

*****

Jack brought Dee lunch at the station after text messages explaining how busy her day was. He hoped to fill her in on the happenings at Jim's, but she barely had time to eat, let alone talk. It could wait. He understood the job. He decided to go back to the café and see if he could be useful there. Maybe do some more research.

Jim helped the kids board up their bedroom windows and taped soundproofing foam to the inside. He sent them off to do the same at their friends' houses, with express instructions that he did not send them. He did not want to get angry calls from parents. With any luck, they would not notice right away. He tried think about how often he went into his kids' rooms. Not often. He worried about Saturday yard work. That was the time discovery would most likely happen. But that was days away.

Billy did not go to school today either. He did not much care about school, his friends, any of the things that used to matter. He stayed in bed most days and barely ate. His mother did not bring him food, and he did not think to get any. He did not watch TV and did not read. Mostly, he tried to sleep. Sleep seemed right, good, what he needed. He did not know his friends were worried. He did not know why his friends would be worried. He thought maybe his friends had stopped by, but he may have imagined that. Getting out of bed was more than he could manage most times, and he wondered if he even cared.

Chris and Alex helped Abigail and Steve board and soundproof their windows. Chris said they had to do Billy's window too. At least the outside. He was still their responsibility. The foursome went to Billy's house, snuck around the back, and went to work. No one came outside, and no one sent them away. Chis thought they might be able to go inside as well. Abigail advised against it. If they got caught, the exterior protection would be taken down. They hoped the boards would be enough. It was all they had.

Dee barely had time to pee. She felt guilty that Jack had brought her lunch and she was only able to thank him and send him off. She knew he understood the job and the requirements, but she also felt like he was pulling all the weight in their relationship. However, she did not have time to think about that. The phones were still ringing nonstop. She had to call in her off-duty deputies to handle the volume. And she still had not heard if Adams and Collins found anything at the Simpson house. This was a Wednesday. What *the fuck* was going on? What the actual fuck? Friday night, Saturday night, those were busy. Middle of the week was always quiet. WTF?

Jill Wilks had decided to walk into town to shop. There were few shops left in Eggers Cove. Fewer that she would want to patronize. She had to do something, and she did love to shop. She found the shops sparse both in inventory and customers. She bought a trinket here, a knickknack there, and a kitchen towel. This day would be better with friends or acquaintances or anyone. She thought about lunching at the café but did not want to see Jack. Or eat alone. She was hungry, and it was only a block away.

Mary Stevens never, never, went out to lunch. She thought it was an unnecessary expenditure, and they did not have money to spare. But today, with her husband throwing caution to the wind and doing God knows what, she decided to treat herself. She had earned it. She worked, cleaned the house, and did the laundry, with little thanks. Today was about her. She would have her lunch, and she would tell Jim that she deserved it. Fuck him.

Mary and Jill reached the café at nearly the same time. Mary held the door for Jill and asked if she wanted to join her. She did not know why this impulse came. Maybe she did not want to eat alone. Maybe she wanted Jim to know that she had friends too. Maybe she was being polite. Jill thanked her for the invitation and agreed to sit with her.

Ray Dobbins noted the multiple vehicles parked near Jane Russel's house. He knew that bitch was messing with him. She enjoyed it. He knew that she wanted him miserable and alone. And tormented. He did not know why Jane Russel, that bitch, wished such misery on him, but it was clear to him that she did.

Jane Russel greeted her Wednesday brunch guests. They would call this "Hump Day Brunch" going forward. They all had agreed. None of the ladies worked, but they all needed to fill their days. And if Jane was willing to host several weekly events, it was the better for them. They would come to Wednesday brunch and book club, now meeting twice weekly, and any other event Jane or any other woman created. The truth was these women were lonely. They were desperate, and they did not mind being used. They were not stupid. They knew who Jane's neighbor was. They hated him too. Whatever their friend needed, and whatever they needed.

*****

Dee was wrapping up her day. She looked at the time. It was already after eight. She had not spoken to her deputies about the Simpson house. She had discussed today's calls with her deputies, and she felt they had put in a solid day's work. Adams and Collins volunteered to handle the night shift. She hoped they got some sleep between calls. She went home—well, to Jack's home—and was grateful for the dinner he had saved for her.

Jim had dinner with his family. Pizza tonight. That was rare. Mary always made dinner. No time to worry about that. His children's lives were at stake. Although, he could not help but notice Mary's dismissive attitude. If Jim was honest with himself, he really did not care what Mary thought or felt. He felt bad about this. It was his wife, but she was such a bitch.

Jill Wilks made dinner for her husband as she did every night. Tonight's dinner was different. Special, even. She had found a friend today, and the dinner reflected her happiness. Charlie was grateful to see his wife happy this evening. He knew she had been struggling to fit in. He hoped she had found a friend or a hobby, something to keep her busy. She was pretty. That's what first had drawn him to her, but he knew there was more there. He just had to find it.

Ray Dobbins noted the cars on his street. Their passengers had all gone to Jane Russel's house. He was collecting evidence, evidence the sheriff could not ignore. This was his street. He had the most money, the biggest house, the most to lose. He could not abide this woman and her idiosyncrasies. This was his charge. He went on Amazon that night. Cameras seemed to be the solution. He would hire someone local to install. Then people would see. Then they would understand.

Chapter 8

Dee spent most of Wednesday night thinking about the creature, how she could find it, kill it, protect the children of her town. She thought about the people who lived in Eggers Cove, who had been here the longest, who would know most about the history. The history of Eggers Cove was loosely documented. She decided she would visit the eldest town member on Thursday.

Maribelle Eggers spent her mornings walking the grounds, feeding the birds, and soaking it all in. She loved the quiet, the routine, the ease of it all. She did not have the life she wanted. Maybe she had the life she deserved. She sat on her porch as she did most mornings, and she thought about simpler times, older times.

✶✶✶✶✶

Maribelle found herself at another party, another place she was merely tolerated. Sure, she had friends, good friends, but most of her peers were more interested in what her family could provide. Other girls were jealous of her many suitors, although they were only seeking fortune and power. She made polite conversation and counted the minutes until she could depart. Tomas Finley caught her eye from across the room. The only boy in town who saw her, really saw her. Maribelle smiled and hoped he would walk over.

Tomas Finley was the youngest of five, the third son, with no hope of inheritance of any kind. His oldest brother was learning the family business, his sisters were married, and his other brother was in college. He had nothing to offer Maribelle and wanted to give her everything. He loved her since they were young children, probably from the first time he saw her. And he hoped she loved him. Tomas crossed the room and offered to walk her home.

They purposely took the long way home, through the humble downtown, past the central park, speaking of the future and dreams. The way young people often do. Tomas declared his love for her that night and promised her a future, a future out of this town. Maribelle never dreamed of leaving the town and her family. This was her home. But looking in his eyes that night, she would leave everything behind. She loved him, she trusted him, and she knew he was her future.

Tomas had a plan. He would join the military and earn a career. He was good with mechanics. Maybe with military training, he could launch that. Maribelle would wait and dodge her parents' incessant meddling. It would only be four years.

Neither of the two predicted the Korean War. Neither of the two predicted he would be deployed. Neither of the two predicted he would not return.

Maribelle greeted Jen Marks (formerly Finley) with a welcoming smile. Jen was Tomas's closest sibling, both in age and relationship. Maribelle's smile quickly faded when she recognized the look on Jen's face. It was of heartbreak, both for her loss and Maribelle's. The two comforted each other on Maribelle's family's porch, and Maribelle knew she would never leave this town. Would never leave this house. Tomas was her future, her only future.

*****

Maribelle sat now on that same porch, many years later, and wondered what her life could have been. She and Tomas would have been happy. They would have had a family, and most likely, they would have been poor. She would not have cared. She would have rather lived a life of modesty with the love of her life over the millions of comforts she inherited from her family. Maribelle's life was lonely, sad. She knew that now more than ever, wasted. Now she just clung to the memories, the memories of her sweet Tomas, the dreams they could have lived.

Dee waved at Maribelle as she approached. She knew she had to tread lightly. She had heard the stories. The crazy woman, the hermit, the lost woman.

"Good morning, Sheriff. Would you like some tea?" Maribelle asked as she stood to greet the sheriff. She pointed at the teapot and cups on her table.

"Expecting company?" Dee asked, noting the two cups.

"You never know. I like to be prepared." As she sat, she offered the other chair to Dee. "Tea?"

"Oh, no, thank you. I'm fine." Dee wondered the last time she had company. Dee knew that Maribelle had people work for her several days per week, but visitors? Probably years. She wondered if she was being impolite, not taking the tea. Too late now.

"What brings you up my way?" Maribelle sipped her tea. "I can't imagine you were just in the neighborhood."

"No, I wasn't. I wanted to ask about the town's history. I figured since you have lived here the longest, you would be a great resource. I've lived here my whole life, minus the few years in college. And as far as I know, you've done the same."

Maribelle looked off into the distance, past her front yard, her driveway, all the way into town. "Yes, I've never left this place." Dee wasn't sure if Maribelle meant the town or this property. "I'm happy to answer any questions you have. But my memory isn't what it used to be."

Dee doubted that. None of the stories she heard ever included the words *senile*, *forgetful*, or *dementia*. People told of her sharp wit, her long memory—mostly of those who wronged her—and her quirks. Dee thought anyone spending a lifetime alone would have to develop quirks, maybe just to survive. She could not imagine that loneliness. It must be all-consuming.

"I'm not sure how much you've heard about the happenings in town lately," Dee started.

"The girls gossip. Not to me but with one another. I hear things, Sheriff. I hear a lot of things." Dee assumed she meant the women she paid to look after the place, run her errands, and other tasks as they arose.

"So you heard about the tragic death of Sally Simpson?"

"Yes."

"Do you remember the tragic deaths from five years ago? The children?"

"Yes."

Dee had hoped Maribelle would be chattier, offer her ideas or opinions, or more than one-word answers. "Do you recall anything else like this? Children or otherwise?"

Maribelle took a few moments to think. She could remember many oddities over the years, times when children died and there were no answers, livestock being mutilated, neighbors killing each other for seemingly no reason. In her eighty-seven years here in Eggers Cove, she did not think there was much she missed. "What do you mean, Sheriff?"

"For instance, I remember around twenty years ago, children were murdered. I remember my friends and I were scared. We were twelve. But I don't remember why. I don't remember if they, my dad, caught the responsible party or parties." Dee was remembering more from that time, but there were a lot of holes in her memory. "Things like that. That's what I'm asking about."

"I'm not sure you're asking the right questions, Sheriff."

"Okay, what are the questions I should be asking?" Dee did not have much patience for this woman. She thought it was the stress, but maybe it was just this woman.

"That's the question now, isn't it, Sheriff?"

Dee thought for a minute. She tried to put herself in Maribelle's shoes, get inside her head. "Do you think or know of a connection between what's happening now and what's happened before?"

Maribelle's face lit up. "Now you are on the right track." She stared off in the distance again. Dee hoped it would not be for too long. "Yes."

"What's the connection? Besides terrible things happening to children while they should be safe and sleeping?"

"The Natives. Can I call them that? Is it insensitive? I'm not sure anymore."

"I believe you can call them Native Americans, Indians, or just use the name of their tribe to be safe." Dee had to admit she had a hard time keeping up as well. But she tried. She thought that was what mattered. She did not want to offend anyone, and she found herself ashamed of her ignorance at times.

"Regardless, they have some folklore you'll want to look into. It may solve or explain the recent vandalism as well." Dee knew there was a connection. She had not brought it up. She knew this woman was holding back. Maybe on purpose, maybe because she was afraid. Afraid of being labeled, again, as the "crazy lady." Afraid of Dee not believing her, afraid of consequences Dee could not begin to imagine.

"Could you tell me? Even just the highlights? Or what I should be looking for?"

"I think you already know. I think you knew even before you came here." Maribelle finished her tea. "I rarely get visitors, Sheriff. Would you like to stay for lunch?"

Dee wondered what could be gained from staying for lunch. Half answers? Riddles? She thought, briefly, she should stay. This woman was alone up here. It would be the neighborly thing to do. Then she remembered she had responsibilities. She had to figure this out fast. "Thank you for offering. Another time, maybe. I have a lot to do."

Maribelle stood to say goodbye to Dee. "You be careful out there. There are monsters everywhere."

Dee thanked her for her time and drove away. She needed to see Jack. She needed to tell Jim and Charlie. She needed to solve this.

*****

Chris and his friends went to Billy's house to try to walk him to school, if he was feeling better. No one answered the door. Chris went around back to make sure the window was still boarded up. He confirmed it was, and it did not appear that the boards had been tampered with. That was something. It was the only thing he could do to help his friend.

As the group walked to school, there were no reports of noises, lights—red or other—the night before. They were hopeful for the first time. Now they just had to figure out Billy. Steve suggested they break in and take Billy to the hospital themselves. He was unclear on the details. None of them were old enough to drive, and biking the twenty miles seemed unrealistic. Abigail thought they should involve Dee. She knew that cops did welfare checks. She saw it on television. They all agreed and nominated Chris to handle it. He immediately sent a text to Dee and told everyone he would let them know.

Steve and Alex walked ahead of Chris and Abigail. They kicked rocks at each other and made jokes at the other's expense. Boy stuff. Abigail and Chris were having a more grown-up conversation. Chris thought they needed to do more, but he did not know what.

They made it to school without a solution but planned to think on it and regroup at lunch. Abigail spent her free period researching on the internet. She tried keywords like *red eyes*, *child murder*, and the town's history of unusual crimes or events. She knew there was much more to do, but she had a start and a backpack full of printouts.

Brian joined them for lunch, so Abigail held back on her findings. They ate lunch like it was two weeks ago. Before Billy got sick, before little Sally died, before some creature started stalking them. It was good for the group to have normalcy, even for only forty-five minutes. Chris looked at his friends laughing, throwing napkins at each other, and he suddenly felt overwhelming sadness. Would they ever be like this again? For more than just lunch? He decided to enjoy this moment.

*****

Dee found Jack at the café and recounted her conversation with Maribelle Eggers. "So what? We scour the internet for local folklore?" Jack asked.

"I guess so." Dee looked at her phone. She had several new text messages, one from Chris. "Chris wants me to do a welfare check on Billy. Not a bad idea. I think I'll call the hospital first. We should ask

Jim to see if he was seen at Doc Reynolds's. Mary still works there, right?"

"As far as I know. Jim and I don't talk about Mary." Jack thought for a moment. "Jim and I don't talk much about anything anymore. Not since I've been back." Dee raised her eyebrows. "Don't say it. We both know why Jim and I aren't close anymore."

"He still trusts you," Dee offered. The truth was, Jim and Charlie's relationships with Dee and Jack were strained. It was easy to blame it on their spouses. Dee did. But maybe there was more. "One crisis at a time. I'm going to head over to the station, call the hospital, get ahold of Jim. Have him ask Mary about Billy."

Jack offered to start the internet search, and Dee was grateful. They promised to keep each other informed about their progress, and Dee headed out. As she left, she turned. "Do you remember how close we all were? The four of us? We were unstoppable." Jack smiled. He remembered those times as well.

Dee called the hospital from the station. There was no record of Billy being seen or admitted. The text messages between her and Jim confirmed Billy had not been seen by Dr. Reynolds either. She called the school, and they confirmed Billy was still not in school. They had not received a doctor's note. Dee relayed the information to Jack then drove to the Johnson house.

When she pulled up to the house, she noticed the blinds were all drawn, the porch light was still on, and Ben's car was gone. She knocked several times and got no response. She called the station and had Dawn dig up a number on Ben. She walked the exterior of the house and noticed the kids had been there. The bedroom window was boarded up. Dee smiled at how ridiculous it looked but was touched by how thoughtful those kids were.

Dawn was able to get a cell number for Ben. When Dee tried it, there was no answer. She left a message asking him to call at his earliest convenience. She had made it back to the front of the house and gave the door another knock. No response. On the off chance it might be open, she tried the knob. It turned. She was in. She called out to Gabrielle, to Billy, and to Ben. There was no response. The house was dark, messy, and there was an odd smell Dee could not put her finger on. It was not death, but it was awful. The kitchen sink was full of dishes, the trash was overflowing, and there was a trail of ants marching across the counter. Dee found the rest of the house in a similar condition. She went down the hall to the bedrooms. The first room she tried looked like a guest room. There was nothing personal in it. The next room was Billy's. She knew by the boarded-up window. She flipped on the light and saw Billy laying in his bed. He was staring at the ceiling and did not flinch at the light. She crossed the room and said his name several times. No response. He was breathing, but it was shallow. She shook him gently. No response. She radioed for paramedics and encouraged them to hurry. In the master, she found Gabrielle sitting in a chair. She had a lit cigarette, and the ash was well passed the time to flick it. Dee called her name. Nothing. She put out the cigarette and radioed the update.

Dee went back to the front of the house and turned the lights on. Paramedics would need to see, and she needed to investigate. She radioed in again and asked for Adams or Collins to come out. Dee waited with Billy for the paramedics. She did not want that little boy to be alone for one more second. She knew he was twelve but looked half of that. He was frail and small, and his eyes were vacant. Dee wiped away a single tear from her face. She was not sure why, but a memory of her mother surfaced, a bittersweet memory.

*****

It was summertime. Dee had been playing all morning with Jack and Jimmy, and she was hungry. She ran home for lunch and found her mother in the kitchen. Her mother was sick, some days sicker than others. Her mother was not bedridden yet. That would come in several weeks, but she had the dark circles under her eyes and the hollowness in her face that often comes with chemo. Her mother had music on and was dancing. She was baking. It was one of her favorite things to do. Dee giggled at the sight of her mother.

Margot turned and smiled at her little girl. Dee was covered in dirt and sweat. She looked like she had had a fun morning. She grabbed her daughter's hand, and the two danced in the kitchen to music that Dee did not recognize. It was old people music. "Are you hungry? You look positively starved."

"Yeah, Mom, I was going to get a sandwich."

Margot told her daughter to sit, and she would make her one. It felt good being up and in the kitchen. Much better than the past few days. She had lived in the bathroom and barely made it to her bed. Her mind told her to embrace these days because her body told her there were few left.

Dee ate her lunch and talked with her mom about school, about her friends, about anything other than cancer. When she finished, she helped her mom bake cookies. She had promised her friends she would meet them, but this seemed more important. The two baked, sang songs, and laughed the afternoon away.

Conor came home to the smell of freshly baked goods. He saw his wife and daughter in the kitchen laughing, flour everywhere. Margot kissed her husband, transferring flour to his face. Dee laughed and threw more at her father. He picked up his daughter and swung her around while throwing a handful of flour at his wife. They were all laughing. It was the best day any of them could remember.

It was the last day Margot baked, danced, or sang. Dee did not realize it at the time, but that was the last day she had with her mother. Her mother did not die for at least a month, but the cancer killed the woman Dee knew after that day.

*****

The paramedics arrived first and took Billy and his mother to the hospital. Neither knew what was wrong with the pair. Adams and Collins arrived within minutes of each other, and Dee had them process the house. She sent texts to both Jim and Jack, asking Jim to tell his kids that Billy was being treated. She went through the house room by room, and other than the things she noted upon arrival, the only thing that was out of the ordinary was missing clothes. It looked like Ben had packed his things and gone somewhere. Maybe a business trip? Maybe a hotel? Dee would find out. She wondered what had gone on in this house. She thought she may never truly find that out.

After the deputies finished, packed away the gear, and sealed the house, Dee told them to talk with the neighbors. Standard questions: Did anyone see anything? Hear anything? Does anyone know the last time Ben was here? Dee told them she would see them back at the station when they were finished.

Dee called the hospital to get an update on Billy and Gabrielle. The doctor said they both had malnutrition, dehydration, and were in shock. They were still waiting on labs. She asked they keep her informed. She took the long way back to the station.

Dawn greeted Dee with messages on her way to her office. Dee asked that Dawn tell Matt and Dylan to come to her office when they got back. In her office, she sat in her chair and seriously considered a nap and a vacation. Both would have to wait. She saw her deputies walk in, and Dawn directed them her way. Deputy Adams knocked on her door, and she invited them in and had them sit.

"Anything of note from the neighbors?"

"A few neighbors said that Ben Johnson hasn't been around for at least a few days," Deputy Adams began. "No one heard anything last night or saw anything unusual."

"There were those kids though," Deputy Collins chimed in. "Same bunch of kids have been coming around. One neighbor said they were boarding up the bedroom window. So that mystery is solved."

"That's the Stevens boys and their friends. They asked me to check up on Billy. Said he'd been sick lately." Dee thought few details were better at this point. "Anything else? Strange people in the neighborhood or cars?"

"It's a quiet street, Sheriff. No one noticed anything out of the ordinary," Deputy Adams explained.

"Okay, let's talk about the house. Aside from the dishes, trash, ants, specifically in Billy's room."

The deputies exchanged a glance. Dee noticed but did not acknowledge it. "Sheriff? Is there something you're not telling us?" Deputy Collins found his balls.

"About?"

"It's the boards, you knowing this kid was sick, Sally Simpson," Deputy Collins began. "It's like you have the answer and you're testing us or something."

Dee thought for a moment on how to answer. "I wouldn't lie to you guys. I hope you know that."

"No, Sheriff, we aren't saying that." It was Deputy Adams's turn. "We're just trying to put it together."

"Me too, guys. Me too." Dee thought for a minute more. "I'm close with the Stevens family. Jim and I have been friends since we were kids. The kids were worried about their friend and asked me to help."

"What's with the boards? We can't figure it out," Adams asked.

"I'm not sure. I'm planning to ask the kids about them. What else did you find in the house?" Dee needed to change focus.

"Nothing, really. Looks like Ben moved out," Adams inferred.

"I've got a few calls in to him. He could just be out of town." Dee remembered the Simpson house. "What about the Simpson house? Did you guys find anything new there?"

"I took some pictures of some symbols on a few trees. Dylan didn't think they were anything. I thought they were similar to the vandalism calls we've had."

"Send them my way. I'd like to take a look." Dee thought this might be helpful, maybe a connection. She was not sure to what, but she felt hopeful. "Good work today. I'm going to cut out early, but I'll be available if I'm needed." She dismissed them and sent a quick text to Jack to see where he was, although she could guess.

Jack was at the café. He said he could leave at any time. She texted him she would be home in a few minutes. She found herself mistakenly calling Jack's home her home more and more often. She stopped correcting it. There was a lot to discuss. Dee did not feel like talking about it tonight. She hoped for a light evening with good food and better company.

Ralph met Dee at the door, whole body wagging and spin jumping, his typical greeting. It instantly elevated her mood. They went out back after Dee changed to play. Jack arrived moments later and received the same enthusiastic greeting from Ralph. Jack loved on him and threw his ball.

"I was thinking salmon for dinner. Maybe some asparagus?" Ralph returned with the ball, and Jack threw it again.

"Sounds perfect." This was what Dee needed, just for a little while. Later, they would discuss what they each found today and go over the pieces again. Try to make sense of it all again.

*****

Abigail told Chris they had to talk after school. She wanted to talk just with him first. Steve would make jokes, Alex was too young, and they did not talk to Brian about anything of importance. Chris told her they could go to his house after school. He would just tell Steve and Alex that she was helping with an assignment. It would not be the first time.

In his room, despite his mother's protests, Chris shut the door and asked Abigail what was going on.

"I spent free period researching," Abigail started as she pulled a stack of papers out of her backpack. "I started with red eyes, child murders, and got way too much information and images. Then I narrowed it to our county. Anything involving children that was unsolved." Abigail reached into her bag and pulled out another stack. "And that's when I found these."

Chris was thumbing through the pages, not sure what he was looking at or for. "Abs, this is a lot. Can you leave these here so I can read it all?"

"Those are yours. I made copies."

Of course, she did, Chris thought and smiled. "Did you see any stories about here, Eggers Cove?"

"They're on top." Abigail paused and looked down. "The stuff from five years ago is first." She looked up and met Chris's eyes. They were sad and scared and angry. She came in the aftermath of the tragedies five years ago. She helped Chris through it then, and she would help him now. He was so busy worrying about everyone else, he often forgot to take care of himself.

The two looked over the papers and pointed out things to one another. Abigail thought this might be what it feels like to work in a law office or in a police department, solving puzzles and solving crimes. There was a light rapping on the door, then Jim poked his head in.

"It's getting late. I'm going to walk Abigail home." Chris looked at his phone. It was late, almost dark.

"Thanks, Dad." Chris hugged Abigail and told them to be safe. "Dad? Is Alex home?"

"Yes, he's been home for quite a while." Chris let out a sigh of relief. Abigail finished gathering her things, and Jim walked her home. On his way back to his house, he could not help himself from picking up the pace. He was jogging by the time he reached his door.

Chapter 9

Brian was unable to sleep. He was thinking about his friends. He knew they were up to something, something he was excluded from. He found that his friends often excluded him from things. He was pretty sure he knew why. His friends did not trust him. He did not trust himself. A couple of years ago, while trying to climb the social ladder, Brian told some kids a big secret. A secret about his friends, and they never forgave him. They still let him hang around, but he was no longer a part of the group. He had accepted this fact and was counting the days until college. He would go out of state, make new friends, and he would not betray them.

He looked at his phone. It was after one in the morning. This was going to be a long night. He was worried about Billy. The last time he saw him, the kid looked like walking death. He did not know what was wrong with Billy. He hoped it was not contagious. One thing he did know: that family had rotten luck. First Tom and now Billy. He heard his parents talking, and it sounded like Billy's parents were getting a divorce. Brian's dad said that Billy's dad moved out. Brian did not blame him. Billy's mom was useless. He thought it would be hard to lose a kid, but it had been five years. He thought at some point, you have to move on.

He heard a noise near his window. He dismissed it as a racoon or an opossum. There were a lot in the neighborhood. He heard it again.

(Scratch, scratch)

A racoon or an opossum never did that. He looked toward the window.

(Scratch, scratch)

He thought maybe it was a prank by one of the high school kids. He did not think he was even on their radar, but maybe...

(Tap, tap)

Brian was starting to get scared. This was really weird. He noticed a red glow in the window. His heart was pounding. He hoped this was a prank, but...

(Scratch, scratch, tap, tap)

That light. He felt a pull in his head. It was tugging, and there was a low voice, almost a whisper, encouraging him to go to the window. Open the blinds, confirm it was just a prank. Brian was getting out of bed. He was walking toward the window. He did not remember making that decision. Yet here he was, getting ready to open his blinds. The red light was brighter. It seemed bigger. He opened the blinds. His eyes met a pair of red. He tried to look away. It was too late. That pulling, that tugging was too strong. Brian's last thought was of his friends. He hoped they were safe. He was not.

*****

Dee's phone buzzed at just after six Friday morning. It was the station. Dee took a deep breath. It could only be one thing. "This is the Sheriff."

"Sheriff, can you get out to the Reynolds's house right away?" Dawn asked. "Collins is already there. He says the Reynolds boy is dead."

"Tell him I'll be there soon." Dee hung up and dressed. She scratched Ralph on the head and told Jack there was another dead kid. On the drive over, she radioed Dawn to send more deputies. Deputy Collins met Dee as she pulled up. He looked scared and confused. Dr. Reynolds was waiting on the front porch.

"What are we looking at, Matt?"

"Mrs. Reynolds went into Brian's room earlier when he didn't answer her knocks. She saw him lying on the floor. He was unresponsive. She called for her husband. He called us." Deputy Collins's voice did not crack. Dee expected it to. She was impressed. These cases were hard.

"Okay, let's go inside. Paramedics on the way?"

"Yes. I radioed for them right away," he answered as they walked toward the house.

"Dr. Reynolds." Dee put out her hand to him. He shook it.

"Right this way, Sheriff," he said, leading them toward the back of the house. "I did a preliminary exam, careful not to disrupt anything. I would say time of death is less than six hours based on the temperature." Dee thought this was not the worst way to respond to the death of your child. Fall back on what you know. For Dr. Reynolds, that meant being a doctor. "My wife is in our room. I gave her a sedative." Dee wished he had not done that. She had hoped to get a statement.

"Is she asleep or just calm?"

"Calm. She was hysterical. I knew you would need to speak with her. I made sure not to knock her out."

They arrived at the door to Brian's room. The doctor motioned for them to enter. He stayed outside. Dee saw Brian's lifeless body on the ground near his bedroom window. He was curled in a ball, facing the wall. Dee did not want to, but she had to look. She had to see his face. His mouth was formed into a silent scream. His eyes were open, huge. If there had been life in them, Dee thought she would see pure terror.

"Sheriff?"

"Yes, Matt."

"The paramedics are here."

"Show them the way." Dee stood and left the room. She asked Dr. Reynolds to show her to his wife. She was sitting in a chair in their room, staring out the window. A cup of tea sat on a table next to her. It looked untouched. "Mrs. Reynolds? I'm Sheriff Halley. Can I ask you a few questions?"

Mrs. Reynolds stared out the window, unresponsive. Dee touched her lightly on the shoulder. "Mrs. Reynolds?"

"Hmmm?" She turned to look at the sheriff, as if she just noticed her presence. "I'm sorry. Did you say something?"

"Mrs. Reynolds, I'm Sheriff Halley, and I'd like to ask you a few questions." Mrs. Reynolds nodded. "Did you notice anything different about Brian's behavior yesterday? Or over past several days?"

"No, he was normal. Went to school, came home, did his homework, went to his room."

"Okay. And last night, did you hear anything during the night?"

"Just animals. Racoons or something." Mrs. Reynolds looked back out the window. She had detached herself again. Dee knew she was not going to get any more out of her, at least not now.

"Thank you, Mrs. Reynolds." Dee motioned for Dr. Reynolds to follow her. She saw the paramedics in Brian's room and asked if they could speak in the kitchen. After they sat, Dee asked, "And you, Dr. Reynolds? Did you notice anything different in Brian's behavior?"

"Nothing unusual, like my wife said. Except he was worried about his friend, Billy Johnson. He asked me if Billy's mom had brought him in to the office. Brian said he looked really sick."

"And last night? Or the past few days? Anything out of the ordinary? Maybe a car or someone you didn't recognize?"

"Nothing like that. But honestly, Sheriff, I'm not home much. My practice keeps me busy."

Dee watched the paramedics wheel Brian's body out of the house and saw Collins on the porch talking with two other deputies. "Dr. Reynolds, is there somewhere you and your wife can go for a few hours? I know this is difficult, but we need to investigate, gather evidence, figure out what happened here."

Dr. Reynolds said he was going to take his wife to the hotel. He did not think they should stay in the house for at least a few days. Dee gave him her card and asked him to call if he or his wife thought of anything else.

"We'll be in touch soon, Dr. Reynolds," Dee said as she walked the Reynolds to their car. They drove off, and Dee went to her deputies.

Dee sent Deputies Nichols and Hagen to interview the neighbors and had Collins and Adams process the house. Dee walked carefully around the exterior of the house, paying close attention to the area outside of Brian's room. Approximately eighteen inches from his window, there was a print, identical to the one outside the Simpson house. Dee photographed it and looked for more. She did not find any more tracks but found several symbols carved into a nearby tree. She photographed these as well. After several more minutes of looking, Dee found nothing more. She decided to call it and let her deputies finish up. She told Adams and Collins she would see them back at the station.

She stopped by the café on the way to the station to get something to eat. She was not hungry but knew her body needed it. Jack made her a breakfast sandwich to go and made her promise to eat it. She promised and asked if he could set up a meeting with their friends. There was a lot to go over, and Dee felt like they were running out of time.

*****

To add to her day, the autopsy came back on Sally Simpson. Inconclusive. Cause of death: unknown. Manner of death: unknown. Perfect. Just like the cases five years ago. To make matters worse, her deputies returned with similar stories as the Simpson case. Regular police work was getting them nowhere. Dee checked her phone. Jack had set the meeting for one again in the park. She was about to text Jack when he appeared in her doorway.

"Someone order lunch?" Jack smiled at her and held up a bag. "I brought some for the troops too," Dee looked out at her happy staff and smiled back.

"Thanks, Jack. They need it today." He came in and sat across from her. As he unpacked their lunch, she asked, "Did you get any pushback from the guys?"

"No. Jim stayed home with his kids today. They were friends with the Reynolds boy. I guess Doc Reynolds called Mary early this morning and said he would not be in the office today. Asked that she go in and cancel his appointments." He took a bite of his sandwich. "I think Charlie is just happy to be included."

"I didn't know they were friends," Dee said between bites. "Why wasn't his window boarded? Guess we'll ask Jim in a little while."

"Guess we will." Jack paused. "You wanna talk about this morning?"

Dee showed him the pictures she had taken near Brian's window. "Just like the Simpson house." Jack looked them over and agreed. "And, Jack?" Dee took a deep breath. "His face. It was just like Sally Simpson."

Jack grabbed her hand and met her eyes. "Guess we'll just have to solve this, won't we?" He smiled at her, and she smiled back. Dee looked at the time. It was time to meet their friends. She let Dawn know she would just be across the street if she were needed.

Dee and Jack crossed the street to the park and saw Jim was already waiting for them at what was quickly becoming their spot. He waved at them as they approached, and Dee saw Charlie walking toward them from the other end of the park. After hugs and handshakes, they all sat, and Dee started.

"Jim, I was wondering why Brian's window wasn't boarded like the other kids. He was part of their group, right?"

"The boys feel terrible. Abigail too. She's been at my house all day. Steve is there too. It's a little fuzzy, but I guess Brian wasn't really part of their group. Something about a broken trust. I don't know, Dee. They're kids."

"I was thinking, and I know its far-fetched, and I'm not sure how we sell it, but what if we put out a statement for all kids' windows to be boarded up? We could spin it like a health issue or an extra layer to keep the bad guys out." Dee was frustrated. She knew this was a stretch. "I don't know, guys. It feels wrong not to share what seems to be working." Dee looked at her friends, hoping for an idea.

"I agree. We just have to get the messaging right." Jack always had her back.

"Would this come from your office or mine? Or both, maybe?"

"First the message. I'm not sure what health issue would require boarding up children's windows." For once, Jim was the voice of reason.

"Animals?" Dee knew she was grasping at straws. "But why would animals only attack children? And leave no wounds?"

"Let's put a pin in it for now. We'll all think on it." Charlie had become a politician. "What about the research we were all going to do? Anyone come up with anything?"

Dee and Jack exchanged a look. "No fair. You two have to share!" There's the Jim they knew. He had started that saying when they were kids. Dee and Jack did not intentionally keep things from their friends, even when they were kids. They just could read each other better and were usually on the same page. Everyone laughed at the juvenile expression.

"I talked to Maribelle Eggers. After some prodding, she suggested I look at folklore of the local tribe," Dee started. Then she went into the similarities of the crime scenes with the tracks and symbols. She told them about the children's faces. She stopped there and awaited input or questions.

"I saw Chris and Abigail going over some research yesterday. It did not look like a school assignment. I'll ask them what they found." The group was hopeful at that. Charlie said he found several unsolved child deaths over the years. Many of them had few details, and a few were sparsely documented. He was not sure if pieces of the files were missing or just never existed.

Jack was the last to speak of his progress. "I think one or a couple of us go up and talk to Willie." Willie was from the local tribe. He lived alone in the woods. Only a few people in town knew how to find him. Jack was one of those people. "He might be a great resource. He would know the stories, heard them as a kid. Probably faster than typing key words into the google machine."

Dee liked the idea. She was not sure why Jack had not shared it with her before. She knew how his brain worked. He probably had not decided until this minute that it was a good idea. "So to recap, Jim is going to talk to the kids about their research. Jack and somebody are going to go talk to Willie. We're all going to think of a good reason to recommend boarding up the windows of children in this town. I think maybe you should ask the kids to tell other kids to board up their windows, Jim. Anyone they can."

Everyone agreed to their tasks. Jim offered to go with Jack, and Charlie said he would look deeper into those cases he found. The group separated, and Jack asked Dee if she really had to go back to the station. She said she did, but only for a few hours. He kissed her and told her to hurry. Dee thought that was the first time they had showed affection in public, other than the occasional hug. She thought she would feel uncomfortable, but she did not. It felt right. She kissed him back.

*****

Chris spent Friday morning consoling his friends. After he got the news of Brian, he called his friends and had them come over. He told them Brian would not have believed them. He would have teased them, and he would not have listened. He told them it was not their fault, and they believed him. He could be convincing because he knew it was not their fault. It was his.

His dad had made them breakfast. No one ate. After his dad left, Abigail suggested they talk about the research she had done as a group. Chris went to his room and grabbed the copies Abigail had left him. He spread them across the dining room table.

"Holy shit, Abs, how long did this take you?" Steve asked. "We don't have to read all this, right? You've got the CliffsNotes?"

"It was just during free period." Abigail stood and started sorting the papers. "Here, these are the ones from our area." She handed each of her friends a stack. "Start reading." After some minor grumblings, they all did as she asked. They usually did.

Chris brought sodas and chips to his friends and began reading. A few minutes in, he had a thought. "Let's tell everyone we can to board up their windows."

"Sure, genius," Steve started sarcastically. "Tell them all some creature is snatching kids' souls through their windows. Yeah, that won't get a laugh."

"We have to try," Alex offered. "We have to try something." They agreed and started dividing up the kids they knew. They decided the message should be based on a rumor they heard or a story, keep it vague, no mention of creatures.

"We're gonna get slaughtered for this. We'll be the biggest dorks in school." At least Steve was optimistic.

"Who fucking cares, Steve?" Abigail was tired, tired of Steve's mouth, tired of the fear, tired.

When Jim arrived home with the suggestion that they spread the word about boarding up windows, Chris told him they already had. He looked at the table. "And that was going to be my next question. What have you all found?"

They spent the rest of the afternoon looking over what Abigail had found. Jim brought out his laptop and began diving deeper into stories that seemed promising. He felt like they were actually getting somewhere, being productive. He hoped Mary did not come home any time soon.

Chapter 10

Charlie Wilks rose early for a Saturday morning. He told his wife he had to go to the office for a few hours. She pouted in her typical fashion. He said he would hurry home, promised a Sunday brunch. He did not want to lie to his wife, but he did not know how to explain that he and his friends were trying to catch the boogeyman. He could hardly believe it himself, but children were dying, and no one had a better explanation. This town was his home, and as mayor, this town was his responsibility.

He arrived at Jack's a few minutes before Jim and was welcomed by Dee. He thought this was an interesting development. They would have to discuss this at a later time. He brought a bag with a change of shoes and sat on the couch to change them.

"Didn't tell the wife what you were up to?" Dee asked.

"Couldn't find the words." He sounded a little hurt. He knew Dee and Jill were not immediate best friends, but he hoped the two would become close over time.

"I get it. I've been tiptoeing around my deputies. You don't want to sound like a lunatic."

Jack came into the living room with Ralph on his heels. "Glad you could make it. Jim should be here any minute."

"Jim's here. He's just pulling up," Dee announced. She opened the door for him, and he asked if she was coming with them. "Not this time. I'm going to the office." Dee wished them luck and watched them drive off. She wished she was going with them, but she was needed here.

Ralph nudged Dee's leg with his muzzle. He needed to go outside. Dee let him out back and grabbed her running shoes. She thought they both could use it. After their run, Dee went to the station. She was pleasantly surprised her phone had been silent all morning.

She greeted Nick and asked if there were any pending calls. He told her that Pickers and Nichols were out on calls, but nothing major. She thanked him and went to her office. She flipped through her stack of messages, many from Ray Dobbins, and set them down. On a whim, she called the hospital to inquire about Billy. He was alert, eating, and perking up. Dee said she would be there soon. She told Nick where she was going and to call if she was needed. As she drove to the hospital, she thought about bringing Chris or the other kids, but this was official business. They could all meet later.

When she first saw Billy, she thought it was a different kid. This boy was not the boy she saw yesterday in his home. This boy was alert, eating, and full of life.

"Hi, Billy. I'm Sheriff Halley. I'd like to ask you some questions, if you feel up to it."

"Hi, Sheriff. How can I help?"

"How are you feeling?"

"Good. How's my mom?"

"I don't know, but I'm sure we can find out. For now, I want to ask you about the last few days."

"Okay." Billy paused and looked around the room. "Do you know where my dad is?"

"I don't, Billy. I've called him and left messages. I hope he returns them soon." Dee sat in a chair next to Billy's bed. She grabbed his hand. "Do you know why you're here?"

"They say I was dehydrated, malnourished, and in shock."

"Yes, I've heard that as well, but do *you* know why you're here?"

Billy looked the sheriff in her eyes, tried to read her. "I guess I was sick."

Dee thought for a moment and weighed her options. "Billy, I've talked with your friends. Jim Stevens and I have been friends since birth, basically. You can trust me, trust that I'll believe you, trust that I won't tell anyone what you say here."

Billy looked at her again. Dee could almost feel him digging around in her brain, trying to get a sense of her. Dee knew he did not believe her. She had to find a way to make him.

"Chris told me about the red eyes," Dee just said it, let it hang in the room. Pieces would fall where they may.

Billy's face went pale, and his breathing became erratic. "What do you know?"

"What do you know? Billy, I'm trying to help you and your friends. You need to be honest with me."

"You know my brother died five years ago."

"Yes, Billy, I know."

"Do you know what happened to him?"

"I'm sorry, Billy. I don't."

"Then you don't know what's happening now." Billy turned toward the window. Dee was afraid he would not talk to her anymore. "Do you want to know what's happening now?"

"Yes, Billy. I want to help in any way I can."

Billy took a deep breath and looked Dee in the eyes. "Five years ago, I heard something scratching at my window. I hid under the covers. It went to my brother's room. He looked." Billy kept his gaze at Dee. "That's what happened, Sheriff. And that's what's happening now."

*****

On the drive, Jack, Jim, and Charlie told stories from the old days, recounting past triumphs and joking about missteps. It was a forty-five-minute drive outside of town, mostly on a dirt road. Then the trio would have to hike the rest of the way. Jack assured his friends that the hike would not take more than an hour and half, two hours max. After two hours and fifteen minutes, Charlie started grumbling.

"You've been here before, right, Jack?"

"Yeah, half a dozen times. It should be just over this ridge." Jack pointed ahead.

"You think he'll be there?" Jim's turn.

"We'll find out, won't we?" They continued walking in the direction Jack insisted was correct. Ten minutes later, they saw the cabin. "See, I told you I knew where it was."

"Pure luck," Jim joked, and Charlie chuckled.

"This, my friend, was all skill." Jim and Charlie exchanged an unimpressed look.

The cabin looked empty. When they looked through the window, it did not look lived in. "Did he move?" Charlie asked.

"Or die?" Jim, the forever optimist.

"Ain't dead," a voice said from behind them. Startled, they all turned around to see a large man holding a rifle. "Not yet." His long dark hair was in traditional braids, and although he wore jeans and a flannel shirt, it would not be hard to picture him in deer hides, a bison cloak, and moccasins. He stuck his hand out to Jack. "Long time, old friend." Jack shook his hand.

"We would have called, but—" Jack smiled as his friend laughed.

"No White man phone for me. People need me, they can come see me." He invited them to sit on his wooden benches, and Jack introduced Willie to Jim and Charlie. Jack asked about the fish and what game he was hunting. Willie told him that he was getting by, and Jack knew to drop it. Jack knew the deer had been sparse the past few years, and he had not been getting many bites when he fished. "I know you are not here to talk about deer and fish. Why are you here?"

Jim and Charlie looked to Jack to start. He knew Willie. They only knew him by reputation. Jack began, "Willie, do you know what's been happening in town?"

"I hear things out here. Sometimes it takes time to hear them." This was Willie speak for no. Jack was used to it.

"A couple of kids were killed in the night. No apparent injuries, no cause of death, no signs of an intruder, and…" Jack started then drifted off. He looked at his friends. They just looked at him. "One kid said something was scratching on his window. Said he saw a red glow."

Willie looked at Jack and then the two men he brought with him. Willie trusted Jack. He was a straight shooter, honest. He was a good man. Willie thought these men with him must be good too. Jack would not be friends with men who were not. "Why are you here?"

"Willie, do you know Dee? She's the sheriff," Jim finally chimed in. Willie nodded. "She went to see Maribelle Eggers." Willie perked up at this. He knew Maribelle. Her family had been here for many generations. "Maribelle suggested we look into old folklore."

"It seems strange things like this have been happening for as long as anyone can remember," Charlie added. "Kids dying with no explanation, livestock mutilated, weird stuff."

"And there's the vandalism," Jim interjected. Willie looked at Jack.

"A few times, Dee has gone to vandalism calls where there are black outlines of eyes with bloodred centers. And symbols like these." Jack showed Willie the pictures Dee had taken at the abandoned buildings and the outside the children's houses.

Willie studied the images carefully. He looked at Jack then into the distance. For several minutes, no one said anything. Jim and Charlie looked uncomfortable. The two kept looking at Jack for guidance. Jack gave them an assuring look. This was the process. "White people see symbols that look like ours, and think they are ours. These are not."

"We didn't think they were yours. We were hoping you could direct us to whose they might be. Or if you've seen any like this before." It was not any of their intention to offend Willie, especially not Jack. "Children are dying, Willie. People are scared. That's why we're here."

"There are always children dying, Jack. There are always bad things happening in your world."

"Yes, Willie, there are. We try to stop them when we can."

Willie nodded at this. He looked Jack in the eyes. "Do you want to hear a story, Jack?"

"I think we all would, Willie."

"When I was a boy, the old women would tell us stories. Stories to make us be good, stories to scare us." Willie paused there and looked at the men. By the look on their faces, he knew they had been told stories as well. "The story you are looking for is about the Creature. It has no White man name. He steals your spirit. His eyes are bloodred. He has long claws. Some say he can fly. Some say he can just disappear."

Willie told the tale of the Creature, which was the closest English translation from their language. He remembered it mostly word for word as it had terrified him as a boy. At the end of his story, Willie explained that there was no pattern, there was no reason. The Creature would come, kill, and leave.

"Do you know how to stop it?" Jack asked.

"Better yet, do you know how to kill it?" Jim asked.

"They did not tell me that. Telling children it can be killed defeats the purpose of telling the story."

"Do you know anyone else we can ask?" Charlie asked, grasping at straws.

"There is no one I know with the answers." Willie stopped the conversation there. He was tired of these men. This was more conversation or interaction than he had had in months.

Jack thanked him for his time and promised to come back in a few months for a hunting weekend. The trio walked back to Jack's truck, mostly in silence. Charlie was the first one to speak. "Anyone else feel like that was a waste?"

"I think we have more information than we had before," Jack said. He knew that Willie had helped as much as he could. If he had any answers, he would have given them.

"What's next?" Jim asked.

"We get to the truck, drive back to town, talk to Dee," Jack answered. "That was always the plan."

*****

Dee waited for the men to return at Jack's. The station was mostly quiet today, so Dee had time to grab pizza and beer on her way over. It was midafternoon when they arrived. Jim and Charlie looked defeated. She offered the pizza and beer, but Charlie only had time to change his shoes.

"I promised Jill I'd only be a couple of hours. She's going to be pissed." They said goodbye and watched Charlie drive away.

"How'd it go? How's Willie?" Dee asked as they went inside.

"Willie's getting by. He looked good," Jack answered. "He had heard the story we were sent to ask about."

"That's great!" Dee let herself be hopeful. As they ate the pizza and drank the beer, Jack recounted Willie's tale. Dee found there was no new information. A part of her had hoped the guys would return with Willie and he would have some ancient weapon. The five of them would hunt and kill this creature that very night. Far-fetched, but a girl could hope.

"The question now is, what's next?" Jim asked, knowing he would not get a good answer. The truth was, they were basically where they had started. Not for the first time, he was thinking about packing up his kids and taking a long vacation.

"I have good news," Dee started and immediately had their attention. "Billy is awake, alert, and I talked with him today."

"What? That is good news. How is he?" Jack asked.

"What did he say?" Jim asked at the same time.

"He looked much better. They want to keep him for a few days," Dee started. "He's scared. He told me that what happened to his brother is happening again." Dee went over her brief conversation with Billy. Jim and Jack both expressed their happiness that Billy was doing better. But this did not answer the question on the floor: What's next?

*****

Mark Sullivan was sleeping peacefully. He had spent the afternoon boarding up the exterior and duct-taping soundproof foam to the interior of his bedroom window. When he got the text from Chris, he thought he was being pranked, but a voice deep down told him to listen. He was not close with Chris. They had a few classes together and had been on the same baseball teams, but he knew him to be honest. He hoped his parents would not ask questions. He hoped his friends would not make fun of him. Mostly, he hoped it worked.

What Mark did not know—and would never know—was that night, as he slept soundly, he was being hunted. The creature approached his house and began to reach out to the young boy's mind. He was dreaming of summer. It grasped ahold of an image and began to change it, to startle the boy awake. As it reached the house, it saw the boards. This window was secure. The creature clawed at the wood. It would not budge.

It left the house, the boy, the meal behind and wandered into the forest. It was hungry, and it could hear children in the distance.

Chapter 11

Ruth Ann felt like time was standing still. The afternoon was dragging. Yesterday after school, she had been invited to a high school party by a sophomore boy. She was fourteen. This was her first invite. None of her friends had ever been invited. She knew this was big. She spent the morning trying to decide what to wear and found all her clothes unacceptable. Some of them were hideous. She went to her best friend's house, and her clothes would not do either. Ruth Ann's mother refused to take her to the city to buy something new. Money was tight, and her mother found her request frivolous.

Ruth Ann settled on an outfit she thought would do. She would not be winning any fashion awards, but she thought she would fit in. With that settled, all she had to do was wait. Wait for the seconds to tick by. Each felt like an hour.

She told her mother she was going to her best friend's house and would be home by curfew. She told Bobby (her date) she would meet him at Dobbins' field. Her mother would never allow her to go to the party, certainly not with a boy. Especially not an older boy. She walked the ten minutes to the field and saw the bonfire already going. Her and her friends had often watched these parties from afar, full of jealousy and anticipation for their turn.

Ruth Ann walked past several clusters of kids she only knew as high schoolers and looked for Bobby. She hoped she would find him soon. She knew she could be discovered at any moment and forced to leave. In utter humiliation. Bobby waved at her, motioning her to come his way, and she smiled brightly. He introduced her to a couple of his friends and their girlfriends and gave her a beer. She had not planned on drinking. For some reason, the thought had not occurred to her. She had made it this far. There was no turning back.

She sipped her beer slowly, but that was soon followed by Jell-O shots and more beer. It was not long before Ruth Ann felt woozy, wobbly, and her vision was blurry. She excused herself and went for a walk to clear her head. She was in over her head. She heard laughing behind her. Ruth Ann knew they were laughing at her. The little girl that could not keep up. She started jogging into the woods. She was crying now. Embarrassed, ashamed, she was sure her reputation was ruined.

Ruth Ann leaned against a tree and slowly slid down to the ground, face in her hands. She did not hear the twig break behind her. She did not feel the claw grasp her arm. She heard a faint voice in her head, telling her to look up. She opened her eyes and raised her head. Her eyes locked with a red pair. She felt an immediate pull in the back of her head, a tugging, a fear. She tried to scream, but no sound came out. Her last thought was *I thought this only happened in your bedroom.*

What Ruth Ann did not know before she ran off into the woods was that the other kids were not laughing at her. They had been laughing at a keg stand gone wrong. One of the seniors, trying to show off, attempted a one-man keg stand and ended up falling, knocking two kids over. Bobby had gone to look for Ruth Ann, to make sure she was okay. He had missed her trail by only fifteen feet. In this darkness, fifteen feet may have well been fifteen miles.

*****

The missing person call was taken by Nick at a little after one in the morning. Her mother had called. Ruth Ann had missed curfew and had not gone to a friend's house. She could not imagine where her daughter could be.

Deputy Adams responded to the house by twenty after one and interviewed the mother. This was not typical behavior for her daughter. She never lied. Someone must have taken her. He asked if anything unusual had happened in the last few days. Her mother said Ruth Ann wanted a new outfit. She threw a fit when her mother said no.

Knowing the town and the teenagers, Adams's first stop after the missing girl's house was Dobbins's field. When he arrived, teenagers scattered like roaches. He was able to stop a couple of them and show Ruth Ann's picture. They had not seen her, or at least claimed to have not seen her. He cornered a few more. Same response.

Adams walked around the bonfire, noted the beer cans and bottles, solo cups, basic teenage party trash, but did not see Ruth Ann. He went to the tree line and called her name. He assured her she would not be in trouble. He just needed to find her. No response. He had shone his flashlight into the woods and did not see any evidence of anyone hiding. He would need help to scour the woods, if she was even here. Or had been here.

Hagen arrived at Dobbins's field to assist. Adams told him to shine his flashlight in the woods and keep calling to the girl. He would be back soon. Adams drove to the house of Ruth Ann's best friend, the house where she was supposed to be. He spoke to angry parents and then a scared girl. She tried to keep her friend's secret. She was loyal, but eventually, she gave in. Ruth Ann had gone to Dobbins's field party to meet a boy, Bobby, no last name. Adams pressed more and found that Bobby was a sophomore. That helped, a little. He thanked the family for their help, left his card, and asked that they call if they heard from Ruth Ann.

Adams called the sheriff directly. They were going to need search and rescue, maybe some volunteers. Dee called the search and rescue emergency number on her way to Dobbins's field. She had Nick call the list of volunteers that were local. Jack, in the seat next to her, called Jim and Charlie. They agreed to help.

Within fifteen minutes, there were almost twenty volunteers at Dobbins's field. Many of those volunteers had at the very least gone to the informal training the sheriff's office offered. Others had participated in a search before. Everyone had a flashlight, a whistle, a partner, and a few had flair guns. The county search and rescue team would take at least an hour to arrive. Dee set the volunteers, including her deputies, in a line a few feet apart from each other and asked them to walk in as straight of a line as possible. Adams marked trees at each end of the line. If they had to make another pass, they needed to know where they had already been.

The group began walking slowly, careful of the terrain. They took turns calling out to Ruth Ann as Dee had directed. They had not been searching for ten minutes when the first scream was heard. Dee told everyone to stay in place through her megaphone while she went to the source of the screaming. Jack went with her. He was her partner; her rule was to stick with your partner.

Dee and Jack found the source of the screaming, which thankfully had stopped. A man was comforting a woman who was sobbing near a tree. Dee did not recognize them. The man pointed to the other side of the tree. Dee and Jack went around it. Dee shone her flashlight on a teenage girl in the fetal position. It appeared that she had soiled herself. Dee did not want to, but she had to look, had to look at the girl's face. She brushed the girl's hair aside. Her face was contorted in the same way as the other children—a silent scream, big empty eyes. She radioed for Adams to come over and tape off the scene. She ordered everyone else out of the woods.

Dee thanked her volunteers, had Hagen get their contact information, and took statements from the man and woman who found what they all assumed to be Ruth Ann. Dee looked at the picture Adams acquired from Ruth Ann's mom, and she was sure this was Ruth Ann. She was also sure the rules had changed.

*****

Hours later, the group sat around Jack's kitchen table. None of them knew what to make of the new information. Leftover pizza seemed to help get their brains working. Jim suggested they meet with the kids later today. He said they had done some good work. The group agreed.

"I'm going to establish a county-wide curfew for sundown. Anyone under eighteen must be in their home or at an approved location by their parent or guardian," Dee announced.

The guys all exchanged glances. "Are you sure we're there?" Charlie, the politician, up for reelection next year, asked.

"Three kids, Charlie. Three, all after dark. Yeah, we're there," Dee asserted.

"What are you going to use for the reason?" Jim asked.

"At the press conference, which will include me and Charlie." Dee looked at Charlie with a look he knew well. He knew better than to argue. Dee would win. She always did. "I'll say it's a matter of public safety. Charlie will agree, and it will be effective today." She received no arguments or pushback.

Charlie looked at his watch. It was late. Jill was going to be pissed. "What time are we calling this press conference?"

"Late morning? Early afternoon? Give people time to prepare."

"Okay, let me know. I have to get home. I promised Jill a brunch. Guess that'll have to wait till next week." Charlie left. Dee knew he was annoyed with her, but she did not much care. Children were dying. It was their job to protect the ones that were still living.

"I'll gather the kids for after the press conference. Where should we meet?" Jim asked.

"Here," Jack offered. "They love Ralph. It's a controlled environment. We control who's here."

They all agreed, and Jim went home. He thought about asking to crash there, still afraid of the dark, but he did not want to get teased. His friends could be merciless. After he left, Jack and Dee continued the conversation.

"I get it now," Jack started. "I get why you've reacted the way you have."

"The way I've reacted? What do you mean?"

"You and Jim from the beginning were ready to grab crosses and holy water, probably silver bullets, and hunt this creature down. I thought it was a strange case, but I thought there would be a reasonable explanation. Maybe the autopsy would show a tiny injection site with something toxic in their bloodstreams." Jack paused for a minute and grabbed Dee's hand. "I was wrong, and I'm sorry."

Dee kissed him. "I needed you to be skeptical. Like you said, Jim and I were one step away from pitchforks and torches. I was hoping for a reasonable explanation." Dee thought for a minute. "We'll have to go back to the scene at first light. We need to look for tracks and symbols."

Jack agreed, and they opted not to sleep as first light was less than an hour away.

*****

First light on a Sunday morning usually found few people moving about in Eggers Cove. The early service at church was not until eight, and outside of hunting season, most men found no need to rise early. This Sunday was not sleepy. There were people bustling about everywhere.

A sheriff and a former cop were nosing around the latest crime scene; a mayor was arguing with his wife over broken promises; a grieving mother was walking down the street, disheveled in her slippers; a couple of paramedics were rethinking their career choices; and the town asshole was plotting against his neighbor.

Dee and Jack found two tracks near the tree where Ruth Ann was discovered and symbols carved on several surrounding trees. They photographed everything they found and went back to Jack's to prepare for the rest of the day.

Charlie was calmly trying to explain to his wife why brunch was cancelled and why he was needed at a press conference. He could not believe how selfish Jill could be. Children were dying, and she wanted a mimosa. He went into the office to make arrangements for the press conference and work out his statement with his press secretary.

Jim made breakfast for his kids and two neighbor kids that had basically moved in. He did not mind the extra kids in the house. He had always wanted a big family. Mary did not. Jim knew that the first pregnancy was a trap and the second was an accident. She was not the nurturing type, and he understood her life had not turned out the way she had planned. He resented her for not understanding that his life had not worked out either, and he had done all the work to succeed. A stupid injury changed his life. Mary made her own choices. He told the kids they were going to Jack's later to discuss options. Chris's face lit up at the prospect of not only being included but participating. He felt that Brian's death was his fault. He needed to make it right.

After Charlie called Dee to discuss the press conference, she called deputies Adams and Collins. She wanted them there as well. After a little back and forth, they settled on having it in front of the mayor's office, which happened to also be the courthouse. Jack said he would go as well for moral support. Dee and Jack went to the café for lunch, and Dee went to the station after.

The press conference was scheduled for one that afternoon. It was just after noon. Dee busied herself with paperwork and ignored messages that needed to be returned. Her top two deputies arrived around twelve thirty with their brass freshly polished. They were in full uniform, and Dee almost regretted wearing jeans. She thanked them for coming in, especially after a long night. They said all the right things, and Dee decided to budget raises for the both of them. They had earned it. Adams deserved a promotion, and Collins was making great strides. Dee was confident they both would go far in their careers, either here or wherever their ambitions took them.

Dee hoped that she and her deputies did not look too menacing crossing the park to the courthouse. They entered through the back and went to Charlie's office first so the group could walk out together. Charlie had included two staffers and the deputy mayor. Dee thought it was overkill. It was likely their group would outnumber the reporters.

Dee was wrong. Not only were local press in attendance, but press from all the neighboring counties as well. Dee thought she saw a van from a station in the city. She shot an accusatory look at Charlie. He shook his head. She would not budge on one aspect of the conference. She would make the announcement. She was implementing the curfew.

Charlie started the conference then handed it over to Dee. She explained the recent events and the dangers and announced the curfew, effective tonight. Several reporters tried to interrupt, and Dee raised her hands to them. "For the safety of our community, for the safety of our children, this curfew is in effect until further notice. Anyone under the age of eighteen must be in their home or approved location by sunset. Anyone under the age of eighteen found outside will be, at the very least, escorted home. Again, let me stress, this is for the safety of our children and our community." Dee did not take questions. She had made her point. Charlie fielded several questions, backing Dee, overtly agreeing, doing all the things he was supposed to do. Charlie was the politician of the group. Dee did not have the patience for his brand of politics.

*****

At Jack's, Dee and Jack prepared for company. Neither was sure what teenagers were eating these days but thought they could not go wrong with snack foods and sodas. Ralph was bounding around the house, sensing the energy of his people. They had transformed the dining room into a workspace. Basically, they cleared the dining room table.

Charlie arrived first. He immediately apologized to Dee again for the press conference. He had instructed his team to only notify local press and could only assume that the others had been tipped off. By whom, he was not sure, but he would find out. Dee accepted his apology. She still thought he was a politician, and politicians could not be trusted.

Jim pulled up moments later with four teenagers in tow. Charlie was introduced to Steve and Abby, and everyone convened in the dining room. Abby and Chris began unpacking their backpacks and making piles of papers. Dee thought this looked like the strangest study group ever—four teenagers and four thirty-somethings. She chuckled at the sight and covered it with a cough.

"Thank you, everyone, for coming," Dee started. "There's snacks and sodas in the kitchen. Help yourselves." The kids helped themselves to sodas, and the adults helped themselves to beer. Everyone settled into their seats. "So what have you found? What do we need to know?"

Chris and Abby exchanged a look, and Chris nodded. "I started googling during a free period at school," Abby began. She explained all the research she did and said the stacks closest to Dee were the local findings. "I narrowed it to our county and over here," she said, pointing to a stack near Jack. "These are from the nearby counties."

Dee, Jack, and Charlie started flipping through the pages. Chris took the opportunity to share his perspective. "Here in town, there was the kids five years ago, including Billy's brother. Around twenty years ago, a bunch of kids died mysteriously. You guys have to remember that, right?"

Dee thought there was something. She remembered they were scared one summer. She looked to her friends. They seemed to be struggling as well.

"Don't forget the cows," Steve interjected. "Those pictures were gnarly." He looked through a stack and handed the pictures to Jack.

Dee looked at them as well. The animals had been mutilated, the article said it happened to a few dozen cattle at three different farms. "I'm not sure how these would be related. All the bodies are unmarked."

"I agree. Let's put this in the strange pile," Jack suggested, "until we can figure out a connection."

"In the early 1900s, a handful of kids died in six days. The article said the causes were unknown, but a doctor said it was probably malnourishment," Abby interjected. "We found more. It's all there. We don't know what is doing it."

"Yeah, and now it's killing *outside* of houses," Alex added. "How do we know it won't start coming inside or during the day?"

The adults all paused. They had not thought of the possibility of the creature coming indoors or hunting during the day.

"We implemented the curfew, which we think will help," Charlie offered. The kids were not impressed.

"This is all great information. You guys have been busy," Dee said. "I went to Maribelle Egger's."

"The crazy lady?" Steve asked, and Abby elbowed him. "What? She's a lunatic. Everyone knows that."

"She's not crazy. A little eccentric, definitely lonely, but not crazy," Dee assured. "She's been in town the longest. I figured she could be a good resource."

"Was she?" Chris asked hopefully.

"Yes. She suggested we look to the local folklore," Dee began. "So these guys hiked out into the woods to speak with Willie, a local tribe member." Dee motioned for Jack to take over.

"Willie and I go way back. I've been hunting and fishing with him for years. We met when we were in high school, and his parents were trying to assimilate him into our White culture. He was a little offended when I asked about the symbols, but we got past it."

"What symbols?" Abby asked.

"Oh, sorry. These." Dee handed out copies of the pictures she had taken. "We found these at the scenes where the children were killed and a couple of vandalism sites. The vandalism also included these big red eyes." She pointed to the pictures of the red eyes.

"Creepy," Abby whispered.

"Yeah," the other kids agreed.

"Look at those claws!" Steve had discovered the pictures of the tracks.

"Not helpful, Steve," Jim scolded. "Let's get back to Willie. Jack?"

"After some prodding, Willie told us a story he was told as a boy." Jack told the tale of the Creature, and the kids' faces paled. "He says he was never told how to kill to it or stop it. It would defeat the purpose of the story."

"That story would scare the shit out me if I wasn't already scared."

"Language, Steve." Jim was beginning to think he was now the father of all teenagers, or at least all teenagers in his eyesight.

"Sorry," Steve muttered.

"I dug into those old unsolved cases," Charlie interjected. "There isn't much there. No notes from the investigating officers. Medical examiner ruled them all inconclusive. The strangest part was the lack of information. It's almost like they were just dropped after a few days. No follow-up, nothing."

"That is weird," Dee began. "Five years ago, I worked one of the cases, not Tom's," she said to the kids. "And it wasn't taken away, but we didn't finish working it. I can't remember why."

"That's not like you, Dee," Jack said, confused. "You're thorough. You do damn good police work. This doesn't make any sense."

"No, it doesn't." Dee tried to think back, not only to five years ago but twenty years ago. There were just blank spots. Not necessarily blank but foggy. "I know you guys were young, and I don't think you were here yet, Abby. But what do you guys remember from five years ago?"

"Besides what I told Dad, just Billy," Chris said. "He was lost, scared, and we helped him."

"You're good friends. I had a group like that when I was growing up," Dee said and smiled at her friends. "Sometimes, we still show up for each other."

"Sometimes?" Jim joked.

"On a more serious note, Abby, Steve, can you talk to your parents about what's going on? How are they handling your boarded-up windows? I'm sure they have questions." Dee wanted to protect these kids. She thought maybe their parents would be useful.

"Not my parents. My mom already smothers me," Steve said. "My dad would listen then send me to the psych ward."

"Not mine either. They're really busy." Abby offered nothing else. Dee instinctively knew not to prod.

"And your windows?" Dee followed up.

"They haven't asked," Steve said.

"Mine won't."

"I've been trying to figure out a way to have all the kids stay together, but Abby," Jim started. "I think it would be hard to sell her parents on sleeping in the same room as three boys."

Abby blushed, Chris looked embarrassed, and Steve cracked an off-color joke. "Do you feel safe at home, Abby? At night?"

"As safe as I can feel with some crazy monster hunting us."

"Here's my card." Dee handed her card to Abby and Steve. "Program my cell in your phone. Call me any time if you need us."

"Us?" Steve asked coyly.

"Cute, kid," Jack retorted. "If you need us, call or text or messenger or whatever it is kids do now."

"I already had a run-in with this thing. There was no time to text or call or messenger or whatever it is kids do now," Steve quipped. "That thing comes, you put your head down and run."

"We're trying, Steve," Jim responded. "We're all trying."

"We know, Dad." Chris gave Steve a look that Steve had seen many times before. It meant shut up.

"What do we do now? We have all this information, but no information on possible weaknesses or time frames or anything that can help us destroy this thing." Charlie was frustrated. They all were.

Jack and Dee looked at each other. "I don't know. I think the kids will be safe with their windows boarded up and soundproofed," Dee began. "Maybe we set a trap." All the kids looked excited at this suggestion.

"I like it!" Steve exclaimed. "We trap this thing and stab it or set it on fire. Just don't look it in the eyes. That thing was poking around in my head, and I hadn't met its eyes. If I had looked in those eyes…" He trailed off.

"Where? How?" Jim asked.

"At Billy's old house. We can set up one of the rooms to look like there's a kid in there. Two of us inside, two outside. Adults only. Sorry, kids. It's too risky." Dee was forming a plan, out loud, before she had time to process it fully.

"You don't want to go to Billy's old house," Chris warned.

"Why?" Jack asked.

Chris looked at Abby. She nodded. "We went in there the other day. We were looking for Billy."

"That poking around you talked about, Steve, I felt it there. But it was like a pulling or tugging deep in my head." Abby looked scared.

The adults all exchanged a look. "It fucking lives there!" they all said at once.

"Tonight?" Dee suggested.

"Do we need time to make plans?" Charlie asked.

"I say we go tonight." Jim was on board.

"Okay, let's get some artificial sunlight, headlamps and flashlights, and weapons. What kind of weapons?" Jack could think on his feet too.

"Anything silver," Chris suggested.

"Or wooden?" Steve offered.

"Maybe just a really big gun," Abby said, and everyone looked at her. No one expected that suggestion from the young girl.

"Jim, get the kids back to your place. Jack, Charlie, let's hit the hardware store and the station."

"It's just after four now. Meet back here in an hour?" Jim asked.

"Sounds good. Abby, do you have any friends that are girls? Anyone that you can tell your parents you're staying the night?" Dee asked. She hated to make a kid lie to their parents, but she needed to keep this kid safe.

"Yeah. I could say I was sleeping over at Beth's." Abby paused, looked at her hands, then up at Dee. "I don't lie to my parents, Dee. But if you think it's the right thing, I will."

"I want you guys together. You'll be safe together. I don't know how I know that, but I do." And she did know. She was sure.

On their way out, Jack pulled Chris aside and said a few words to him. Dee wondered what he said and made a mental reminder to ask later. After.

*****

After Charlie broke brunch plans that were his idea, Jill reached out to Mary. She hoped that Mary was free and they could grab a bite, become friends. Jill was hopeful. Mary said she would love to meet for brunch or for whatever passed as brunch in this town. The two women met at the café just after eleven. While they were there, they saw Jack and Dee come in and go to Jack's office. Dee left a little while later, eventually followed by Jack.

"They didn't even see us," Mary noted.

"They don't care about us." Jill was becoming increasingly annoyed with Charlie's friends. None of them bothered to get to know her or make plans to include her.

"Welcome to my world. I've been excluded for years," Mary complained. "And don't get me started on that Dee. What a bitch!"

Jill did not think Dee was a bitch. She found her unapproachable, distant, and a little masculine, but not a bitch. "I don't think she knows how to have girlfriends. From what I've heard, her mom died when she was young."

Mary dismissed that comment with a wave. "I've heard that my whole life too. Poor Dee, lost her mom, doesn't know how to be a girl. Blah, blah, blah."

Jill was beginning to think that Mary had been drinking prior to their brunch. But this was the first friend she was close to making. She would keep her mouth shut. They spent the afternoon drinking champagne, which they were both surprised to find at the café, and talking trash about Dee. Neither woman could figure out what made her so special. Why did their men want to spend time with her over them? Jill was not insecure about her marriage. She was only insecure about her place in this town. Really, in this world. She thought Mary was just looking for a way out. If Dee was having an affair with her husband, then Mary could leave, clean.

After the women were basically cut off at the café, some teenager told them she needed the table. The women headed back to Jill's. She had champagne, wine, and vodka. They could make a real party of it. Jill asked Mary if she wanted to invite anyone. She did not. Apparently, Mary did not have friends either. The women spent the afternoon and evening uncorking bottle after bottle of wine. Sometime late in the afternoon, Jill opened the tequila. Neither could remember how many shots they did.

Charlie stopped in, before monster slaying, to see how his wife was. She had not responded to any of his text messages. He found Jill and Mary drunk and angry. Jill berated him with questions about where he had been, where he was going. Mary chimed in with a crack about Dee. He did not have time for this. He barely recognized his bride. He changed his clothes and left, telling Jill he would be home late.

Chapter 12

Dee and Jack were the first to arrive at Billy's old house. They were going through their gear when Jim pulled up, followed closely by Charlie. As they geared up to hunt, Dee looked around the neighborhood to see if anyone was watching. She was not sure how she would explain it, the group getting ready to infiltrate an abandoned house, hunt, and hopefully kill a monster. It appeared that no one was watching. Dee thought people probably stopped watching this house years ago.

"What exactly is the plan?" Charlie asked.

"I say we stick together," Jim suggested.

"We could cover more if we split up." Jack's years of being on the job were showing.

Dee thought they should at least split into pairs, one in front and one in back. She also knew that Jim and Charlie did not have police experience. Maybe sticking together was the way to go. "Let's go around back. We'll stick together. Jim, Charlie, you two will be behind us." Then to Jack, "We'll clear it room by room. I don't think we need to worry about it going out the front. The sun hasn't quite set yet."

Everyone agreed, and the group went through the side gate into the backyard. The window in the back door was broken, and it was slightly ajar. The group entered cautiously into the kitchen and went through each room systematically. Besides some empty boxes, newspapers, and beer bottles, the group came up empty. They felt the heaviness of the air, smelled the dankness that Chris and Abby described. Dee was not sure, but she thought she could hear a low voice in the back of her head. It smelled and felt the worst near one of the bedrooms. Dee suggested they look in there again.

Instinctively, she went to the closet. Everyone knows that monsters hide in closets. Jim and Charlie exchanged a doubtful look. Dee felt around in the closet, the walls, the floor. She noticed the carpet was pulled up slightly in one spot. She shone her flashlight on the spot and pulled on it. Beneath the carpet was an access panel to under the house. Jack was standing over her. She looked up and smiled at him.

"Guess where we're going." The idea of crawling around under the house was less than appealing to Dee, but she was excited at a possible lead.

"I knew you were going to say that," Jack smiled back at her. "Let me get into position then pull it open." Jack adjusted himself in case something came from under the floor. Jim and Charlie took a few steps back. He motioned for Dee to open it. She did and took a half step to the side, gun and flashlight pointed at the opening. Nothing emerged.

Dee holstered her weapon. "Shine the light for me. I'm going in." Jack shined his light in the hole, and Dee hoisted herself down. She clicked her flashlight back on and shone it around the immediate area under the house. "I'm good. Looks clear," she called up. The space was cramped, and Dee had to squat as she walked around under the house. The light from her flashlight illuminated several of the symbols she had found at crime scenes carved into the wood. Jack had joined her under the house, and she was grateful. It smelled and felt much worse down here.

About fifteen feet from where they entered, they discovered another door in the ground. Dee opened it in the same fashion as she did the closet door. Nothing emerged. Her flashlight revealed what appeared to be a tunnel. Jack looked at Dee, and she nodded. Jack called up to the guys to come down. After some grumblings, the two men joined their friends at the new opening. From what they could see, the tunnel looked tall enough to stand up in and only wide enough to walk single file.

"Let's find out where this goes," Dee said, already climbing down the wooden ladder.

Jack was not thrilled at the idea of Dee leading. Despite her skills and job, a part of him still wanted to protect her. Now was not the time to for that conversation. He would set his feelings aside. He knew she could handle it. He was next down that ladder. At the very least, he would provide the best backup. Once they had all made it into the tunnel, Dee had them turn on their headlamps, and they began walking.

"That smell!" Charlie complained. "It's worse down here."

"Yeah, and the air," Jim started. "It's so thick."

"Heavy," Dee corrected. "It's heavy, the air." She looked back at her friends, careful not to blind them or herself. "We should be quiet unless necessary. We don't want to give it a heads-up."

After fifteen minutes of walking, the tunnel forked. Dee stopped and consulted her friends. They agreed to go right, and they marked the tunnel with spray paint. The paint was Jack's idea, a last-minute decision at the hardware store. Dee agreed to the purchase but insisted the color be blue. Around seventy-five feet later, the tunnel forked again.

"Anyone else think we should turn back before we get lost down here?" Charlie asked.

Dee glared at him. "We'll just go right again, mark it, and it'll be easy to find our way back." The group continued and took two more right turns, Dee was about to turn back when she saw another wooden ladder leading toward a door. Jack took a position of cover as Dee opened the door. She shined her flashlight around. They were in another structure. It looked abandoned or vacant. She climbed the ladder. The others joined her.

It appeared they were in a back room. There was old office furniture, trash, and dusty cobwebs. No creature. Dee noticed a desk on its side. It looked familiar. She looked at the other side. There they were. The symbols. They were downtown, across the park from the station.

"We're downtown, in one of the vacant buildings. This is one of the vandalism sites," Dee explained. The group cleared the rest of the building and tried to decide what to do next. It was after ten. They were all covered in dirt, cobwebs, and other filth from both tunnel and the vacant places. Jack suggested they go back down and follow the tunnels to the left.

"I'm not going back down there," Charlie proclaimed. "Not tonight."

"Guess we're walking then." Dee looked at her friends. "But not like this." She pulled her equipment bag off her back and set it on the ground. "Headlamps, flashlights, firearms, all of it in here."

The group walked back to Billy's old house and their vehicles, mostly in silence. They were all tired, drained, and felt defeated. Charlie did not have the energy to deal with his drunk wife and her new friend. He hoped Jill was already passed out and that Mary had left. When they arrived at their vehicles, they made plans to meet up the next afternoon.

"Hey, Jim?" Charlie pulled his friend aside. "If your wife isn't home, she's most likely passed out at my house. I guess the ladies spent the day drinking together." Jim rolled his eyes and thanked his friend for the information.

Dee and Jack watched their friends pull away then drove off themselves. "Jack?" Dee asked.

"Hmm?"

"What did you say to Chris earlier at your house?"

Jack looked at Dee. "I told him that if something happened and we didn't make it back, he was to take Ralph and his friends and leave town."

*****

While Dee and her friends were exploring underground tunnels, an orderly in the psychiatric ward discovered Victoria Simpson dead in her room. She had tied one end of her bedsheet to the bedframe and the other end around her neck. Then she simply leaned forward. No one on the staff expected it. Victoria had been smiling earlier in the day. She had even said a few words.

Earlier that morning, Victoria had decided to kill herself. She did not want to live without her Sally. She felt immediately calm and at ease with that decision. She enjoyed her breakfast and lunch, waiting for the window she needed. She had been in the hospital long enough to learn the routines. In the afternoon, she would have the time. Her last thought was of her daughter's smiling face. She could not wait to see her again.

Chapter 13

Dee went to the station early Monday morning. She texted Charlie to see if he could find any old records of tunnels under town. She received the message that Victoria had killed herself and that Billy was improving. They hoped to discharge him today, if they could locate his father. Gabrielle was still mostly unresponsive and unable to care for her son.

"Dawn?" Dee called through her intercom. "Have we gotten any call backs from Ben Johnson? Billy's dad."

"No, Sheriff. I haven't heard from him."

"Thanks." Dee tried Ben Johnson's cell again. Straight to voice mail. She then put in a call to his firm and asked for someone to return it when the receptionist was not cooperative. Another piece of the puzzle, but Dee did not know where it fit.

Charlie received Dee's text while he was still at home, and he was glad for the task. Jill was still sleeping. He would be able to leave before she woke, and they had the inevitable fight. He left more than an hour earlier than usual.

Jim got the four children under his ward fed and off to school. Mary was still passed out on the couch. He was pissed at her for driving in her condition. He had already checked her car for damage. He cursed her under his breath as he left the house. He would need to make an appearance at the office today.

Jack went to the café early as well. He greeted Bob and Tug and got a quick rundown from Susie. It was a typical morning, only the usuals with a few to go orders. He said he would be in his office if things picked up. He had brought the stack of research Abby brought to his house, the stack pertinent to their county. He was determined to solve this puzzle. He just needed to figure out where the pieces went.

Ray Dobbins woke early. He had a plan. A plan to end his suffering, at least in his neighborhood. He would just have to wait for the right time. He had a feeling it would be coming soon.

*****

As Dee was heading out to meet her friends, a call came in regarding mutilated cattle. She stopped in her tracks. There were at least nine injured or dead. Dee had Dawn send Adams and Collins with strict orders to update Dee after they assessed the scene.

The group met at Jack's, and Dee told them about the cattle. "I don't know if it's related, but it's a hell of a coincidence."

"Guess we're moving those articles into the relevant pile," Jack said as he flipped through the stacks still sitting on his dining room table.

"Make some space. I found some old city plans, tunnels included," Charlie said, pointing to rolled-up papers in his arms. He spread them out across the table. He had already marked Billy's old house and the vacant building downtown. "If you start at Billy's and follow this line, you end up at the vacant building. The main tunnel branches off several times to the left. It leads to land outside of town near the river and two other houses on the east and west sides of town. Then there's the other tunnels."

Jack and Dee exchanged a surprised look as they looked at all the tunnels running under Eggers Cove. None of them had expected to see this many. They hoped they would not have to explore them all.

"Maybe we can just go the entry or exit points and not have to explore them all," Dee suggested. "Wait, is there a central point where they all meet?"

Charlie's face lit up. "I thought you'd never ask. It isn't central, but all the tunnels lead here." Charlie pointed to a place on the map.

"The Dobbins's place?" Jack asked.

"Yep. It's unclear if there's an opening to the house or an out-building or just outside somewhere. He did a lot of work on that property."

"Of course that's the center of all evil," Dee said, not realizing she was speaking out loud. Jack smirked, and Jim held back a laugh. They all knew Ray Dobbins. He was the ugly stain on an otherwise beautiful community. "Whatever. He's an asshole."

"How do we get on his property?" Jim asked.

"A girl just died on his property. Part of it is already a crime scene. I'll just expand it."

"Think he'll go for that?" Jack asked.

"I can be pretty persuasive when I need to be." Dee smiled at him. "Let's see if we can gauge where the opening might be before we go over there. It looks like it's not at the main residence, and fairly close to the tree line." Dee looked at her friends and smiled. "This could be easier than we anticipated. If it's close enough to the main scene, he might not even notice."

"We could enter from the woods here," Jack pointed at a spot on the map. "If he asks questions, we're volunteers."

Dee's phone buzzed. "It's Adams. I have to take this." She answered the phone and listened to his assessment of the scene. He had counted twelve cows so far, all mutilated, some eviscerated. He took photos and sent them to Dee. He said some of the cattle had symbols carved or burnt on their corpses. She asked for pictures of those as well. "Can you and Collins handle this?" He said they could. After Dee hung up, she shared the pictures from her phone that Adams had sent.

"Cattle from before looked a lot like this. No symbols though," Jim commented.

"They might not have been visible from the angle they took them," Dee offered.

"Probably," Jack started. "We gonna do this or what?"

"Let's go," Dee said.

They drove to Dobbins's place in two vehicles. After discussion, the group decided three was too many, and one was not enough. They parked on the edge of the woods, geared up, and hiked in.

Charlie had pictures of the map on his phone, and they were using it as a guide. Fortunately for the group, Ray Dobbins was not currently at home. He was in the final stages of his plan, which included a trip into the city. They made it through the woods and saw an outbuilding thirty feet away. It was a good place to start.

The door was not locked, so Dee opened it with Jack covering. The building was the size of a toolshed, and mostly empty. On the back wall, there were some garden tools, a small workbench on one side, and a lawn mower. Near the back wall, there was another door in the floor. Dee motioned for Jack to come in so she could open the door. They opened the door in what had become their traditional fashion. They found another wooden ladder. Dee called for Jim and Charlie to join them, then she descended the ladder.

In the narrow tunnel, Dee waited for the others. The air seemed heavier here, the smell much worse, and that voice was back. This time, she was sure. She could not quite understand it and thought trying to would be a mistake. She was working on pure instinct. Letting that voice in further seemed dangerous. It was then she noticed a slight pull, maybe a tug, deep in her head. She tried to push it out, away.

"Dee!" Jack was shaking her. "Dee!"

She blinked twice and reoriented herself. "I'm fine. Let's move."

"What was that? You were just staring off."

"I don't know. It's gone now." She gave him an assuring smile and started forward.

Jack was worried. He knew now was not the time. Dee was stubborn, strong, and capable of making her own decisions. They would discuss this later. For now, he would just stay close. The group moved forward through the tunnel. Around twenty feet, they entered a large open space. They shone their flashlights on the walls and saw the symbols they had become familiar with everywhere. There was almost no empty space on the walls. There were additional tributaries in four directions.

"Do you think it lives here?" Charlie asked.

"I think it definitely spends time here," Dee said. "A lot of time."

"Unless its invisible, it isn't here now," Jack said without a hint of sarcasm. At this point, he could believe almost anything.

"It must have heard us, right?" Dee asked. "Or sensed us?" she remembered the earlier visitor to her mind.

"Okay, so now what?" Jim asked. "If it can hear or sense us, how can we find it and kill it?"

"I don't know, Jim. I just don't know." Dee sounded as defeated as she felt. "Let's photograph as much as we can. These mean something. If we can figure that out, maybe we'll know how."

"Do we explore this tunnel system more? Maybe get lucky?" Jim asked.

Jack and Dee looked at each other. "I don't think so," Dee started. "I don't think we'll find anything more today."

The grouped finished photographing the room then headed back to the entrance. After escaping the tunnel and Dobbins's property unscathed, the group went back to Jack's. They discussed what they found, and more importantly, what they did not find. Copies of the pictures were handed out after Jack figured out how to work his printer. Jim promised to share his with the kids. Maybe Abby could work her googling magic. Everyone agreed to keep the others posted with anything they found. For now, they would hope for a peaceful night, a quiet night. And for Dee, maybe a bath.

*****

Ray Dobbins did not go to the city often. In fact, he avoided it. Online shopping had all but eliminated his need to go there. What he needed today required the trip. There was a time where he could have just sent his assistant on this errand. After moving to Eggers Cove, he no longer had an assistant. He was unlikely to find anyone competent in Eggers Cove to fill that position.

He had to meet his contact in a part of the city he was even more unlikely to be. Unsavory characters made this part of the city theirs. He did not think he was racist, but he could not help but notice the number of minorities in this part of town. He double-checked that his doors were locked. He parked in an alley and waited.

He saw the car he was waiting for pull in behind him, so he popped his trunk. He exited his Mercedes and handed the guy an envelope of cash. The guy placed his requested items in the trunk. They both drove away. Ray Dobbins back to his home, and his contact back to whatever hole he crawled out of. He thought for a moment about having a nice dinner while he was here. Eggers Cove's choices of fine dining were a cheap café and a pizza parlor. It would be nice to have caviar, or maybe duck. In the end, he opted against it. He would treat himself another time. After.

Chapter 14

Charlie had not spoken to his wife since her drunken tirade Sunday afternoon. He had spent most of Monday away from home, away from her. Monday evening, he had come home, made himself a sandwich, then shuttered himself in his office until late. He knew he was being a child, but he did not have the mental capacity to fight with his wife. There was too much going on, real problems, real fears, real consequences. His pouty wife could wait. She would have to.

Mary was not speaking to Jim. He had moved two more children into their home, one of which was a girl. What would the neighbors think? A teenage girl sleeping in the same room as three teenage boys? She had protested. She had lost. She always lost. She had married a selfish man. Five more years, then Alex would be off to college, and she could leave. She wanted to leave now but feared her boys would choose Jim. She rarely admitted this to herself and would never say it out loud, but she knew it was true.

Dee and Jack woke early Tuesday and took Ralph for a walk around the neighborhood. They used to run together before Jack moved to the city, but after his knee injury, it was no longer possible. Dee did not mind walking. They were still spending time together, and there was Ralph. On this walk, they did not discuss the creature, the deaths, or any other madness. The two just enjoyed each other's—and Ralph's—company.

Ray Dobbins was in the final stages of his planning. Today or tomorrow, his nightmare would be over. Jane Russel had another book club gathering Tuesday morning. She was having people over most days now. She knew it was small and petty of her, but she no longer cared. Her favorite new hobby was annoying her neighbor.

*****

When Dee arrived at the sheriff's station later that morning, two of her deputies were waiting for her. She hoped they just wanted to talk about the cattle mutilations, but she knew better. They were smart guys. They were becoming good cops, and they had good instincts. They knew she was hiding something—or several some-things—from them. Dee told them she would see them in a few minutes and prioritized her messages. She was surprised none were from Ray Dobbins. She briefly thought about sending a deputy for a welfare check then dismissed that idea. A mistake that would later haunt her.

She motioned for her deputies to join her in her office and had them sit. "What's up?"

"Sheriff," Adams began. "We've been comparing notes."

"Notes?" Dee asked.

"Yeah, this vandalism, the girl, the cattle." Adams took a breath. "We think there's something going on, Sheriff. You see all the calls, or most, I guess. We figured you would notice the patterns. Hell, you probably already put it all together."

Dee took a moment. She did not want to lead them. She wanted their opinions. She had teamed them up purposefully. She wanted them to investigate without her prejudice. Kind of like a double-blind study.

"So what do you guys think?"

Collins looked at Adams. "A cult, maybe?" Collins did not sound confident.

"Why a cult?"

"The symbols are carved and spray painted everywhere, like someone is trying to take credit, ritualistic mutilation… I don't know what else to think, Sheriff." Collins had done some googling too.

"Did you look into cults? See if those symbols showed up any-where else?"

This time, Adams spoke. "All we could find was local tribal art that looked similar."

Dee felt a little discouraged. She did not think these deputies would solve the problem. She just hoped they would have found something more than her friends. "Anything else?"

"I started looking into drugs that might not show up on an autopsy capable of killing. There are quite a few, but none of the autopsy reports show needle marks. The drug would have to have been ingested. That would mean the parents or someone with access to the kids."

"Did you find any links between the deceased? Someone from the community, maybe?" Dee knew this was not a great lead, but it was a lead.

"No, we came up empty. And we thought it was a stretch to begin with." Adams scratched his head, an endearing quality he had that Dee had noticed early on. He had done it once during his interview and another time on his first day. Dee figured it was a tick he was not aware of. "We think you might have a better idea or at least a direction to go in."

"I don't think Victoria Simpson killed her daughter," Dee began. "And I'm positive Doc Reynolds didn't kill his son."

Collins looked at Adams for a response. He just shrugged his shoulders. "I don't think so either," Collins said finally.

There was a long silence. None of them made eye contact, then Adams suggested, "What if it's something else?"

"Like?" Dee asked.

It took a moment, then Adams looked up from his hands and met Dee's eyes. "I don't know the right word, um, paranormal?"

Collins looked from Adams to Dee, trying to read them. He had talked with Adams about this theory, but they were not going to present it to the sheriff, not yet.

Dee studied them both. Adams had been known to be a joker. He did not appear to be joking now. "Can you expand on this paranormal theory?"

At that moment, Collins knew that the sheriff had a similar theory. He knew she would believe them. "I found an old tribal tale about a creature that kills kids, kids that misbehave. They just called it the Creature."

Perfect, Dee thought. "I found the same thing."

*****

After her enlightening conversation with her deputies, Dee went to the café to see Jack. She thought this was a good news, bad news situation. The good news was that now they had more help. The bad news was that this was real. She recapped her conversation with her deputies and waited for Jack's thoughts.

"More resources, I guess," Jack said. "The question is, how far do we let them in?"

That's the question Dee had been asking herself since day one. She had hoped to keep them out of it, protect them. "As far as we have to."

"We should loop Jim and Charlie in. I'll text them that we need to meet."

The group met in their usual spot in the park, and Dee told them about her deputies. "And just so we're clear, they came to me with this. I didn't tell them anything."

Charlie looked as if he did not believe her. He knew Dee to be truthful, but that was years ago, and people change. "Can we trust them?"

"Absolutely. We'll only include them if we have to, if they're needed." Dee was not sure if she was reassuring them or herself.

"I say it's not the worst thing to have a couple more badges on this, with their training," Jack added.

"Did they find anything more than what we have?" Jim asked hopefully.

"Not that they told me, but I didn't push."

"If we're all caught up here, I have a meeting," Charlie announced, looking at his watch. The trio said goodbye to him and watched him walk toward his office.

"I gotta go too. I gave copies of the pictures to the kids. Maybe they'll find something we've all missed." Jim walked away. Dee noticed his shoulders were slumped. This was wearing on him. She understood. She could not imagine having kids during this time.

*****

Chris and his friends spent their Tuesday afternoon looking at the pictures his father brought them from the cave. Abby was googling and printing everything she could find that looked remotely like the symbols found in the cave. Chris and the others were comparing them to the pictures, trying to find a pattern or more similarities. They did not notice when Mary came home and found her way into the dining room where they had set up.

"What's all this?" Mary asked, picking up a few papers and flipping through them.

The four kids, surprised by this intrusion, froze for a moment. "School project, Mom." Chris finally came up with an excuse or reason for what his mother was observing.

"Looks tribal. What class is it for?"

"American History. It's a group project. Alex said he would help."

"Okay then. Make sure you clean it all up when you're done." And with that, Mary left the room. It was then that Chris noticed she was staggering a bit, and she had a glass of wine in her hand. That was a worry for another day, another time. His fourteen-year-old self was already maxed out.

A few hours later, Abby noticed a repeated symbol, and it resembled a symbol from the local tribe. She was so close to solving it. It was just out of reach. She kept this information to herself, not because she wanted the credit of solving it but because she could not find the words to describe what she was seeing. She would think on it. Maybe she could talk to Dee.

Chapter 15

Emma Wilson turned ten the previous Saturday. She had wanted a princess-themed party, complete with a bouncy castle. Her parents obliged as they always did with their sweet Emma girl, but no one from school came. She had given out invitations three weeks prior, and all the girls in her class said they would come. She had picked out the perfect princess dress and tiara. Her mother had a stylist come and do her hair and makeup. It was going to be the best birthday ever.

The party started at one in the afternoon. Emma was ready by noon. One o'clock came and went, and no one arrived. Then two o'clock. By half past two, Emma was inconsolable. Around three, her mother began cleaning up. By four, her mother had called every parent from Emma's class asking why no one came. The parents were not aware of the party. Their children had not told them.

Around five that evening, Emma went to her social media page. She found a thread that explained everything. Emma learned that she was a baby, having a baby party, and how lame was that? She was a year younger than her classmates. She had skipped second grade. She genuinely thought that the girls in her class were her friends, that she was at their level. Emma's mother found her daughter looking at the thread, crying, unable to stop scrolling. She took Emma's laptop away and tried to explain that kids could be cruel, but it would get better. Emma did not believe and swore she would never go to school again. She did not.

On Monday morning, Emma faked a stomachache, which her mother saw right through, but she allowed her to stay home. Tuesday morning found Emma still sick, and her mother allowed her one more day at home, insisting she would go to school Wednesday. Tuesday night, Emma went to bed at her usual time, but the knots in her stomach were keeping her from sleep. She knew everyone was going to make fun of her, the stupid baby with the stupid party. She did not understand why her mother would not let her homeschool.

It was after one the next morning, and Emma was still awake, fretting over the next day of school. She was trying to come up with a survival plan: keep to herself, try to go to the library at lunch. She figured the rest of her days at school would be that way, avoiding contact with others at all costs.

She felt better having a plan. She was relaxed now and began to feel sleepy. Emma was starting to drift off, and she thought she heard a quiet voice deep in her head. She could not make out the words, then...

(Scratch, scratch)

A noise at the window. She thought she was imagining it. Then a scarier thought crossed her mind. What if it was kids from school? What if they had come to torture her more by scaring her? What if...

(Scratch, scratch)

This was her life now. No escape from torment. She was trying to muster the strength to go to her window, to tell those kids to leave and to leave her alone.

(Tap, tap)

Maybe she could just roll over and ignore them. They would give up. But that voice, it was getting louder, stronger. And there was a new feeling, a pulling, tugging.

(Scratch, scratch, tap, tap)

Emma looked at her window. There was a red light now. She was sure it was not there before, and more pulling, tugging at her. The red light, if felt warm somehow. Maybe she would just take a peek. Emma crossed her room to her window. The voice told her to open her blinds. She did. She looked out her window, expecting to see mean girls from school. Instead, she saw large red eyes. She tried to scream. Nothing came out. Her last thought was that the mean girls had won. They had beaten her, all because she wanted a princess party.

*****

Dee's phone buzzed just before six Wednesday morning. It was the station. She was needed. There was another deceased child. Ralph nudged her leg with his muzzle. She stroked his head and scratched his ear. Somehow, dogs always know when they're needed. Jack kissed her and promised to bring her breakfast later.

As she was leaving, she looked him in the eyes. "Jack, we have to figure this out. I can't take anymore calls like this."

"We will."

She arrived at the Jones's house and saw Adams on the porch with the mother. He walked over to Dee when she pulled up. "Same as before, Sheriff. Mom found Emma this morning when she went to wake her for school. No forced entry, no signs of foul play."

"Thanks, Dylan. Can you radio Dawn for more deputies? Make sure one of them is Matt." Dee crossed the yard to speak with Mrs. Jones. Olivia Jones was sitting on her porch swing, slowly rocking, staring east toward the sunrise.

"It's beautiful, isn't it?" she asked Dee.

Dee looked over her shoulder and admired it for moment. "Yes, it is." Olivia offered Dee a nearby chair, and Dee accepted. "I'm Sheriff Halley. Do you mind if I ask you a few questions?"

"Would you mind if I just sat here for a few minutes? It really is beautiful." Olivia continued to stare at the sunrise, and Dee excused herself.

Dee motioned for Adams to come with her into the house. He showed her to Emma's room. The walls were pink. She had a canopy bed and butterfly curtains over white wooden blinds. The perfect little girl's room. Dee crossed the room and saw Emma's body in a ball near the window. She looked so small, helpless. Dee leaned down and brushed the girl's hair out of her face. The same tortured face with the silent scream, big eyes once full of terror, now empty.

Dee stood and looked at Adams. "Did you radio Dawn?"

"Yeah. The deputies will be here soon. Paramedics just rolled up. Coroner too."

"Show them the way. I'm going to try to talk to the mother." Dee went back out to the porch and asked Olivia if she would like to go inside to talk.

"No, let's just sit here." Olivia was still staring at the sky.

"Is there anyone we can call for you?"

"I called my husband. He works in the city. He said he would come after his nine o'clock meeting."

Dee took a second to process that information. She wondered what was more important this morning than his family. "Can you walk me through last night and this morning?"

"She's been upset the past few days. It was her birthday Saturday," Olivia began. Her voice was monotone. She showed no emotion. Dee thought it was shock. "None of the girls came to her party. She was heartbroken. I kept her out of school Monday and yesterday. The last thing I told her was that she was going back to school today."

"Did any of the kids threaten her?"

"No, nothing like that. They teased her relentlessly on social media, I had to take away her phone and laptop. Kids can be so cruel. I don't know why they do that." Olivia was still looking at the sky. The sun had long since risen, but she still looked toward it. Then she looked at Dee. "We should have known better. A princess party with girls a year older? We just didn't think."

Dee felt bad for this woman. Her daughter was gone, her husband was absent, and she was beating herself up over a birthday party. "I'd like to look at the posts and the comments. I'm sure it's not related, but I would still like to see them." Olivia nodded at Dee. "Was there anything else going on? Did you notice anything strange in the neighborhood?"

"No, this is good neighborhood. We all watch out for one another. Our kids play in the street. It's always been perfect."

"Is there somewhere you can go? Maybe just for a night or two? We need to investigate. We need to find out what happened to Emma."

"I've already packed a bag. I thought I would stay at the motel."

"Is there someone that can stay with you until your husband arrives?"

"I thought I would go to a neighbor's until." Olivia looked at her street for the first time. The sidewalks were full of clusters of people looking her way. She knew they were speculating about what was happening in her home. "Maybe not."

The paramedics wheeled Emma's lifeless body out of the house. Dee waited for Olivia's breakdown. It did not come. The other deputies had arrived, and Dee excused herself to talk with them. She put Adams and Collins on the house and Hagen and Nichols on canvasing the neighborhood. As she was assigning duties, one of Olivia's neighbors approached the house. Dee looked to Olivia to see if she wanted this guest. Olivia motioned for her neighbor to come over.

Nora Watts was Olivia's closest friend on the street. She hugged her friend and sat beside her. The two women spoke briefly, then Nora ushered Olivia off her porch and headed toward Nora's house. The women paused to speak with Dee. Dee gave Olivia her card and asked that she call if she remembered anything. The two walked off, Nora's arm around her friend's shoulder, Olivia standing tall. Dee liked Olivia, thought maybe the two could be friends under different circumstances.

Dee walked the exterior of the home and found several tracks and symbols carved into trees. She photographed them all, and for the first time, she showed Adams and Collins. They reported the usual findings from the interior. None. She left the scene in their capable hands and went to the station.

At the station, there was a message from the city police. They had located Ben Johnson and gave him the news about his family. He was not returning to Eggers Cove. That explains the lack of returned calls, Dee thought. She could not understand how a man could just walk out on his family. Dee left a message for the social worker handling Billy's case, asking her to return. She wondered if Jim could take in one more stray.

Jack arrived with breakfast as promised for Dee and Dawn. They were both appreciative. He stayed only for a few minutes, long enough to get the details from the latest victim. On his way out, he volunteered to text the rest of the group. Dee thanked him and waited for her deputies to return.

Adams and Collins were the first to arrive. They had nothing new to report. Awhile later, Hagen and Nichols came in with their witness statements. These looked remarkably similar to the canvases from previous incidents. Dee was not surprised by either of these reports. It was exactly what she had expected. She spent the afternoon googling the symbols and local tribal folklore. There was a piece they were missing, a vital piece. Dee hoped they could figure it out. Just after three that afternoon, she received a text from Abby. She wanted to stop by the station.

Minutes later, Dawn was on the intercom announcing a visitor. Dee went to the lobby to show Abby to her office. After the two were settled in and exchanged pleasantries, Dee asked, "What's up, Abby?"

"We were looking at the pictures and trying to find patterns, and I think I found something. I don't know though. I can't quite see it." Abby looked a little embarrassed to admit this fact.

"Can you show me what you were looking at? Do you have it with you?" Dee knew this was a dumb question. She thought Abby might sleep clutching her research.

"We need a big table. Do you have one here? Like a conference room? My dad has one at his office."

"I have an interrogation room. We could go there."

Abby's eyes widened. She was excited to see an interrogation room. "That'd be great."

Dee smiled and led her young friend to the interrogation room. "You can spread out here." Dee gestured toward the table.

Abby looked around the room. It was not like what she saw on TV. It looked like a regular room with a large mirror and a few chairs. The only thing missing was a window. "Is that a two-way mirror?"

"Yep, but no one is watching now."

Abby gave her a look that asked if she was sure. Dee nodded. Dee knew her deputies respected her. They would not invade her privacy. Abby began pulling various papers out of her backpack. Some had been cut, and others had been marked up. Dee noticed they were all numbered. Smart girl. "So first, I noticed these symbols looked like these." Abby pointed at copies of the pictures and her downloaded pages. "Then I turned the pictures from the internet sideways." Abby turned the pictures clockwise, and Dee saw it.

"They are related," Dee said, almost in a whisper. She was concentrating, trying to get the connection. She could see it, but like Abby, she could not quite touch it. "We have to get Jack over here now." Dee texted Jack. He arrived minutes later.

Jack knocked on the door and entered. He said hello and then, "What's going on here?"

"I think Abby solved a big piece of the riddle," Dee said, and Abby blushed. "Go ahead. Tell and show Jack."

Abby went through her process again, more excited this time, talking faster. Dee focused on Jack. She could see his mind working. He had always been better at puzzles. She was glad he was on their team. "I get it. We need to find the cipher. One thing—or place—to start. What repeats the most?"

Abby sorted through the papers. "This one," she said, pointing at a symbol from the pictures. "And it goes with this one." She pointed at a googled page.

"Great. This is where we start."

Chapter 16

The group was gathered at Jim's Wednesday evening for dinner and a discussion about what Abby had discovered and where it had led Jack. Mary had made an appearance and quickly excused herself to their bedroom. Dee noticed she was staggering a bit and looked inquisitively at Jim. He shrugged his shoulders. After they ate, Abby walked the group through her findings. Jack jumped in at the end with his.

"Wow, this is really great, Abby," Jim said and patted her shoulder. "I would never have seen this. And, Jack, I knew you would figure it out. You've always figured shit out before me."

"Okay, now what?" Charlie was less appreciative of the findings.

"Now we decode it. The way I figure it, the underground cave is the creature's writings. It's descriptions of conquests or whatever. The symbols at the houses and woods, those are like, forgive me, crop circles. Mapping out where it's been," Jack said, working through his thoughts as they came. "At least that's what I think now."

"You think it's writing its own history? Like the Egyptians?" Chris asked.

"Could be. It's my current theory."

The group was quiet. Dee was happy Charlie was not talking. He had become less than helpful. She thought about the cave, the writings. She wondered how long it would take to decipher. She looked out the window. It was already dark. "I have a separate but related topic."

They all looked to Dee. "What?" Jim asked.

"Billy. He's ready to be discharged. Gabrielle is not going to be released anytime soon, and Ben is not returning from the city." Dee looked at Jim. "I was hoping we could find somewhere for him to go."

Jim looked at Dee. He should have seen this coming. She was always trying to get them to take in strays. When they were kids, it was dogs and cats. Now that they're grown, it's kids.

"Dad, we have to. He's my responsibility," Chris asserted.

"We'll make it work. What do I need to do? Be a foster parent? Or?"

"I know the social worker. We'll figure it out," Dee promised. "I think Billy will be grateful. He doesn't have a lot right now."

As they were leaving, Charlie grabbed Dee and asked if they could talk privately. They stepped into Jim's study. "What?" Dee asked, clearly annoyed.

"I'm trying to clear the air. Obviously, you're pissed at me, and we need to talk about it."

Dee noted his perception. "I am."

"Is this still about the press conference? I told you I had nothing to do with the turnout."

"That's one thing," Dee began. She was not in the mood to get into this with Charlie, not tonight. "There's a lot going on right now. Can we just table this?" Dee turned from him and began to walk out.

"Dee," Charlie began. "You are one of my best friends. I know there's a lot going on right now. We need to be together, solid."

"Okay, Charlie. I don't trust you right now. You're different. You've become a politician. You see things differently now."

"You realize you're a politician as well?"

"Maybe, but I don't act like it." Dee knew this was a lie. How many times had she catered to the Ray Dobbins of the county, hoping for reelection. She felt like her scenario was different, like her fight was righteous and his was a power play. "And I don't feel like you have our backs anymore. To be honest, it breaks my heart. That's what you're feeling, my disappointment."

"Wow. What am I supposed to do with this, Dee? I don't know how you became the leader, if we have a leader, but I want a recount," Charlie demanded then realized his mistake. They were best friends since childhood. That does not happen often. "Dee, I'm sorry. I'm under a lot of pressure, at work and home. I don't think my head has been in this."

"Well, your head *needs* to get in this. I love you, Charlie, but you've been an asshole lately. And I know I can do better too." Dee paused for a minute, thought about his marriage. "Can I help? With Jill?"

That was the Dee Charlie knew. In the middle of a fight, she asked how she could help. He guessed they all had that in common. "She's just not fitting in. She hung out with Mary a few times. That was a disaster."

"My advice, between you and me, keep her away from Mary. I'll try to make an effort after."

"Are we good?" Charlie asked, hopefully.

"We'll get there, Charlie. We always do." The two friends hugged it out and said good night.

On their way home, to Jack's home, Jack asked Dee about her conversation with Charlie. "He's been a dick lately. I called him out on it. We're fine now." In the back of her mind, Dee wondered if they were actually fine. For now, they had to be.

*****

Ray Dobbins woke early Thursday morning. He was excited to start his day. This day, this was his day. The day he would right the wrongs. At least in his little world. He had spent the late night hours the night before putting everything in place. Now he just had to wait for the right moment. His moment. He found himself positively giddy. He had not felt this way in years. Typically, the festivities began at Jane Russel's house around nine in the morning. He thought half past nine would be perfect. He had four hours to kill. He looked out his window, down on his neighbors. The street would never be the same.

The minutes ticked by slowly. There were several times he almost pushed the buttons. He had maintained his willpower over the years and felt it would serve him well today. It did. Although the morning did not go as planned for Ray Dobbins, the outcome was what he had wanted. As nine approached, he found himself doing a jig in front of his window. Then nine fifteen came, and he was rubbing his hands together. To an outsider, he would look like a villain. But in his story, he was the hero. From his vantage point, he could see into Jane Russel's house. It was bustling with people. Another book club meeting, he supposed.

Right before nine thirty, Jane Russel remembered she had forgotten the book for her book club in the car. Book club was just an excuse to have people over. They rarely talked about the books. Still, Jane thought she should at least have the book out. To make it official. She excused herself and walked outside. She had made it two steps out the door when she heard the noise. It was loud, and she felt like she was flying. The loud noise she heard was followed by several others. Jane could not be sure how many.

There were six loud noises. Two came from Jane Russel's house, and the remaining came from cars on the street. Neighbors ran from their houses when they heard the first noise. They wanted to see. Some wanted to help, if it was needed. Most just wanted to see. Nora Goldman was the first to approach Jane. She was lying near the street. The blast from her house had thrown her at least twenty feet. Nora patted out the fire on Jane's body and called for help.

As Jane lay in her yard, she remembered how children teased her in school. She had been chubby, still was. And although she was not ugly, she was only marginally attractive. The children mocked her endlessly about sharing the name of a beautiful actress. "I only have one *l*, she would argue. I'm not named after her." Children are cruel and, as Jane found, relentless. They teased her all through high school.

Nora was asking her questions she could not understand. All she could remember was those kids, their cruelty, her misery. "I only have one *l*," Jane said with her last breath. Nora started CPR and did not stop until paramedics relieved her. She looked around her street. It looked like a war zone. Not the street she and her husband had planned to raise their family, walk their dog, and have barbeques on the weekends. This was not a place she wanted to live. Not anymore.

Dee and Jack were having coffee at the café when they heard the first bomb explode. They both knew what it was. Then they heard the others. They could see the smoke from a couple of streets over. They were in Dee's truck before either said a word. When they arrived at what appeared to be the center of the bombing, they sprang into action. Paramedics had not arrived, but sirens could be heard. Dee and Jack split up, trying to help where they could. Dee was doing triage to the best of her limited abilities when the first ambulance pulled up. The firetrucks arrived next.

As the first responders did their work, Dee could not help but look toward Ray Dobbins's house. She saw him sitting on his porch, drink in hand, smiling. She knew in that moment he was responsible. She did not know if she would ever be able to prove it.

*****

The body count was fifteen. Twelve more were critically injured, and ten were treated for minor injuries. Eggers Cove was rocked. People arrived at the high school gym, where a makeshift shelter had been set up with blankets, clothes, food, and medical supplies. No one could believe that this could happen in their town. There was endless talk of terrorists, although no one could determine why they would strike here.

Dee's group was all present and accounted for at the gym, helping where they could. Dee spent every free minute calling the arson investigator, hoping for evidence. She spent the rest of her time questioning people from the street. As was typical, no one saw anything. Jack brought burgers and fries for everyone and sandwiches for later. He said it was the least he could do.

When the group had a moment to gather, Jim asked if this was related.

"Nope, it was Ray Dobbins," Dee announced as fact. "I saw him on his porch, smiling while his neighbors were dying."

"The creature lives on his property. Maybe it is related," Jack offered. He did not think Ray Dobbins was capable of such cruelty. He was an asshole, for sure, but not a cold-blooded murderer.

"Regardless, I know it was him," Dee reaffirmed. "That bastard has been gunning for Jane Russel for years."

"We need to kill this creature before it does any more damage," Jim said. Dee noticed he was pale. He had dark circles under his eyes.

She put her hand on his shoulder. "We will, Jim. We have to."

*****

Later that night, Dee found herself sipping wine with Jack. He had made a fire, and Ralph was soaking it up. She smiled to herself and thought this must be what heaven was like. Sipping wine and watching a dog live his best life in front of a fire. And the man she loved sitting next to her. Recent events had Dee remembering things long forgotten from her childhood. Specifically, the summer when she was twelve kept popping up. They had gone through something that summer, her group. She knew she needed to remember. She thought somehow, it would help.

*****

Dee and her friends spent most days at the river during the summer. This day was no exception. They had fashioned a rope swing and took turns swinging and jumping into the river. The idea was to one-up the previous turn. Jim was doing flips, Jack was hanging upside down from the rope, and Dee was laughing. The smartest part of her brain told her to remember this day, these times. These were things you had to remember. The good times.

Charlie had become increasingly quiet and distant, scared of the imminent separation. Dee had been pestering him for days about it, but he refused to tell her what was wrong. She talked to Jack about it. He did not know what was wrong. Dee asked if it could be school. Charlie did not have any friends his own age. The pair decided to be as inclusive with him as possible, show him he would not be forgotten.

Later, the group went for slices and then a two-dollar movie. The theater in Eggers Cove never showed new releases, but it was cheap and kept kids out of trouble. Summer was winding down, and the group was determined to enjoy every second of it. It was starting to get dark when they left the theater, and the boys offered to walk Dee home.

"Bullshit. *I'll* walk you guys home," Dee said, full of confidence and a smile. Her friends laughed but knew better than to give Dee much grief. She could handle herself—and them. The group ended up taking their usual route home from downtown to Mulberry Street, where Jim and Charlie went right, and Dee and Jack went left. Promises were made to meet after breakfast.

The next morning was the beginning of the day the group had worked hard to forget. It was the day they almost lost Charlie. Jack was waiting for Dee on her porch early that morning, backpack full of gear. Dee smiled and asked what he was up to.

"You'll see." He smirked. "Let's go meet the guys." The pair walked to Jim's house and found Charlie already waiting. "You knock yet?"

"Nah. Just got here a minute ago."

Jim's mom waved at them from the kitchen window and stuck up one finger. Jim would just be a minute. Moments later, Jim bounded out the door. "Sorry, guys. Mom insisted on a big breakfast."

The group teased him a bit then headed toward the river. First stop, their spot, formerly known as their fort. Jack unloaded his backpack on the large tree stump they used as a table. It appeared he had the whole day planned. He had brought Charlie's favorite games, snacks, and left a few surprises in his pack.

They played games for the rest of the morning. It was the last Saturday before school started, their last moments of freedom. When you are young, September is the most dreaded month, June the most anticipated. The summer months fly by. The school months drag. When they tired of games, they took the short walk to the river to cool off.

The rope swing one-up game turned into dunking each other then the breath-holding game. The idea was to stay underwater longer than any of the others. Dee was the first above water. She abhorred this game. Jack followed. Dee suspected he was trying to let

Charlie win. Jack won more often than not. The pair continued to tread water while they waited for their friends.

"It's taking too long," Dee worried out loud.

"No, we've been down longer."

Seconds later, Jim emerged, gasping for air. The three looked around, expecting Charlie to appear victorious. Seconds passed. Dee could not wait any longer. She dove underwater and looked for Charlie. Jack and Jim followed. They swam around, frantically looking for their friend, their responsibility. Jack spotted him first. He was on the bottom, and his leg was stuck.

Jack swam to the surface for air and asked his friends to follow him back down. Charlie's right leg was stuck between two rocks. Dee thought he must have tried to sit on the river bottom to stay under longer then moved wrong. They pulled and pushed on one rock until it moved enough to slip Charlie's leg out. Jack put his arm around him and swam to the surface.

Charlie was not breathing. They got him on the beach, and Dee began CPR. In her family, this was a requirement. They all knew CPR. After what felt like forever to the scared kids, Charlie began coughing up water. They turned him on his side. He finally sat up and was breathing normal. Dee hugged him.

"Shit, man, you don't have to almost die to win," Jim joked nervously.

"And that's as close as you'll ever get to making out with Dee," Jack added. They all laughed. Charlie blushed.

Charlie looked around at his friends. Then something caught his eye. "Guys, what's that?" He pointed at a nearby rock. On a large rock on the bank they seldom used was symbol etched into it. It was a symbol the group would all see again, many years later.

Chapter 17

Friday morning, Dee awoke feeling more determined than ever. Determined to find and kill a monster, determined to prove Ray Dobbins was responsible for the tragedy the day before, determined overall to win. Over coffee, she asked Jack if he remembered the summer when they were twelve.

"Some of it, sure. Why?"

"Do you remember the day we almost lost Charlie? He almost drowned?"

Jack thought back. Much of his childhood was just images and feelings now. Then the memory that he had fought so hard to repress came flooding back. Dee noticed Jack teared up slightly. "Yeah, that was scary. I thought he was dead." Jack paused a moment. "Why are you bringing it up now?"

"Remember after, after he was back, he pointed at a rock?"

Jack looked puzzled, then realization came over his face. "The symbol! I can't believe we forgot about that."

"I was going to take a field trip down to the river today. Interested?"

"Yeah. Should we invite the guys?"

"Which ones? Our guys, my guys, some variation?" Dee realized that their once small group had increased significantly. "Maybe just Jim and Charlie for now. They were both there before."

"Is this an after-breakfast trip or later today?"

"I have to go to the station this morning, deal with the aftermath of yesterday. Let's plan for after lunch. Can you set it up?"

"I'm on it."

"You're the best." Dee kissed him. "I'll see you later."

*****

At the station, Dee reviewed the preliminary arson report. There was no new information. Multiple devices, triggered remotely. The largest device was placed under the porch of Jane Russel's house. It supported her theory but was not enough to charge Ray Dobbins. Dee tossed the report on her desk, frustrated. She had her best deputies, Adams and Collins, at the scene scouring for evidence. They had orders to look for evidence related to the bombs and evidence out of the ordinary.

She was sorting through witness statements, knowing that not only were they unreliable, but these also had no information. Like her other open cases, no one saw anything, heard anything, or even smelled anything. Dee looked to see which deputy asked about smells. Collins. She smiled at that. Collins was coming along.

Dee's phone buzzed. "What's up, Matt?"

"Um, Sheriff, we think you'll want to see what we found out here."

"I'm on my way." Dee let Dawn know she was headed over to the scene. She parked close to the roped-off block and walked in to meet with her deputies. They were exactly where she thought they would be, in front of Jane Russel's house. "What do you have for me?"

"This way." Adams led Dee to the side of Jane Russel's house that was still mostly intact. Dee saw what they found immediately. She pulled out her phone to photograph the symbols carved into the wood. There were at least half of a dozen that Dee spotted immediately. "There's more." Adams led Dee to the back of the house. "See." There were dozens of symbols, some Dee recognized, some looked new.

"Have you seen anything like this before?" Collins asked.

Dee had almost forgotten Collins was with them. "Yes." She took pictures of everything she could see. "Any more surprises?"

"This is it, but we haven't made it very far," Collins said. "We thought you would want to see this right away." Collins paused, took a breath, and said quietly, "In case it disappears."

Dee looked at Collins. He could not quite meet her eyes. "Good thinking. Two weeks ago, I would have laughed. Now I just expect anything." She put a comforting hand on his shoulder and squeezed. "Good work. Keep looking." Dee was about to walk away. "I'm going to go have a conversation with Ray Dobbins. If you can, try to get a look around his property while I distract him."

"You think he's responsible, don't you?" Adams asked, more like stated.

Dee shrugged and tilted her head slightly. "Just going to ask him about yesterday." She walked toward Ray Dobbins's house and saw a curtain move in a front window. He had been watching them. Before she reached his porch steps, the front door opened.

"Sheriff." Dee supposed that passed as a greeting in Dobbins's land.

"Morning, Mr. Dobbins. I was wondering if you had a few minutes to answer some questions."

"I've already spoken with your deputies and the fire marshal. I've answered all of their questions."

"I know. I just have a few others."

"If you must." Ray Dobbins motioned for her to sit on a nearby chair. Dee obliged.

"I know you were asked about the past few days. I'm more interested the past few weeks," Dee began. This got an involuntary eyebrow raise from Ray Dobbins. Dee noted it, pretended not to see it. "Anything new or different on your street?"

"Besides the influx of cars and visitors at the Russel house?" Dee noticed he tried to keep the distain out of his voice. He was unsuccessful. Dee nodded. "Nothing else of note."

"How about something not of note?"

Ray Dobbins gave her a look that was part inquisitive, part speculative, and all suspicious. He knew she was questioning him about more than the neighborhood. He realized he was her primary suspect. He had anticipated this, taken precautions. He would just answer carefully. "I'm not sure what you mean, Sheriff."

"Maybe something small, barely noticeable. You may have dismissed it without a second thought?"

"Nothing like that. Now if you will excuse me, Sheriff." Ray Dobbins stood and tried to usher Dee off his porch.

"One more thing, Mr. Dobbins." Dee stood as well and met his gaze. "Yesterday, when your street was on fire, people were screaming. Why didn't you do anything? I saw you on your porch, watching."

His eyes first filled with joy then switched to outrage. "How dare you. What was I supposed to do? I'm an old man."

Dee had asked for his response. She knew he was responsible. This confirmed it. "It's just that I saw people of all ages and abilities lending a hand where they could. I was just wondering why you did nothing."

"I believe we're finished here." He pointed at his steps, as if Dee did not know how to exit a porch.

She stepped off his porch and walked to the sidewalk. There she stood for several minutes, pretending to mess with her phone. She was buying time for her deputies. As long as she was standing here, Ray Dobbins would not look anywhere else. She saw Adams and Collins peek around from the side of Jane Russel's house. They had completed the search of the Dobbins's property. She texted Adams to fill her in at the station. She did not want to speak to them now. No need raising any more suspicion with Ray Dobbins. Dee looked at the time. Almost two. She texted Jack that she was on her way. She would meet them there.

*****

For the first time, Dee was the last to arrive. She found her group gathered on the other side of the river near the rock. She greeted her friends and apologized for being late. They climbed down the bank of the river to the beach. As had become the norm, Dee went first. She made her way to the rock and saw the symbol she had seen so many years ago.

"It's still here," she said, mostly under her breath.

"Where'd you think it would go?" Charlie asked.

"Shit keeps disappearing. I'm just as surprised when it doesn't." She took pictures of the symbol and walked around the rock, looking for more. "Maybe we should split up and search the area."

"We'll go this way. You two the other," Jack suggested. Not waiting for a response, he and Dee walked north along the bank. After fifteen minutes of looking high and low, nothing new was discovered. They walked back to the beach. Jim and Charlie were waiting. They had similar results.

"This wasn't a total bust. At least we were able to see that symbol," Charlie said, pointing to the rock from their youth.

"You guys want to see why I was late today?" Dee asked, pulling pictures up on her phone. "These were taken at the back of Jane Russel's house." She showed her friends the pictures from the house.

"This looks like the cave," Jim said. "That's a lot of symbols."

"And I had a conversation with Ray Dobbins."

"Shit, what'd he say?" Jim asked.

"It wasn't what he said. It was his reaction. I'm sure he bombed his street. He knows I know. I think he predicted that, probably planned for it."

"Anything on the arson report?" Jack asked hopefully.

"No, nothing more than what we already knew." Dee looked at the time. She needed to get back to the station. "Jim, can we meet at your place later? Talk to the kids. I'll bring pizza."

"Yeah, the kids would like that. They like feeling included."

The group decided on six at Jim's, and Dee went back to the station. Charlie left next, leaving Jim and Jack standing on the beach, looking at the river.

"You okay, man?" Jack asked. He, too, had noticed Jim's paleness and the dark circles under his eyes.

Jim looked at his oldest friend, his best friend. "Just stressed. Worried about the kids. My marriage is over. Mary has become a drunken mess…" Jim trailed off. "A lot going on, that's all."

"We're all here for you, you know that." Jack put his hand on Jim's shoulder. "Anything you need."

Jim turned and hugged his friend. "I know. Thanks."

After their field trip, Jack went to the station to see Dee. She was finishing up with her deputies when he arrived. Dawn had him wait in the lobby. It was still hard for him, being on the sidelines. He missed the job. He was grateful Dee included him as much as she did. A few minutes later, Dee emerged smiling. She took Jack back to her office and closed the door.

"Just wanted to check on you. See what you held back earlier." Jack smirked at Dee. Sometimes she hated how well he knew her.

"I asked Ray why he just sat on his porch and watched while his neighbors were dying," Dee began. "His eyes lit up, Jack. They fucking lit up. I'm not sure if it was pride or satisfaction, but he was pleased with himself. With his actions."

"I didn't think he was capable of such evil."

"Nothing surprises me anymore." Dee sighed. She was exhausted. "Can you do me a favor and pick up the pizza for later? I have an errand I have to run."

He said he would. He hugged Dee and left. Dee was out the door right behind him. She needed to hurry, or she was going to be late for the second time today. She was the last to arrive at Jim's but knew she would be forgiven.

"I hope you don't mind. I brought a guest," Dee said as she entered. "Come on in."

Behind Dee, a boy small for his age, with the eyes of an old soul, walked through the doors. "Hey, guys. Miss me?"

"Billy!" his friends yelled in unison as they rushed to hug him. Chris reached him first.

As the kids hugged each other and laughed, Dee filled the adults in. "I got the call earlier today that he was ready to be released. I just got back from picking him up. There's some forms you'll need to sign," Dee said to Jim. "But we can do that later."

Jack came over and gave Dee a hug. "This was your errand." He smiled and kissed her head. There was a new energy in the air. It was hope mixed with victory. Hope that they could win this, victory in that they saved one of their own.

*****

149

After they ate pizza, drank sodas and beer, they began to fill Billy in. He had missed a lot while in the hospital, but he had his own information to share. They showed Billy the symbols and the patterns they had discovered so far.

"I've dreamed of those," Billy said, pointing to a cluster. "Every night since this started again."

"Those are the ones we've seen the most," Jim started. "Specifically this one." He held up a picture of a symbol.

"It's also the one that disappears the most," Dee added. "That and the tracks."

"I think these," Jack said, pointing to the symbols from the local tribe. "Are either a warning or a counter to the others."

"That makes sense. If this thing has been around, or at least a version of it, for over a hundred years, they probably would have developed something as a protector or to combat it," Dee agreed. "Now if we can just figure out how to use them."

"I liked your idea from before, Dee," Charlie chimed in. "Where we trap and kill it. We know where it lives or where it spends time. It shouldn't be too difficult."

"Just blow up its home," Steve added. "That would solve everything."

"Where it lives, where we think it lives, is under the town. We can't blow that up," Jim lectured. "We're not burning it either." Jim knew Steve well. He figured that would be his next suggestion.

Steve rolled his eyes at Jim but did not speak. He was out of ideas.

Chris looked around at the adults. "How would we trap it?"

"Not *we*, kid. The adults. You're planning stages only," Charlie stated.

Although Dee agreed with Charlie, she felt his delivery was poor. "I think what Charlie meant is that you guys are being hunted. We can't put you in danger like that." She put her arm around Chris's shoulders. "But we're open to any ideas you have. Besides the ones involving destroying the whole town." Everyone chuckled at that. Steve blushed slightly. "Abby, have you found anything new? Or pieced anything more together?"

"Not really. I've been researching how to break codes. Too much math. I'm trying the look for patterns and method and hope for the best." Abby felt like she was letting everyone down. She had not found anything new. She had worked really hard though.

"I've found that sometimes, you can just see patterns, Abby. Keep looking. You discovered the first pieces. The rest will come together," Jack offered. Abby smiled at him.

"Can I see the cave?" a small voice asked. It was Billy. His head was down. He was looking at his feet. He looked up slowly, eyes scanning the room. He locked eyes with Dee. She could see he thought he needed this, thought somehow, he could help if he saw the cave.

Jim was the first to speak. "Buddy, I don't think that's a good idea. We're trying to keep you kids far away from that creature."

"Billy," Dee started. "You almost died. I think that thing was feeding on you in your house. We can't let you anywhere near it." She read his face. There was fear and disappointment. "I'm not trying to scare you any more than you already are. It just isn't safe. I'm not putting any of you in danger."

This statement almost broke Billy and his friends. Especially Chris. In his mind, he was going to find this cave, the creature, and kill it. Possibly with his bare hands. He did not let any of this show on his face. "You guys are right. We shouldn't go near where it lives." Abby gave him a look that begged him to stop. Steve nodded at him. They had their own language. Abby, who had been trying to learn it, took the exchange as a positive. She would ask Chris about it later.

Charlie got a text from his wife and had to leave. Dee and Jack followed moments later. "Billy, I'm glad you're here, safe," Dee said as they were leaving.

"Thanks," Billy said. Then quietly, "Do you know where my dad is?"

Dee looked at Jack. He shook his head slightly. "No, I'm still looking." Dee lied. They would have that discussion another time when he was safe, when they all were safe.

"You think he knew I was lying?" Dee asked Jack back at his house.

"Probably, but if he does, he knows you're doing it for his own good. That kid is beyond his years."

"I'm sure you're right. I just hate lying. Especially to kids." Dee laid her head on Jack's shoulder.

Jack lifted her head and kissed her lightly. "Don't beat yourself up. It was the right thing. You'll—we'll—explain it to him later."

They went to bed soon after, and Dee dreamed of her mother. Her mother before she was sick, before those last few nights. As a child, Dee prayed that she would remember her mother before her illness, not the monster she had become.

*****

As the sickness progressed, Margot Halley became less and less like herself. She snapped easily in conversation, she wailed in the night, and she had become mean. Dee had only known her mother as kind and loving. She did not recognize what she had become. Dee was scared. She was young, and she was incapable of understanding the toll cancer could take on not only its main victim, but secondary ones as well.

Dee would cry herself to sleep. She hated what her mother had become. She knew it was not her mother, not the mother she knew. She called this one the "Cancer Mother." Cancer Mother or Cancer Mom was a shadow of Real Mom. Cancer Mom's eyes were filled with pain, rage, and sadness. The hands that were once full of warmth had become cold and bony. Dee feared that if one of those hands grasped her for too long, she would become like her mother.

One night, near the end, Margot called for her daughter in the night. Dee tried to ignore it, hoped the calling would stop. It did not. She slowly walked down the stairs to the living room where Cancer Mom's hospital bed had been set up. The air in the room was damp, cold, and it smelled of rotting flesh. She saw Cancer Mom's hand stretched out towards her. She called her daughter's name again. Dee felt a shiver down her spine.

"Mom?" Her voice was barely above a whisper.

"Deirdra, you wretched little girl, come here." Her arm seemed to stretch closer to Dee. She could not be sure, but Cancer Mom's fingernails seemed to be growing. She felt the cold clutch of death on her arm. The nails dug into her skin. This had to be a nightmare. Cancer Mom was not—could not—be real.

"You're hurting me," Dee cried as she tried to pull away.

Cancer Mom's grasp tightened. Her cold eyes locked onto Dee's. "It's coming for you too," Cancer Mom warned.

Dee pulled away and ran out of the room. She ran to her parents' room. She needed her father. He was not home. He was working. Dee was alone in the house with Cancer Mom. She went to her room and put a pillow over her head, hoping to block out her mother's (Cancer Mom's) screams. It did not. Dee wished for it to stop, for it to be over. She wished for Cancer Mom to die.

Chapter 18

Chris woke early on Saturday. He had plans for the day. He had discussed them with Abby last night. She was game. He knew Steve would go along, and Alex would do whatever he told him. The question that both he and Abby had was whether to include Billy. Neither thought it was safe for him. Chris suggested they leave him and Alex behind.

"We'll call it a scouting mission. Tell them they can come for the real thing," Chris said.

"I think we tell them nothing. Billy will want to come. He'll follow. Alex too." Abby was right, and her friends agreed.

When he was sure his parents were gone, Chris went to their room to retrieve an item. His mother had not said goodbye to him this morning, and Chris was not sure she had been home the night before. Another issue he would worry about later. They were beginning to stack up. He had done a quick check of the house to make sure his parents were gone. He did not need them surprising him.

Chris, Abby, and Steve left soon after convincing Alex and Billy to stay behind. Chris—with a little help—had convinced Alex and Billy to stay and review the symbols. Billy was new to this information, or at least the information they had. They needed him to look. And as Chris expected, Alex did what he was told.

Once they were blocks away from Chris's house, sure they had not been followed, Steve asked where they were going.

"Billy's old house," Chris stated. "They might not tell us where the cave is, but I bet we'll find answers there."

Abby shuddered at the thought of going back to that house. She feared the voice would still be there. She knew she could not say anything to her friends. They needed her. She had to be brave. It was hard being a girl hanging out with boys. She was always a little afraid she would be excluded for being too much of a girl.

As if Chris could read her mind, he grabbed her hand in his. "It'll be okay, Abs. I promise." She smiled at him.

"Who's gonna hold my hand?" Steve joked. It earned him a slug to both arms.

The trio arrived at Billy's old house and entered through the back door, which had become the main entrance lately. Steve was the last to enter and immediately expressed his distain for the place. "Let's make this quick. I don't want to spend one extra fucking second in this hell."

Abby was not exactly searching for the voice she had heard before, but she was listening. She was a fan of horror stories, and inevitably, mind control was involved. The main character would try to build a wall in their brain to keep out the predator. She wished those parts of the books had been better explained. She was having a hard time trying to figure out how to build walls.

Purely on instinct, the trio went to Billy's old room first. The only thing they knew for sure was that a tunnel opened somewhere on the property, so they proceeded to stomp on every inch of floor. They pulled at the carpet, knocked on walls, and found nothing. Steve suggested they search elsewhere when Abby stepped into the closet.

"Here," she said. "The carpet is folded." She pulled at the carpet and revealed the door the adults had found previously. After the immediate cheers, reality sunk in. They exchanged worried and scared looks.

Chris opened his backpack and pulled out flashlights, one for each of them. "I figured the tunnel wouldn't be lit," he said sarcastically. He reached in again and pulled out an item wrapped in cloth. He unwrapped it. Abby and Steve took a step back.

"Shit, man. What's that for?" Steve asked.

"What do you think?" Chris responded, tucking his father's .9mm in his waistband. "We're not gonna hug it to death." Both Chris and his brother had taken hunter safety classes and were raised with a respect of firearms. They knew they were not toys; they were tools. Tools for hunting, tools for protection. He looked to Abby to see if she was going to protest. The look on her face suggested she would not. She looked almost relieved.

"Let's go," Abby said, pulling at the door.

"Wait," Chris said, pulling Abby back. "I'll go first." Abby agreed, and Chris opened the door and shined his flashlight into the open space beneath the house. Chris climbed down and was followed first by Abby then Steve. They followed the path the adults had taken just days before and reached the door leading to the tunnel.

When they arrived at the first fork, they saw the blue paint. "They went right," Chris said. "Let's go left." The others agreed. At the next fork, they went left again, deciding it would be easier to find their way back if they kept turning the same direction.

"Or we'll go in circles," Steve said sarcastically. "We should have thought to bring spray paint."

"Too late now." Abby sighed.

After three left turns, the passageway narrowed, and the ceiling was lowering. Within twenty feet, the trio was crawling. Abby was about to suggest turning back when they came upon an opening to a large room.

Chris shined his flashlight around. "It's the cave," he declared, voice barely more than a whisper.

"Do you think it's the same one?" Abby asked.

"I don't know. Probably. How many caves could there be?" Chris reasoned.

As they shined their flashlights around the cave at the symbols covering every wall, Abby began to feel the familiar tug. She tried to push it out, to ignore it, but it's grasp got tighter. Then the voice, small at first, not even a whisper, then louder. "Chris? Do you hear that?"

"What?"

The voice was much louder, yelling. No words, just noises. Abby grabbed at her head. "Make it stop!" she screamed. Her body began to tremble. Chris and Steve tried to hold her. She fell to the ground and began thrashing, still screaming.

"What do we do?" Steve asked, panicked.

"I don't know," Chris said. "We have to get her out of here." Chris looked around the cave. There were multiple ways out. He did not think they could drag her the way they came, but the other ways were unknown. They could get lost in the labyrinth under their town. A voice, his own, inside said to take the tunnel on the right. He trusted it. "Grab her legs. We're leaving." Chris grabbed her under her arms and started toward the tunnel.

"That's not the way we came," Steve protested.

"We can't carry her the way we came."

"Shit." Steve did not like this plan. He was scared they would die down here, in the dark, and no one would ever find them.

The boys struggled to carry a screaming and flailing Abby and flashlights through an unknown tunnel. The fear of death was growing in them both. They were not sure how far they had gone when Steve said he saw a ladder. They set Abby down, and Chris climbed the wooden ladder and opened the door at the top. Bright light blinded him momentarily, and he realized he found the surface, the outside. It looked like they were in the woods somewhere.

Abby's screaming had stopped, and her body was still, too still, Chris thought. Fortunately for the boys, the ladder was more of a step ladder, with only four steps. Fortunately for Abby, her friends were strong. Steve was able to sit Abby against the ladder then pushed as Chris pulled her through the open door. Once out, they carried Abby away from the tunnel to a small clearing. They laid her down on the ground, and Chris checked to see if she was breathing. It was shallow, but she was.

Chris brushed Abby's hair out of her face. There was dried blood around her nose and one of her ears. She needed a doctor. They needed to figure out where they were. He pulled out his cell-phone. He had one bar. It would be enough to make a call or a text, maybe enough to use GPS.

"Check your phone," Chris instructed Steve. "See if you have reception."

Steve pulled his phone from his pocket and checked. "One bar, man. About twenty percent charged."

While Chris's GPS loaded, he looked around and listened. "I think we're near the river. I think I hear it."

Steve was quiet for a moment. "Yeah, I hear it too. That way." He pointed to his left.

"Go check. I'll stay with Abs."

Steve ran in the direction of the river while Chris stayed behind and prayed. Steve returned a few minutes later, winded. "We're near the bridge. I called Dee."

The boys carried Abby toward the bridge and arrived just as Dee pulled up. She was alone, and Chris breathed a sigh of relief. He did not need the lecture he had earned from his father right now.

"Paramedics are a few minutes out," Dee called as she ran toward them. She began to assess Abby. "What were you doing? And what was she doing before losing consciousness?"

The boys exchanged a look Dee could not read. She knew they were about to lie. "We were just goofing around, and she started screaming, and then she fell down. Her body was like spasming or something," Chris explained. He did not want to lie to Dee, but he did not want to tell her the whole truth either.

Dee met his eyes. He was holding back. She would deal with that issue later. The paramedics had arrived. Dee and the boys moved back to let the paramedics work on Abby. After a few minutes, they loaded her into the ambulance and took her to the hospital. Dee and the boys followed in her truck. She texted Jack on the way, asked him to tell Jim. A few minutes later, she radioed into the station and had Dawn notify Abby's parents. She had almost forgotten them. Dee was not sure she had ever met George and Lily Thomas. She certainly had not seen them with Abby since this started.

*****

Jack found Dee and the boys in the ER waiting area of the hospital. Jim and Abby's parents had not yet arrived. Dee briefed him on Abby's condition and on her suspicions. She told him she was waiting to hear about Abby before interrogating the boys. Jim was next to arrive. Dee kept her suspicions to herself with him, and he had Billy and Alex with him. Dee noticed that Chris did not ask why his mother had not come along. Abby's parents arrived next. Lily Thomas was frantically seeking answers from anyone who appeared to work at the hospital. Her husband was failing to calm her.

"Mrs. Thomas, I'm Sheriff Halley." Dee thought she would give it a try. "I'm close with the Stevens family. We're all over there if you and your husband would like wait with us." Dee gently ushered the pair toward her party.

"Thank you, Sheriff," George Thomas said as he shook Dee's hand. "We understand you found her."

"Not exactly. She was with Chris and Steve, and they called me. I called for the paramedics. They arrived minutes after me and transported her here. She was breathing, but unconscious."

"And the doctors? Have they said anything?"

"Sorry, not yet." Dee made introductions where they were needed, and they sat, Lily reluctantly.

The group sat quietly, waiting for information. Lily Thomas was googling causes of seizures in adolescents and possible diseases. George Thomas was pretending to not notice. A doctor came out and explained that Abby was awake and responsive. They were running tests and were going to keep her overnight for observation. She could have visitors, but the number should be limited.

Relieved, Lily and George went first. George returned a few minutes later and asked for the boys. They came back in less than five minutes. Lily was playing security guard and taking her duties seriously. Dee, Jim, and Jack were next. Dee needed to see Abby, even if only for a moment.

Abby was sitting up in her hospital bed. The blood had been cleaned from her face, and her natural color had returned. Dee grabbed the girl's hand. "You gave us a scare, Abby."

"Sorry, Dee. I'm feeling better now."

"Rest up. We'll talk soon," Dee said and left the room. She had other children to interrogate. This one could wait.

*****

Late Saturday afternoon, the group reconvened at Jim's house. Mary was nowhere to be seen or heard. Dee deduced she must be out, again. Charlie arrived with apologies for not going to the hospital. Mayor business had kept him busy. Jim had already asked Chris and Steve what they were doing earlier in the day and did not get any real answers. Dee took the boys into another room to see if she could get answers.

"It's really good news that Abby appears to be okay. Hopefully, she'll be released tomorrow," Dee started. "But earlier when I asked what you guys had been doing, you didn't really answer me." Dee looked at the boys, who were exchanging nervous looks. "It's important, guys. I need to know."

Chris met her eyes. Dee was sure she could see fear in them. "Are you going to tell my dad?"

"We'll see. But most likely."

Steve gave him a look that Dee read as *don't say anything*. "We went in the tunnels."

Dee's first instinct was to grab and shake them both, screaming about how stupid they were. The logical part of her took control. "Tell me everything."

They did. Chris left nothing out, even the choosing of the tunnel they used to escape. "We're sorry, Dee. We wanted to end this."

"I get it. Don't do it again." She met both of their gazes. "I'm serious." They believed her and made their promises. Dee hoped they kept them.

Back in the dining room, which had become their official meeting area, Dee asked the kids to leave so she could speak with the adults. "So the good news is that we now know three different ways to get to the cave." Dee wanted to start on a positive note because Jim was not going to like her news. The guys exchanged puzzled looks. "The kids went on their own mission this morning. They promise to never try anything like that again."

"What did they do?" Jim asked, obviously concerned.

"They went to Billy's old house and found the tunnels. They went the opposite direction we did and ended up in the cave. After Abby's episode, they went out a different direction because they couldn't carry her the way they had come in. They know exactly where they came out and can show us."

Jim took a deep breath. He was pacing around the room. Dee could tell he was ready to yell and punish the kids. There was also a look on his face beyond the anger and rage. It was hurt and pain. Dee thought maybe it was the thought that his boy did not trust him. Maybe it was that it could be his boy in the hospital. Maybe it was both.

"We'll be having a conversation later. What can we do with this information?"

"Trapping the thing just became easier," Jack said. "We have three access points. That's three places we can block or station people. There's just one more." He looked at his friends. He knew this was not going to be received well. "I think we should see where the last tunnel goes."

Before Charlie or Jim could object, Dee said, "I agree." "The more information we have, the better we can plan. The more likely we will succeed."

"When do we go?" Charlie asked reluctantly.

"It's too late today. Tomorrow morning?" Dee suggested. The group agreed to meet at Jack's after sunup.

Chapter 19

Sophia Harris was a well-liked popular eleven-year-old girl. Her social calendar was always full. She played team sports and was a good student. Her parents appeared to have a good marriage, and her siblings seemed to be well-adjusted. On the surface, her life was perfect. She knew some of the girls were jealous of her, even befriended her despite—or because of—it.

Saturday night, she was home and without a friend for the first Saturday in many months. She had not felt like going to a friend's house, and she did not want a friend to stay over. Sophia did not have the vocabulary to explain what was wrong with her. She just felt sad. It did not make sense to her. There was nothing in her life to cause her sadness. She thought about discussing these feelings with her parents, but they were busy. They both had stressful jobs and worked long hours. She did not want to be a burden. She would figure this out on her own.

She tried googling "sadness for no reason." All she discovered was a new word—*melancholy*. She watched her favorite show and cried instead of laughed. She put her laptop away and lay quietly in the dark. Sophia must have drifted off because a scratching noise woke her. She rubbed her eyes and looked around her dark room. No one was there.

(Scratch, scratch)

Again, the noise, coming from her window. She wondered what could be scratching her window. It was on the second floor of her home.

(Scratch, scratch)

Her first instinct was to call for her parents, but she did not want to bother them. She thought about crossing her room and look-ing out the window, but her gut told her not to.

(Scratch, scratch)

Whatever it was, it could not be good. When she was younger, she would crawl under the covers at night when she was scared. Like most kids, Sophia believed blankets had magic powers. They could hide you and protect you from monsters. Before she could pull the blankets up, she felt a tickle in her brain. Then a low voice.

(Tap, tap)

The noise had changed. She was sure of it. But it no longer mattered. Only the voice mattered. It promised to end the sadness, even to ease the stress of her parents.

(Scratch, scratch, tap, tap)

She felt the carpet on her feet before her brain had registered she was getting out of bed. She moved slowly, as if a part of her knew it was wrong, dangerous. But she moved forward. An image of her running through a field of flowers as a young child entered her mind. Happier times, the best times. She reached the window. She lifted her blinds and looked into the darkness. Or what she thought would be darkness. Instead, her hopeful blue eyes locked with a pair of red ones. She could not scream. It was too late.

Around seven thirty Sunday morning, Susan Harris went to her daughter's room to wake her. It was odd that Sophia had not been downstairs yet. She was typically the first of the children to rise. She knocked lightly a couple of times before entering. Susan had teenage boys and learned knocking was essential. She opened the door and found Sophia's bed empty. She looked around the room and found her daughter crumpled on the ground near her window. Susan rushed to her daughter, calling her name. She fell beside her and grabbed her daughter's lifeless body. She brushed the hair out of Sophia's face and screamed again.

Mitch Harris heard first his wife calling for their daughter. Then he heard his wife scream. He had never heard his wife scream like that. It was a combination of fear, horror, and deep sorrow. He dialed 911 as he ran up the stairs.

*****

Dee received the call moments before she and her friends were to descend into the tunnels. "I'm on my way," she told Adams. Then to her friends, "We need to postpone this. Another child was killed."

Jack pulled her aside "Are you sure? We can go without you, just to look around."

"I don't know, Jack. I'd prefer to be there." Dee looked at Jim and Charlie. Both looked nervous at best. "You're call. I have to go. If you do go down there, let me know."

When Dee arrived at the Harris home, Collins was waiting for her and said that Adams was inside with the family. "You're about to warn me. What do I need to know?"

"How—" Collins started then dropped it. He had been working for the sheriff long enough to know that she just knew things. "Susan Harris, the mom, is basically catatonic. Mitch Harris, the father, is sobbing on the stairs. Their two boys are sitting at the kitchen table, staring out the window. No one is speaking."

Dee took a deep breath. "Thanks for the heads-up. You want to start searching outside the house while I go in and deal with the family until the paramedics get here." He agreed and began his search. Dee hoped the paramedics arrived soon.

While Dee was handling, or trying to handle, the Harris family, her friends had decided to go underground without her. Jack took the lead, which felt natural to them all. They were entering near the river where the kids had exited the day prior. It had been difficult to find even with directions from Chris. The group had made it to the general area but did not see a visible door. Charlie, convinced they were in the wrong spot, wanted to leave. Jim argued against him, and they kept looking. Dee thought it was dumb luck when she stumbled upon it.

"Here," she called, moving a plant she could not identify. "I found it."

The guys met her at the entrance. Charlie had a baffled look on his face. "I looked here. How did you see it?"

"I don't know. I don't care. We have an entry." She walked away to take her phone call.

Now as the last to enter, Charlie could not shake the feeling that the discovery of this entrance was different, wrong in some way.

He thought about Billy's old house. Dee had found that entry. Dee had known where to look at Ray Dobbins's place. Dee had known which way to turn in the tunnels. Going down here without her was dangerous. He wished he had had this epiphany earlier. They were in it now.

They were armed with headlamps, flashlights, and .9mms. Jack had also brought his shotgun. His philosophy was to be over pre-pared when possible. Charlie felt like M-16s would not be enough. He hoped this tour was quick, painless, and fruitful. If they had to be down here, he hoped it was not a wasted trip. He hoped no one got hurt, or worse.

When Jack arrived at the cave, he paused to shine the light around. It was a reflex, maybe from his time on the job, maybe just his personality. It looked clear. No six-foot rats. He motioned for his friends to follow. He shined his light down each tunnel, securing the area as much as possible. Then he met his friends at the only unex-plored tunnel.

"Let's see where this goes," Jack said as he stepped up into the tunnel.

Charlie, again, brought up the rear. And again, the doubt was tugging at him. This was wrong. They should not be here. He wanted to scream at them to stop, to turn around. He wanted to run. Jim nearly jumped out of his skin when he felt a hand on his shoul-der. Keeping ahold of his bladder, he whipped around to find it was Charlie's hand.

Jim was several inches taller than Charlie. His headlamp only illuminated the top part of his head, leaving what Jim thought were creepy shadows on his friend's face. Charlie's face was pale despite the artificial light, and his eyes were wide. Jim suddenly shared his friend's fear.

"Jack, wait," Jim said, his voice barely above a whisper. He only wanted Jack to hear, not "other" ears.

Jack turned and walked back toward his friends. "What's wrong? Why'd you stop?"

"It's wrong. We have to get out of here," Charlie said. Jack thought he heard a slight tremble.

"Jim?" Jack was asking what he wanted to do.

"Move forward. It's early enough in the day. That thing seems to be a night creature. Maybe we get lucky, find something."

"Let's go." Jack turned back around and led his group, a little more cautious than before. If that was possible. He trusted his gut. He always had. When he was on the job, his gut had saved him more times than he could count. Most likely, it saved him times he could not count.

They progressed through the narrow passageway. It seemed to Jack the tunnel would go on forever. He had lost track of time and distance. Then they came upon a fork. Last time they went right, they found nothing. The kids had gone left and found the cave. He looked back at his friends for suggestions. Jim shrugged his shoulders, and Charlie looked at the ground. Jack grabbed a can of green spray paint from his bag and chose the right fork.

The voice in Charlie's head was now accompanied by images of his friends, bleeding, screaming, dead. He could not take much more of this. Every bone in his body was begging him to turn around, to leave and never come back. He was typically a logical person. He believed in things he could see and prove. The rational part of his brain was being drowned out by the new crazy voice.

As they went farther down the tunnel, Jack's legs felt heavy. Every turn felt and looked the same, as if they had been going in circles. He knew they had not come to any forks. They could not be walking in circles. He pulled out his phone to check the time. The screen was dark. It had been fully charged when he left his house this morning. The early stages of claustrophobia were setting in. The tunnel seemed to be shrinking in size. The thought that they were lost would not leave his head. Panic was beginning. He shook it off. He still had control of his rational self.

While his friends were dealing with their voices and fears, Jim was experiencing issues of his own. He felt like they had been down here for hours. His wife's nagging voice in his head was making him crazy. She had not been home much in the past few days, and Jim was grateful for that. She had become increasingly angry, mean, and bitchy. If he was honest with himself, he had stopped liking her years ago. He was not sure there was ever any sort of love there. For a time, in the beginning, he had liked her. Of that he was sure. Now her voice was like nails on a chalkboard, and it seemed to echo in his head.

There was movement ahead. Jack was sure of it. It was large and moved quickly. He would almost call it a scurry. He picked up the pace. He did not want to lose whatever it was. He heard his friends muttering complaints behind him. They seemed far away, not just on his heels.

"I saw something. Hurry," he called back to them. He was at a jog now, his knee reminding him that he was no longer a runner with every step. He ignored the pain and quickened his pace. Protests from his friends continued, now much farther away. Then it struck him. His rational self was not in control. He stopped and turned to see darkness.

Jim and Charlie had lost sight of Jack. For a guy with a bum knee, he was fast. They had been almost yelling for him to stop, but he did not seem to hear them. Jim could see a faint glow of light ahead. He encouraged Charlie to move faster. Jim was pulling him along. He did not want to get separated from Charlie too. The glow was getting bigger, brighter. Jim resisted the urge to yell out. A small voice in his head told him not too. What if it was not Jack?

Jim let out a sigh of relief when he saw it was Jack, but he was unresponsive. He was standing in the center of the tunnel, staring into the darkness. Jim shook his shoulders. Still nothing. "Grab his other arm. We're pulling him out of here."

Charlie grabbed Jack's other arm, and the two began to lead him to what they hoped would be the end of the tunnel. After around fifty feet or so, they, too, could no longer judge time nor distance. They saw a door. Jim forced it open, and daylight poured in. It was almost blinding.

"Where are we?" Charlie asked.

"I don't know. I can hear the river." Jim was looking around. They were surrounded by trees. He had two immediate priorities: figure out where they were and get Jack back. He pulled out his phone and noticed Charlie had done the same.

"We're near the mill, I think." Charlie said while studying his phone.

"I think you're right. It's that way," Jim said, pointing. With one problem solved, he focused his attention on Jack. He snapped his fingers in front of Jack's face, shook his shoulders, and was about to slap him when Jack blinked a couple of times and asked where they were. "Near the mill. How are you feeling?"

"Strange. I don't know what..." He trailed off while rubbing the back of his head. "What time is it?"

Jim and Charlie exchanged a glance. "That's the weird thing. We were only down there for around forty-five minutes."

"It felt like hours or days," Jack began. "Did it mess with your heads too?"

Charlie looked at his shoes. "Yeah, I was terrified. None of it makes sense now, but it was real."

"Do we call Dee?" Jim asked.

"I'm sure she's neck deep in shit right now. She won't be done for hours." Jack looked around the forest. "We're near the mill?" His friends nodded yes. "My sister can give us a ride. She should be there."

The guys took off their headlamps and placed them, their flashlights, and guns in Jack's bag. No need to scare the mill workers. Then they made the short hike to the mill. Bitsy, Jack's sister, was surprised but happy to see her brother. They hugged, and she asked what he was doing there.

"We need a ride please. Our hike went awry." Bitsy gave her brother a sideways look. He knew she was not buying it.

"Sure. Just give me a few minutes," Bitsy went back into her office. The questioning would happen at another time.

Jim gave Jack a puzzled look. "I'll get it later. She knows I never ask for anything unless it's important. The car ride will be full of small talk."

As Jack predicted, the car ride was full of small talk. Bitsy asked after Jim's kids and Charlie's wife. When she asked about Dee, Jack said she was working. The topic was dropped.

Elizabeth "Bitsy" Murphy was older than Jack by eleven months. Irish twins. Their father, Frank, had called her Itsy Bitsy when she was a baby. She was so tiny in his large hands. He had begun calling her that on her first day home from the hospital. His wife, Allison, found it adorable, so it took. As an adult, it had never occurred to her to go by anything different.

Bitsy and Jack did not hang out much as children, but they formed a strong bond as adults. She was nervous when their father began grooming her to take over the mill, but Jack had never showed interest in the business. He had always wanted to go into law enforcement, and he was genuinely happy for her. When she dropped them off at their vehicles parked near the bridge, she asked Jack to call her later. He promised he would.

Jack texted Dee to let her know they had made it out and they would talk when she was available. The guys headed back to Jack's place to discuss what happened and try to come up with a plan. Or at least pieces of a plan. Jim called his kids on the ride over. He needed to hear their voices.

*****

Dee was relieved to get Jack's text. She could not wait to get the details of their field trip, but she was still at the Harris house. She would be able to leave soon and let her deputies investigate and question the neighbors. She was just waiting for the paramedics to leave. Susan Harris had to be transported to the hospital. She was still unresponsive. Her husband and boys were going to follow. Mitch Harris had finally composed himself.

She finished at the Harris house and asked her deputies to call if they found anything. Otherwise, they could discuss it tomorrow. She called the hospital to check on Abby. She was doing well and set to be discharged in a few hours. Dee wanted to talk with Abby. She knew her mother would be hovering at least for today. She texted Abby to let her know she was thinking of her and was glad she was doing well. She ended it with "Talk soon," hoping it was light enough. She did not want Abby to be guarded when they did get a chance to speak alone.

On the drive to Jack's, she hoped Charlie and Jim were still there. She wanted all accounts. She also hoped there would be food. She was starving. Mostly, she hoped they found answers or a step toward an answer. She did not want another family to experience what the Harris family experienced today. Dee knew death was inevitable, but not this kind of death. Children died, sometimes tragically, and she hoped to minimize as many as she could.

Ralph did not greet Dee when she walked through Jack's front door. He was sitting next Jack, head in his lap. He looked in Dee's direction when she came in but immediately focused back on Jack. Between Ralph and the condition of her friends, she knew the tunnel exploration did not go well. At least they were alive. They recounted their stories, what they could remember, and what they could fill in for holes in other's memories.

"The clearest memory I have is that you were supposed to be there," Charlie said to Dee. "I knew, somehow, that without you there, it would go terribly wrong."

"Maybe we should have waited for you," Jack said.

"Maybe, maybe not. Maybe if I were down there, it would have been worse." Dee looked around at her friends. "Bright side: we know where the last tunnel leads."

Jim shook his head and chuckled a little. "There's that." It lightened the mood, color returned to pale faces, and Ralph braved moving his head from Jack's lap. "I need to get home and check on the kids. I don't know where Mary is."

"Is that something we need to worry about?" Dee asked.

"Another time," Jim said as he rose from the couch. He hugged his friends and left.

Charlie followed, muttering something about Jill worrying. Dee did not ask if she should worry about his marriage.

With their friends gone, Dee asked Jack if he was okay. He said he was, but there was something new in his eyes. Fear was not the right word, but it was as close as she could get.

"I'm not gonna lie. It was scary, Dee. Really fucking scary."

Chapter 20

Dee woke Monday morning unrested but determined to tackle the day. Jack had barely slept, but he was in better spirits. He let Ralph, who had slept next to the bed on Jack's side, out for his morning business, fed him, and began breakfast for the humans. The smell of coffee lured Dee out of bed. She found her guys waiting for her in the kitchen. Jack was at the stove, and Ralph was sitting near his dishes, tail wagging. She sipped her coffee and tried to enjoy this moment. History warned that her phone would ring any second. The call would take her away. It always did.

Breakfast was enjoyed in mostly silence. They were still processing the events of the previous day. "I'm going to try to stop by and see Abby today," Dee casually mentioned.

Jack raised an eyebrow. "You think her parents will let you? Lily was pretty protective at the hospital."

"I don't know. They let their daughter basically move into Jim's place. I'm thinking the hospital was not normal behavior."

Jack stood to clear the dishes. "Well, good luck. Let me know if you need me."

"I will." She kissed him on the cheek and scratched behind Ralph's ear. "I'm off to the station. Are you going to the café this morning?"

"Yeah. There's a few things I need to catch up on. I'll drop by later."

"Great. Bring lunch." Dee smiled at him at left. She was dreading the day of listening to her deputies repeat the same reports of no findings. And after yesterday's events, Dee felt further from the answers or even an answer. She sighed and reminded herself to think positively. Today was going to be productive. There were going to be answers or more evidence.

As expected, Adams and Collins presented the same findings as every other scene with similar circumstances. They found the same symbol carved into several trees near the girl's room, and neighbors saw and heard nothing. Dee was skimming their notes, half listening to her deputies, and did not hear Collins's question. She realized she missed it and asked him to repeat.

"I was just asking how many kids live in this town?" Before Dee could answer, he continued his thought. "We could scout out their properties. See if there are any symbols carved into trees."

"There are probably hundreds. That's a lot of houses. How would we explain that to anyone who asked?" Adams did not want to shoot down the idea entirely, but it did not seem feasible. They did not have the manpower and could not explain it to volunteers.

"It's not a terrible idea. We could plot out all the places where the creature has killed. See if a pattern emerges…" Dee trailed off. She was close to a plan, a solution. She could feel it. "Matt, get a large map of the town. Mark the scenes. Mark the vandalism in another color." *And I will mark the tunnel entrances*, she thought.

"And the mutilations? Mark those too?" Collins asked.

"Yes, those too. A different color." As her deputies rose to leave her office, Dee remembered one more thing. "Make two copies." Adams and Collins exchanged a look, but neither questioned their sheriff.

Jack stopped in with lunch while Collins and Adams were working on the assigned art project. They were happy Jack had brought them lunch as well and thanked him. "Is it arts and crafts day?" Jack asked as he sat down in Dee's office.

Dee looked at him, puzzled for a second. "Oh, they're plotting all the crime scenes on a map. They're making us a copy too. We can add the tunnels to ours."

"Clever. I guess we'll be reviewing that this evening with the group?"

Dee smiled with a mouthful of cheeseburger. "Good plan, right?"

He nodded. Another thing he loved about her. How proud of herself she was when she had a good idea. They finished their lunch, and Jack went back to the café. He volunteered to organize the group for later.

*****

New map in hand, Dee left the station and drove to Abby's house. She thought to call ahead but decided it would be harder to say no if she were standing at their front door. Lily Thomas was surprised to see the sheriff at her front door and could not immediately think of a polite reason to ask her to leave.

"Just for a few minutes. She needs her rest," Lily Thomas instructed as she let Dee in.

"Of course," Dee said with a smile and followed her to Abby's room.

Abby was happy to see Dee and gave her a hug, "I'm so glad you're here." Abby waved her mother off. She wanted to speak with Dee alone.

"How are you feeling?"

"Better. I wish I wasn't stuck in this room."

"Yeah, me too. We need your help." Dee smiled at her. "Can we talk about the tunnels?"

The light Dee brought left Abby's eyes. Her face paled. "It was in my head again," she said quietly. Dee held the girl's hand, and Abby continued with her story. There were large chunks missing, just like the adults. "It was so scary, Dee. I thought I was going to lose my mind down there."

"I know. We're going to do everything we can so you aren't in that position again." Dee hugged her young friend. "Do you feel safe here?"

Abby nodded. "My parents let me keep the boards and foam up. I told them it helped me sleep."

"Good. I have to get over to Jim's. We have a new project." Dee stood and walked toward Abby's door. "Maybe we'll even find some answers."

After exchanging a few pleasantries with Lily Thomas, Dee drove to Jim's. Jack was already there. Charlie arrived moments after Dee. Jim and Chris took the mirror down from the dining room wall so Dee could hang her new map.

"Scenes where kids were found dead are marked in red. Vandalism is marked in green, mutilations in orange, and the tunnel entrances slash exits are in blue." Dee explained the map as she pointed out the various markings. "Steve, I thought we could mark your house in purple. You were a target."

Steve tried to think of a clever retort, but the terror of that night washed back over him. He said nothing. The group studied the map for several minutes.

"Shouldn't my old house be blue *and* red?" Billy asked. "My brother did die there." Billy looked at his feet. "Purple too. I was a target."

"We should go back to five years ago. Mark all of those scenes too," Jim suggested, glossing over the uncomfortable feeling that had just entered the room.

"I'm not sure we need to do that," Jack started. "All the red marks are close, within a block or two, to the blue ones. It doesn't look like this thing travels far." He pointed at the map.

"What order did they occur in?" Charlie asked.

Dee numbered them on the map. "We only know when the vandalism is reported, not when it happened. And we don't know the creature is responsible."

"Then who?" Jim asked. Dee shrugged her shoulders.

"It appears random," Jack said, more to himself then the room. He was studying it closely and did not hear Chris's question. "Hmm?"

"What do you mean, *appears* random?" Chris asked again.

"Not sure yet. It might be intentional."

"Maybe," Dee said, looking at the map differently. After a few minutes, "I'm starving. What's for dinner?"

"Pizza will be here soon," Jim said. "I also have beer."

The group ate and talked about Abby. She was missed. The kids had stopped by to see her but were ushered out by Lily Thomas after only five minutes. "At least she's still got her windows covered," Chris said. Everyone could see the guilt on his face.

"She'll be fine, Chris. She's smart and capable," Dee offered. She understood the sense of responsibility he felt. She was burdened with the same. After dinner, they all studied the map more. "I'm going to have my deputies scout out the areas around the Harris house and the Simpson house tomorrow. Maybe you guys can look around your neighborhood after school," Dee said to the kids. "If we get lucky, we can determine the next target."

"Just be careful," Jim added.

It was decided the map would stay in its place. Jim's house had become their command center. The other adults took pictures so they could study it on their time. They all said their goodbyes and wished each other luck. When Dee and Jack were home, he casually mentioned Bitsy would be stopping by for a drink.

"What are you going to tell her?"

"As little as possible. She'll be skeptical and probably think we're crazy if we tell her everything."

"I'll follow your lead," Dee said as there was a knock at the door. Ralph greeted their guest as Jack, Dee, and Bitsy exchanged hugs.

"I didn't realize you would be here," Bitsy said to Dee. She gave an approving look to her brother.

"Dee's been spending a lot of time here. Want a glass of wine or something stronger?" he asked as he offered her a seat in the living room.

"Wine sounds good," Bitsy said as she sat. "How have you been, Dee? It seems like ages since we've seen each other."

"You know, just busy with work. You?"

"Same. I knew taking over the mill would be a lot of work. I just hadn't prepared to be there every day."

"No luck finding a good manager to replace you?"

"Not yet. No one I trust."

Jack arrived with a bottle and three glasses. He poured wine and then took a seat. "She'll never find *her* replacement. She'll have to settle for a mere mortal," he joked. Bitsy had been devoted to the mill since high school. She had spent every afternoon and weekend at the place learning the business.

"Did you hear my brother has taken up hiking?" Bitsy asked Dee, smirking at her brother.

"Watch out, Dee. The inquisition is coming."

Dee remained quiet. She had known Bitsy her whole life, and she knew the siblings' relationship. Holding her tongue would be prudent.

"No, just curios how you ended up filthy, dazed, and miles away from your vehicle."

"We wanted to try something new," Jack stated as if it were fact.

"Mm-hmm." Bitsy scoffed while taking a sip of wine. "Dee, you want to fill me in?"

Dee looked at Jack for help or guidance. He shrugged his shoulders. "I had to work."

Bitsy took that piece of information and ran. "So you were helping Dee with a case. Anything to do with the children?"

Dee had forgotten Bitsy was both smart and cunning. She knew Jack had helped Dee before. She should have kept her mouth shut. Jack jumped in before Dee could think of anything to say. "After that girl died in the woods near Ray Dobbins's place, we thought it couldn't hurt to scout out other parts of the woods."

"For what? From what I read, no one knows what happened to that girl." Bitsy shifted her gaze to Dee. "Not that anyone is blaming you or your department. There just aren't any answers being reported."

"We don't have any," Dee said, somewhat defensive but mostly defeated.

"We were just looking for anything that shouldn't be there. Then we got turned around, and the only thing we could see besides trees was the mill." Jack skipped right past Dee's doubt. He did not want to draw attention to it. He knew Dee was under a lot of pressure, both self-inflicted and from the town. Bitsy was right. There were no answers reported, and the community would not tolerate that for long.

Bitsy seemed satisfied with Jack's explanation. She knew if he could tell her more, he would. She shifted gears and began questioning the relationship between Jack and Dee. She wanted to know where it was headed. Was Dee moving in? How long had they been back together? Typical sister stuff. The pair ducked and weaved and avoided her questions. These were questions they had not asked each other. They did not have answers for Bitsy.

They said good night and promised to have dinner soon. Dee and Jack spent the rest of the night discussing the map and next moves. Dee had already given her orders to Collins and Adams with the excuse that they were doing further investigation into the deaths if anyone should ask. She was going to take a closer look around the Dobbins's place for more bombing evidence and signs of the creature. Jack had found some promising information online and planned to dig through it tomorrow.

Dee's subconscious had been chewing on her conversation with Abby earlier. The girl had said the creature was in her head again. Dee wondered if it had ever left. And if that were true, was it digging around in her head as well?

Chapter 21

Late autumn mornings were brisk in Eggers Cove. This Tuesday was no different. The sky was gray with the promise of winter approaching. The once bustling little town had become quiet, friendly waves had been replaced with suspicious glances, and young children once allowed to run free had become tethered to their parents. The casual onlooker would not notice these differences, but Dee was not a casual onlooker. These changes were devasting. She hoped they were reversible.

On her way to the station, Dee stopped by the café for coffee and a quick chat with Susie. Susie was not only good for gossip, she also noticed things most people did not. Susie greeted Dee, but she was not her usual bubbly self. Dee sat at the counter and ordered a coffee. Susie brought the cup and went about her work.

"Hey, Susie?"

"Yeah?" Susie asked, not looking up from the counter.

"Where are the guys?"

Susie looked up. "I'm not sure." She seemed surprised they were not in their normal seats.

"Odd. Tug and Bob are always here," Dee noted.

"I guess."

"Can you come here for a sec?" Susie reluctantly dropped her rag and walked over to Dee. "What's wrong?" Dee asked, grabbing the girl's hand.

Susie blinked a couple of times and shook her head slightly. "What? Oh, I dunno. I guess I'm not myself this morning."

"What about yesterday?"

"Huh?"

"Were they here yesterday? And were you feeling, I don't know, *off* yesterday?"

Susie searched her memory. It was hazy. "I'm sure they were here. They're always here. Every morning." She looked around the café. "I don't know. It's a blur, Sheriff."

"That's okay. Can you get me a to-go cup please?"

Susie went to the kitchen to get a cup. She had not stocked behind the counter in days, and she handed it to Dee.

"Suze, you're wearing two different shoes."

Susie looked down at her feet and blushed. "Oops. Like I said, I'm not really feeling like myself today."

"Hope you feel better," Dee said as she left. So much for digging up information from that particular plot.

On her way into the station, she crossed paths with Adams and Collins. They were headed to conduct further investigation on a couple of recent crime scenes. She made sure they knew what to do and what to say if asked. She stressed that they stay together. It was daytime, but she had discovered daylight was no longer completely safe.

As they were walking away, Dee called out to them, "Hey, guys?" They turned back toward her. "Don't go underground. If you find anything that looks like a tunnel or passageway, call me. Do not investigate." Her deputies looked puzzled but agreed.

Dee went through her messages and reports from her other deputies. She felt like she had been lacking in her day-to-day responsibilities. She was prioritizing, as she always did, and she knew it was the right thing to do, but she hated to think things could be slipping through the cracks. Nichols had finally ticketed the speeder from Mulberry Street. That was a piece of good news. Small but good.

After she felt like she had put in enough time at the office, Dee let Dawn know she was headed into the field. "Sheriff?"

"Yes?"

"We're getting more calls from reporters. Not just the locals anymore."

"Stick to the script. We don't have any other information to release."

"Sure thing."

Dee started out the door then turned back. "Dawn, I'm sorry you have to field those. If I could shut it down, I would."

"I know. It's my job, Sheriff."

"And you're great at it." Dee smiled and left.

*****

Dee parked her truck in front of Ray Dobbins's house. She had no intention of speaking to him, but she wanted him to know she was there. She hoped he would think she was investigating him. People tended to trip up when they thought the law was closing in. Sadly, she was not closing in on him or the creature or any other matter pressing the town of Eggers Cove. As she stepped out of her truck, she looked at the street. The remains of the Russel house were still taped off. The cars that had been damaged had long since been towed away, and most of the debris had been removed from the street and sidewalks. The neighboring yards would probably never recover unless they dug them out completely and started over.

She walked around the Russel house. The markings were gone. No surprise. She looked at the trees in the backyard. Several had carvings of the same symbols that had appeared all around town. The fences were sparse on this street, and Dee was able to move to the neighboring house's backyard with ease. Their trees appeared to be untouched. She went back to the Russel house and looked around more. She glanced a few times at the Dobbins house. She was being watched. A slight movement of the curtain gave him away. She busied herself at the Russel house for longer than she had intended, keep him guessing.

Eventually, she wandered down the street looking for houses that maybe homes to children. She looked in backyards as she could but had come up empty. As she was wrapping up, a voice called to her. Dee turned to see a resident of the street waving at her to come over. She had seen the woman around town and several times on this street when she had responded to calls. Dee braced herself for the questions.

"Hi there, Sheriff. Would you like a coffee or something?" the woman asked as Dee approached.

"No, thank you. I'm fine." Dee looked around the yard and complimented her on the landscaping.

"Well, I'm retired. I have a lot of free time."

Dee smiled. "How can I help you?"

"I don't want to speak out of turn, but I notice things. Things on this street."

Dee did not doubt that. She looked the part of neighborhood busybody. She was only missing the curlers in her hair. "What sort of things?"

"Things like that Dobbins fella skulking about. Late at night."

Dee tempered her excitement. This could be idle gossip or a wild imagination, but a little part of her hoped. "What night? Or nights?"

"A few weeks before the street exploded, I saw him a few times after midnight. He was looking at Jane's house." She paused and blinked back a few tears. "She was a good woman, a better friend."

Just looking at a house was not a crime. If he were on her property, it would still only be trespassing with this statement. She needed more. "And the nights leading up to the tragedy?"

"Yes, the night before. I saw him near the street in front of Jane's house. It looked like he had been kneeling and had just stood. He looked around quickly and hurried back to his house."

Dee was taking notes of the conversation and had several questions. The most pressing was "Did any of my deputies question you that day or the days following?"

"Yes, ma'am. That Nickels fella." Dee stifled a sigh. Nichols dropped the ball again. His training period had been extended twice, and he still barely made it through. Dee often wondered if he should have passed.

Dee thanked her and wrote down her contact information. Her office would be in touch. Her phone buzzed with a text from Jack. She took it as an excuse to leave and walked back to her truck, reading his message. He had found something. She smiled and looked up from her phone. The smile faded quickly when she saw Ray Dobbins standing by her truck.

"Mr. Dobbins," Dee said as she approached her truck. She opened the driver's door, hoping to avoid a conversation.

"Saw you nosing around there, Sheriff."

"It's called investigating, Mr. Dobbins. Now if you don't mind, I'm very busy."

"Not at all, Sheriff. Not at all." Dee could not help but imagine him twisting his moustache like a villain in an old black-and-white movie.

Dee drove away. Ray Dobbins watched her. He wondered what she had found. She looked like the cat that caught the canary. He had been going over his crime. He had been careful. He was sure there was nothing linking him to any of it. His confidence was waning. Maybe he had made a mistake.

*****

Jack waited for Dee at his house. He was excited to show her what he had pieced together. It was more information, and more information was good. He knew it was not enough to stop or kill the creature, but it was another piece of the puzzle. He opted to show Dee first. He felt like this was their task—his and Dee's—and the rest of their group were supporting cast. He loved their friends and respected them, but they were not responsible in the same way. Dee and Jack had devoted their lives to service. And although Charlie was the mayor, *that* was different.

Dee came bounding through the front door with an extra bit of confidence and energy. She had found something as well, Jack thought. She was normally confident and sure of herself. She had an ego only matched by Jack's. He loved her smile, especially at times like these.

"What'd you find?" Jack asked her. He could tell she was ready to burst.

"You first."

Jack led her to his dining room table. Dining room tables seemed to be the first choice among the group when sharing information. There were pictures from the vandalism, the cave, and the crime scenes.

"We all agreed that this symbol is used most," he started, pointing at the symbol that appears in all the photographed areas. "And I couldn't get what Abby found out of my head. That these other symbols were counters or anti the other symbols."

"Okay," Dee said, following along. "So what'd you find?"

"This. Look at these pictures from the vandalism." Dee did. "What do you see?"

"What am I looking at..." She trailed off. "There's more than one artist."

"Exactly. Someone or something is, was, warning or trying to counter the creature. We haven't seen these other symbols at the murder scenes because there's only been one artist. The creature."

"And this other artist, we think he—it—is, I don't know, good?"

"If Abby's theory is correct. And there's more."

"What?" Dee asked excitedly.

"I was finally able to identify the counter or anti symbol for the creature's symbol. According to some scholar, it means *an end* or *the end*, or very loosely translated into *death*."

"Which would mean the creature's symbol is *beginning* or *life*?"

"That's what I think. It fits."

"Yeah, it does. This is good. We'll have to tell the group. Especially Abby. I think she could use this right now."

"Agreed. Now what's your news? What did you find?"

"Me?" Dee asked coyly. "Only found a possible witness that placed Ray Dobbins in front of Jane Russel's house the night before the bombings. He had been kneeling near the car."

"*That* is great news. Why possible?"

Dee described her witness and their interaction. "It could be what I was looking for. At the very least, it gives me more to use against Ray Dobbins."

"Your deputies find anything today?"

"I haven't heard anything. I'll text them and see how it's going." It was immediately returned with a call from Adams. "Whatcha got for me, Dylan?"

"Hi, Sheriff. The first area was a bust. We looked around on the street from the first incident, then the neighboring streets. We fielded a few questions from some neighbors and were careful on the other streets to not draw attention."

"And the Harris neighborhood?"

"We're still here. There's something you need to see. It's a few doors down from the Harris house, in a backyard. It could be a tunnel, and there's carvings on a few trees."

"Text me the address. I'll be right there." She filled Jack in. "Wanna go for a ride?"

"My car or yours?"

Dee and Jack arrived at the potential new scene. All evidence suggested children lived there. There were toys scattered about, along with a bicycle and a scooter. Perfect targets for the creature. It did not appear that anyone was home. Perfect. The deputies led them to their discoveries. First the trees then the possible tunnel. The opening was hidden behind juniper bushes. The casual observer would not see it. There was a large rock blocking the opening. It had been moved slightly, enough to show a possible tunnel.

Dee looked at Jack, and he nodded. "Okay, you guys stay here. If anyone comes home, let them know you're investigating the Harris death. Ask questions, stall. We're going in."

"Sheriff?" Collins was the first to speak. "How many of these, uh, tunnels have you found?"

"Several. I'll fill you in after. We don't have a lot of daylight left, and we need to get down there before its gone."

Collins and Adams exchanged worried looks as Dee and Jack geared up. Dee had never wanted to go spelunking. She had never heard Jack express a desire either. She thought when this was over, she would never want to go underground again. Adams and Collins moved the rock and watched their boss and her boyfriend—what else could they call him—descend into darkness. They hoped for their safety. They hoped for answers. They hoped the two would emerge before the homeowners.

Dee and Jack reemerged from the new tunnel around forty-five minutes later. They were dirty but unharmed, and her deputies had questions. She explained that there was no time now. She would brief them tomorrow. The sun was going down soon. She was not sure she had enough evidence to stake this house out. The tunnel connected to the tunnel from Billy's old house. They saw their original blue paint on one of the tributaries. She excused her deputies and scheduled time with them in the morning.

Jim received a text moments later that Dee and Jack were headed his way. They would reach out to Charlie too. Dee wanted to find out what, if anything, the kids had found. She wanted Jack to share his discovery and get some input. She and Jack could fill them in on the new tunnel, but her piece of news would stay between her and Jack for now.

Charlie was late to arrive at Jim's that night, but he was immediately forgiven. He came bearing pizza, beer, and much to Dee's delight, salad. The group was whole again as Abby was in attendance, and this made the mood brighter. They ate and joked, and for a few moments, it was as if they had forgotten the extreme stress they were under. Reality slapped them in the face, and discussions began. The kids recounted their expeditions around their neighborhoods. They found carvings only around their homes and none around Abby's. Dee could not decide whether that was a good sign or bad. Her gut said bad, and she was relieved to hear Abby had moved back into the Stevens house.

As Jack filled the group in on his discovery, Abby listened wholeheartedly. She agreed with his findings and wanted to help translate the other symbols based on them. He welcomed the help. Everyone agreed it was good news. No one knew how it would help, but more information was good. This had been their mantra. Dee felt this was a good time to let them know about their small field trip as well.

"Jack and I went into a new tunnel this afternoon," she started as she marked the spot on their map. "My deputies found it a few doors down from the Harris house."

Charlie and Jim were relieved to have been excluded from that excursion. "Do they know about the others?" Charlie asked.

"They know they exist, but not where they are. I'm going to brief them in the morning. I instructed them to call me if they found anything that looked like a tunnel. I didn't want them stumbling on them and investigating without warning."

"We all knew we were going to have to bring them in at some point," Jack said. "I think they can be useful."

"Okay, but we're not bringing them *all* the way in, right?" Charlie asked.

"Like I said before, only as far as we need. I trust these men with my life and the lives of everyone in this county. Keeping them excluded as much as we can is for their safety," Dee said, somewhat annoyed. She was not in charge of this group. They all followed her, but she was not in charge.

Jack, sensing her frustration, broke in. "Abby, here's a copy of the translations for the local symbols," he said, handing her a stack of documents. "If you want to get started on the other translations—after your homework, of course—then we can compare tomorrow."

"Yay." Abby was excited to contribute. "I don't have any home-work." She was smiling.

Chapter 22

Mary awoke hungover for maybe the fourth day in a row on Wednesday morning. She reached for the vodka bottle stored in the fridge's freezer in her motel room. Empty. She took several deep breaths and began triaging her body. She would need to get out of bed, and she needed to know how her body would respond. Her stomach was upset, but she did not think vomit was on the horizon. The debilitating pain in her head would be her biggest obstacle. With eyes closed, she clumsily searched for her sunglasses on the nightstand. With them securely on her face, she braved opening her eyes. The pain was bad, but the sunglasses were helping. She rose from her bed and searched for any form of alcohol. She needed it. Half a can of warm beer sat alone on the dresser. It would have to suffice.

After gulping it down, she went to the bathroom, relieved herself, and splashed water on her face. "You look like hell," she said to the woman in the mirror. She no longer recognized that woman. There were new wrinkles that she swore were not there last week. Her hair, usually perfectly styled, was knotted and greasy. When had she last washed or combed it? She reached into her makeup bag and retrieved a hair clip. She dismissed the rest of its contents.

With her hair up and a clean shirt, she left the motel room and walked to the store. Her grocery list included frozen foods, chips, vodka, and wine. She walked the other aisles aimlessly, mostly out of habit. A voice called to her. It was familiar, but she ignored it. A moment later, Jill was standing in front of her.

"Hi, Mary." She looked at her friend's condition. "You look like hell. What's going on?"

Mary, an instinctively manipulative woman, saw an ally before her. "I left him," she said, voice cracking slightly, eyes filled with tears.

Jill wrapped her arms around her. "I'm so sorry. What happened? Do you want to go somewhere and talk?"

She wiped her nose on her sleeve. "Please." Mary, planning ahead, purchased her groceries and brought them and Jill to her hotel room. "Sorry for the mess," she said as she kicked dirty clothes out of the way.

Jill, dumbfounded, looked around the sad room. There was trash and dirty clothes everywhere. She could not believe her friend had been living like this. "It's okay. You could come stay with us," she offered without thinking. A trait Mary loved about her.

"Oh, I couldn't possibly." Mary wanted—needed—her as an ally, but she also needed privacy. She needed to drink alone without judgment.

"Promise me you'll think about it." Mary nodded. "Should we go get something to eat?" Jill asked. She felt her friend could use some real food. Those frozen dinners were not going to cut it.

"Sure. I'll just put on some lipstick." After deliberations, they decided to go to Jill's. The café was out. Jack could be there, and the pizza place would not open for a few hours. Jill drove Mary to her house and made brunch for them. Mary sold Jill on her tale of woe, how mistreated she was, how awful Jim was, how Mary's life could and should be so much better. She, of course, took no responsibility for her part in the state of their marriage. Mary would always be the victim. Jill listened and said the things she was supposed to say and kept her mouth shut where required.

The part that really bothered Jill was that Mary had left. She had children, and she left them there. If Jill were to believe Mary's assessment of Jim's character, he was not fit to be a father. Jill tried to ignore these *facts*. Mary was her only friend in this small town, and Jill needed her. Mary asked for champagne to celebrate her freedom, and Jill obliged, promising herself she would have only one glass.

Two bottles later, Jill opened the red wine. Charlie called and asked her to lunch. She declined. Any other day, she would be delighted at the thought of lunch with her husband. Not today. Today, she had the toxicity known as Mary in her home, sucking the joy out of life. The wine turned into margaritas, which turned into shots of tequila. Charlie called about dinner, and Jill ignored his call. She and Mary were busy demonizing the men in their lives, and the women. Jill had not realized how bad her marriage was until Mary pointed it out. Jill had known how terrible her life was until Mary pointed it out.

*****

Mary was not the only person in Eggers Cove to wake feeling less than perfect. The sun was buried behind clouds, as if it, too, did not want to get out of bed. There was not a lot of optimism left in town. Parents feared for their children, children feared monsters more now than ever, and business owners feared closure as fewer people were patronizing their shops. Dee and her friends feared failure. Dee woke with a feeling of despair. She felt like their window was closing. If they were not out of time, they were in the neighborhood. She wanted to go for run, burn off some of this energy, but the sense of a deadline overpowered her.

She left for the station with a to-go cup of coffee and a quick kiss goodbye. Dee was the second to arrive, beaten only by Dawn, but her shift started at six. She had time to go through messages and gather her thoughts for her briefing. This briefing had been discussed after Jack and Dee were home, sipping wine. They decided to fill the deputies in—everything about the tunnels, the kids, the symbols, all of it. Their thought process was that more minds, more law enforcement minds, could be helpful.

Adams and Collins arrived within minutes of each other, and Dee asked them to the interrogation room. "Bring the map." Collins brought the map as he had become its custodian and pinned it to the wall. Dee marked the map to match the map at Jim's. She marked the newest tunnel last. She gave them a few minutes to look over her additions. Dee explained the additions—houses that were targeted but no deaths, tunnels, and she pointed out the approximation of where the cave was. "Questions?"

"Do you know what it is?" Collins asked.

"We call it the Creature, from tribal folklore. We really don't know what it is. We just know it's killing the children of Eggers Cove."

"You've explored these tunnels?" Adams asked. Dee nodded. "With who? Jack?"

"And a few friends."

"Sheriff?" Collins asked timidly.

"Yes?"

"Why are you including us now?"

"Honestly, we need the help. I tried to keep you guys out of it for as long as I could. I'm pretty sure we're going to have to do some things that may be borderline at best. I wanted to protect you."

"As far as I'm concerned, Sheriff, I'm here to serve you and the people of Eggers Cove, however you see fit." Adams stated. "If that means we gotta go on some night ops with your friends off book, I'm in."

"Yeah, Sheriff. Whatever you need."

"Thanks, guys. What I really need now are ideas. Jack may have cracked the code on those symbols, which could really be helpful, but we also need a plan to attack. To kill. I have no desire to capture."

"Sheriff, who else knows?" Adams asked.

"My friends, a group of kids, you two, and Willie."

"Willie?" Adams asked. "From out in the—"

"Yes," Dee interrupted. "Jack knows him well. He's a good source of knowledge."

"The symbols?" Adams asked. He was putting it together.

Dee nodded.

"Can you tell us more about the tunnels, the cave?" Collins asked. Dee gave as much information as she had. She included the incidents with both the kids and the adults. "You want to try to trap it there, don't you?"

She smiled. "Ideally, yes. We're just not sure how to lure it." They brainstormed ideas for several minutes, then there was a knock on the door. Dawn was announcing Jack, and Dee asked that she show him in.

"I brought breakfast and coffee," Jack said, setting bags down on the table. "Hungry?" he asked, smiling at Dee.

"Starved." She smiled back. "Can you stay awhile? We're strategizing." He closed the door and took a seat.

*****

Abby had stayed up too late going over Jack's notes. Subsequently, she found Wednesday morning more difficult than most. To say she was tired was an understatement. She had never had a cup of coffee, but today, she understood the allure. She rubbed her eyes and dragged herself from the guest room to the kitchen. Her friends were already there, dressed and eating breakfast. Greetings were exchanged while she grabbed a cup of coffee. She took it black. It seemed more grown-up. Jim raised an eyebrow but said nothing. Who was he to judge how anyone, including the kids, responded to recent events? They had been forced to tackle adult issues way beyond their years, and he had yet to hear a complaint. He was proud of his children, more so now, and of their friends.

"Geez, Abs, you look like hell," Steve said, always with a compliment. She punched him the arm as she walked by.

She sat at the table and took a sip of coffee. It was bitter and awful, and she hoped her face did not show it. Jim put a plate of bacon and eggs in front of her, and she thanked him. As she pushed her food around, she could not focus. There was an almost formed thought in the back of her mind. She could almost touch it. She knew it was key. She did not know what it opened, but it was key. After a few bites and painful sips of coffee, she went back to the guest room to dress for school. It seemed unnecessary, but the adults in her life insisted she and her friends go to school. Their whole world may be ending, they could all die, but they would do it educated.

The boys goofed around on the way to school. Abby stayed quiet. Chris tried to include her, but his attempts did not elicit the response he wanted. Chris knew her well. He knew when to press and when to shut up. Her face said it was time for the latter. As Abby gnawed away at the inner part of her mind, Chris masked the overwhelming sense of urgency he was feeling. He had woken to an unsettling feeling. It took him until the walk to school to realize what it was. They were running out of time. He knew it. He just knew it. To make matters worse, there was no plan or even the beginnings of a plan. He was scared. He hoped he was hiding it.

As Billy walked with his friends, he, too, was quiet. He had woken not feeling like himself, not feeling right. This feeling was growing stronger. If he were even just a few years older, he would know a word—*empath*. With the right emotional maturity, he would identify himself as one. For now, he was a scared kid, too small for his age, and feeling even smaller. He felt a sense of urgency and confusion, and he was trying to grasp a thought. He had no knowledge of what the thought was supposed to be or why it was so urgent he find it.

"Stop poking around." It was Abby's voice. Billy was sure she had not spoken aloud. It was coming from his mind.

"Abby?" He pushed back, unsure if this was a two-way street.

"Yeah. Get out of my head. You're freaking me out."

"Sorry." He mentally focused his efforts to leave. He hoped he had. And now he had another word—*telepath*. He looked at Abby apologetically and shrugged his shoulders. He wanted her to know it was not on purpose. He spent the rest of the day trying to remember how he had snuck into her mind. He wondered if he could do it to others. He wondered if he could do it without their knowledge.

*****

Charlie got the text from Jack moments after his wife declined lunch. It was easy for him to reply that he was, in fact, available this afternoon. It was not easy for him to admit why. He was sure she had been drinking. He was also sure Mary was with her. Mary was a parasite, more now than ever, and he did not like her influence on his wife. He understood his wife was desperate for friends, and he understood Mary's desperation for an ally. It was a dangerous situation, and he did not have the time or mental capacity to navigate it, not well. He briefly thought about putting it off and dealing with it after. He feared there may be no after. He feared he was losing his wife. He feared there was nothing he could do.

He called his wife to let her know he would be late for dinner, and she ignored it. He texted her, and she did not respond. The group was to meet at Jim's, and he hoped he could find a delicate way to ask for help. Mary was Jim's wife. Estranged or not, Jim knew her better than anyone else. Charlie would pull him aside at an opportune moment, provided one presented itself. And he would speak with Dee again and impress upon her the urgency of the situation.

Charlie went to Jim's early, hoping to get a few minutes with him ahead of the group. It seemed his luck was changing. The kids had not yet returned from school, and only Jim's car was in the driveway. He knocked on the door and was greeted by a surprised and disheveled friend. Jim ushered him in, apologizing for his appearance. He had not slept much and was trying to nap. Maybe his luck had not changed.

"Sorry. Can I help?"

"We just need to get past this crisis and then work on the rest." Jim seemed to be towing the party line. How often had Charlie heard those words uttered from his friends?

"That's where we disagree, Jim," Charlie said as he was led to the kitchen. "I think our other problems may have intersected." Charlie gratefully accepted the beer he was offered and asked that they sit outside. It was a brisk afternoon, but the sun was shining.

The two clicked bottles in their customary fashion, and each took a swig. "Mary?" Jim asked.

"Yep." Charlie needed to tread carefully. He knew Jim did not love Mary, but she was his wife.

"She dig her claws into Jill?"

Charlie nodded.

Jim sighed. "Maybe you're right. Maybe we need to walk and chew gum at the same time." He took a big gulp of his beer. "The others will be here soon. Can you stick around after? We can put our heads together." Jim paused a moment, then, "Are you going to include Dee? Ask for her help?"

"Jill is desperate for friends. We both know Dee isn't the typical girl, but I think if she got to know Jill, she would like her."

"Good luck. I can count on one hand the girl friends Dee has had over the years." Jim chuckled. "Seriously, she'll help if she can. You know Dee. She loves us. She would do anything for us, including shopping with one of our wives." They both laughed at that and went back inside, ready to greet the group.

The kids arrived moments later with heads down, as if the whole world rested on their backs. Jim thought that maybe it did. He would gladly take their place if he could. "Snacks and sodas in the kitchen," he said as he greeted each one with a hug. He had raised his kids to show affection and not be embarrassed by it. The polar opposite of the house he had grown up in. He was proud that his house had always been the house where his children and their friends congregated. He knew he was mostly responsible for this. Mary had always taken a more hands-off approach to the rearing of their children. In the deepest, darkest part of his mind, he knew she had never wanted them. It was something he never said out loud, even to himself, because it broke his heart. He would protect his children from this for as long as he could. Mary's absence was making it more difficult.

The school day was discussed without much enthusiasm, and the kids ate their snacks. Jim noted their reluctance and made a note to discuss it later. Later tonight, not later after. Charlie was right. They needed to address major issues now and not wait. His marriage was over, probably since before it started. He could not fix that, but he could help save his friend's. And he could help these kids be kids and have a childhood.

Dee and Jack arrived next with company. No one had expected it, not out loud anyway. Fortunately, the deputies had worn civilian clothes and not their uniforms. Jim was sure that was Dee's idea. To make them more approachable and acceptable. This was a tight group. It did not trust easily. Along with their casual attire, the two brought beer, a crowd winner for this crowd.

Introductions were made all around, and beers were refreshed. Jim thought it odd when the deputies opted for water over beer and filed it away. There was casual talk among the adults, and the kids just watched silently. These were new adults, untested. They were not sure how these adults would receive them.

Dee was the first to speak. "Jack and I met with Dylan and Matt earlier today. They had an idea of what was happening. I filled them in." She paused to read the room. She thought she saw betrayal on a couple of faces, but she pressed on. "We may have a plan. We think we need to pick some target houses and set up a stakeout. Watch and see if the creature shows up. Meanwhile, the rest of us—adults—will be underground."

"Wait, what?' Charlie asked. This was all moving too quickly.

"You're suggesting we go underground at night when this thing seems to be most powerful?" Jim was reluctant as well.

"What did you expect? We would just fight this thing from your dining room?" Jack was annoyed. He knew they had a good plan. He needed his friends to trust that.

Everyone began speaking at once, except the kids. They remained quiet. Dee broke in. "Listen! Let me walk you through the plan. Let's discuss it, iron out the rough edges."

While Dee and Jack laid out their plan to the group, Billy used this time to try to peek into the adults' heads. He tried Charlie's mind first. He found anger and confusion about Jill. Billy did not think Charlie was paying attention to Dee at all. When he peeked into Jim's head, he was overcome with fear. It was not fear for himself but for his children and his friends. Billy stayed away from Dee's head. Somehow, he knew she would sense him in there. He was feeling proud of his new abilities and the ease of how he used them. He finished snooping and noticed Abby glaring at him. She knew. He did not feel her in his head, but she knew what he had been doing. She did not approve. Billy dropped his eyes from her gaze and looked at the floor. He felt ashamed.

Dee noticed the exchange between Abby and Billy and decided to ignore it for now. They were kids. It could be about something small. The look on Abby's face suggested otherwise. "As far as we can tell, the attacks, for lack of a better word, seem to occur in the early morning hours. This gives us plenty of time to set up."

"Tonight?" Charlie asked, bemused. "We can't possibly—"

"We're out of time, Charlie," Jack interrupted. "We have to do this now."

Charlie knew Jack was right. They were out of time. He had sensed it. He felt a kind of countdown. He was unsure of what it was counting down to. He was sure he did not want to find out. His thoughts drifted to Jill. He hoped she was okay. He knew every minute spent with Mary was trouble. She was poison. His mind came back to the present, and he heard the tail end of their plan. He did not like it, but he reluctantly agreed.

Jim agreed as well, more reluctantly than Charlie. He was scared for his children. He did not want to leave them in the care of his wife. Jim was not a coward and had never been accused as such. He always rose to the occasion. It was strange for him not leading the group. He led on the field in high school and college until his injury. He led in the workplace and at home. Jim was a leader, but he also knew how to follow. He could not think of better people to follow than Dee and Jack. "Should we eat first? It could be a long night."

"We ordered pizza. They should be here soon," Jack said.

As the adults continued discussing strategy, the kids snuck off to Chris's room. Chris was having doubts about the adult plan. It seemed outrageous. He quickly found his peers shared his doubts. As Steve mocked the adults, Chris worried about his dad. He knew his dad was strong and reasonably intelligent, but he was also injured. As much as Jim had tried to hide it, his boys saw him struggle to even play catch. One thing his injury had done was made his boys accurate at throwing any ball. They hated to see their father wince when he ran for an errant ball. They both had natural athletic ability, and Jim encouraged it but was careful not to demand it. His childhood dreams were ruined by injury. He did not want to see either of his boys suffer that fate.

Chris glanced at Abby and did not like the look on her face. Something was wrong. "Abs?"

"Uh, yeah?" she asked, almost startled.

"What's wrong?"

She begged him with her eyes to drop it. Then she said it in his mind. They would talk later. "Nothing. Just thinking about the crazy adults."

Chris received both of her messages. The first one startled him, but he did not let it show. He, like his adult friends, was tired of *later* and *after*. His mind drifted to early summer, before Billy was hospitalized, before kids started dying. He thought about swimming and riding bikes and Steve giving everyone a hard time. Steve had always been his best friend, but Abby was a close second. If he was being honest with himself, she was more than just his almost best friend. Chris sighed. Being fourteen was hard in normal times. These were not normal times.

"Chris?" It was Alex breaking Chris from his thoughts.

"What?"

"What are we going to do? We have to help them."

"What can we do?" Steve asked. "We can't go with them. We can't stop them. They're determined to go underground, at night, into this creature's lair and what, surprise it? Yeah, good plan, old-timers."

"I just have to think…" Chris trailed off. He believed there was a way to help, to save his friends and the adults who were also his friends. Much like Abby and Jack with the puzzle they were working on, he could feel the answer just at the edge of his mind. Just out of reach. He heard his friends talking. He did not hear their words. He knew *he* had the answer. He had to solve this.

As Chris was trying to solve all their problems, Steve continued to mock the adults. Abby and Billy were quiet, and Alex remained terrified. Alex had known his parents did not love or even like each other since he was very young. He merely tolerated his mother, and his biggest fear was living with her alone. He loved his father and had been preparing himself to tell a judge his mother was unfit. He had not spent any time preparing himself for his father's death. As this became more likely, his fear intensified. It was not just the prospect of living with his mom that was scary. It was the thought of his father no longer around. He did not know what he would do without his father. His only hope now was that his brother made it out alive.

Steve had completed one of his famous monologues without realizing his friends had not been listening. In truth, he was not even sure what he had said. He knew one of his major roles in this group was distractor. He could tell a joke or a funny story or just make fun of something, and his friends would laugh. They would forget, at least for a few seconds, the awful things they were dealing with. He could not forget, but he could do this for his friends. His friends were closer to him than his own family, and he looked at Jim like a second father. He was scared. He knew his closest friends could not survive the death of their father. He was not sure he could survive it either.

Billy worked on his apology to Abby. He thought he should apologize to her. He was not sure. He resisted the urge to jump into his other friends' heads. He wanted to know what they were thinking. From experience, he could figure it out without telepathy. Chris was probably solving the world's problems. Alex was probably scared about his father's involvement. Steve was not taking anything seriously, and Abby was disappointed. Disappointed in him. At that moment, she locked eyes with him. She was not in his head, but she sensed his confusion and fear. Abby was always good at reading them. She knew exactly how they felt.

None of the kids heard the first or second call for dinner. They were all too deep in their own thoughts. Jim had to come and knock on Chris's door. "Hey, guys. Pizza's here."

As the group ate—or picked at—their dinner, conversation was minimal. They were all lost in their thoughts, hoping for the best but fearing the worst.

After dinner, Charlie tried to call his wife again. There was still no answer. He left a message. He told her not to wait up. He would be late, and he told her loved her. He did love her, and he would save her. Charlie knew that somehow, saving her was as important as saving this town. He knew he could not save only one, both must be saved, or he would be a failure. Worse, not just a failure, he would be complicit. The logical side of his brain tried to explain the flaws in his argument. The emotional side could not hear it. He would be blamed, and he would deserve it.

*****

Jill heard her phone, saw it was her husband, and ignored it. Mary had opened her eyes. With Charlie, she came second, or maybe third. She deserved better. She deserved more. She had been sucked deep into Mary-land, an evil place where happiness could not exist. Mary had hinted at a past tryst between Charlie and Dee. Jill dismissed it at first. Now it became clear. He was always spending time with her. He claimed he was with the group, but Mary knew better. And Mary explained it to Jill. For the first time in her adult life, Jill was jealous, suspicious, and she wanted to do something about it. She listened to the message from Charlie. *Don't wait up*? she thought. It confirmed all of Mary's accusations. And she needed to confront him. Now.

The two women had been drinking for hours. Jill's first instinct was to get into her car and drive until she found the pair. Fortunately, the sane and rational part of her knew she could not drive. She could get a cab or a rideshare. But that would only highlight her humiliation to a stranger. It was not quite dark yet. She could walk. They lived close enough to Dee's. It would only be a ten-minute walk. If they were there. Charlie claimed he was at Jim's with the group, but Mary told her he was lying. Said she could hear it in his voice. She had experience with liars. Her husband was one.

As the women continued to brainstorm, Jill had one constant thought deep in her mind: Charlie was not a cheater, he was not a liar. Mary was doing her best to quiet that voice for Jill, but Jill could not dismiss it entirely. Mary's ideas became increasingly violent and destructive, Jill thought they seemed reasonable. On her own, Jill would have never thought to spray paint the word WHORE on someone's house, but Mary made it seem not only possible but appropriate. She drew the line when Mary suggested they throw all of Charlie's things in the driveway and set them on fire. That was too far, even in her enraged drunken state, Jill knew that was too much. Jill refilled their drinks and tried to change the subject. She was beginning to regret inviting Mary over. Jill hoped Mary would pass out soon; they would not act on any of their plans today, she needed a sober mind to maneuver this situation.

*****

At Jim's, dinner was finished in that everyone stopped pretending to eat and walked away from the table. They still had some time

199

before they needed to head out, and Charlie took the opportunity to steal Dee away for a talk. Jim looked at Charlie and gestured whether he should come along, but Charlie shook him off. He wanted to try on his own first, only pull in Jim if necessary.

On the back porch, Dee asked what he wanted. Charlie could tell she was distracted. He understood, but he was going to need her attention. "I'm in trouble, Dee."

"What's going on, Charlie?" He had her full attention now.

"Mary has dug her teeth into Jill, Dee. She's turning her into a person I don't recognize." He paused. "I'm losing her. I know it."

Dee's interest wavered. "It sounds like we might be able to wait on this issue. We're dealing with slightly bigger issues, Charlie. I'm not insensitive. I'm just not sure this is the right time. Can it wait until after?"

Charlie grabbed Dee by the arm and met her eyes. "No. This cannot wait another second. We have been putting things off for too long. We have to deal with things now, not after. If we wait until after to handle stuff, it may all be lost." He realized how ominous his tone was, felt it was fitting.

Dee read Charlie's face, his body language, his eyes. He was obviously hurting. He appeared to be at his wit's end. Dee wanted to help. She just did not know how. "I'm not sure what you want me to do. It's no secret I despise Mary, always have, but beyond that…" Dee trailed off.

"I need you to talk to Jill. I think she'll listen to you about Mary. She won't listen to me. She says Mary is her only friend."

Great. Not only did she need to kill a monster, but she also had to babysit Charlie's wife. A woman she had nothing in common with, except Charlie. "Can I do this tomorrow? I'm a bit distracted tonight."

"Tomorrow might be too late. She's with Mary now. They've been together all day."

"Unfortunate timing," Dee muttered, not meaning to say it out loud.

"I know," Charlie whispered. "Please, Dee."

"Dammit, Charlie." She could not say no to any of her friends, not when they needed her. "I'll call her."

Charlie hugged and thanked her and waited nearby for the results. Dee found Jill in her contacts, a little surprised to find her, and called. After several rings, it went to voice mail. "Hey, Jill, it's Dee. Listen, I was hoping we could get together and talk. Give me a call back." She shrugged at Charlie. She tried. The pair walked back inside and were met with a quizzical look from Jack and a hopeful look from Jim. Dee was not surprised Charlie had gone to Jim for advice. He knew Mary best. For better or worse.

*****

Jill's phone buzzed. It was Dee. She ignored the call. The message confirmed her fears. She did not tell Mary. She could not go back down that particular road of crazy. Instead, she held back her tears and had another cocktail. She would begin packing in the morning. She would go back to the city. Back to her old life, her life before Charlie. Her life before she was so unhappy.

She had conveniently forgotten how miserable and empty her life had been in the city. She was always busy, always had plans, always with her friends. Her friends were empty, shallow shells of humans. Jill had not had real friends or a real life in the city, but her loneliness in Eggers Cove made her reimagine her life in the city. She only remembered fond memories she had reframed in her mind. It was possible she may not be able to experience happiness anywhere. It was possible she would remain lonely for the rest of her days.

*****

Just after ten Wednesday night, the adults left Jim's house in several vehicles. They all had their assignments and knew where to go and where to meet after. None of them knew or had even an inkling that another group left the house just after them. Five kids had piled into Jim's car and were set on helping or stopping the foolish adults in their lives.

Chapter 23

Deputies Collins and Adams set up near the newly discovered tunnel opening. Their assignment was to watch the opening and report any activity. Neither of the men thought they would see anything tonight. They respected Dee and believed her on a basic level, but they could not honestly conceive of a monster living under their town. The children's deaths were unexplained, the circumstances were unusual, but they thought there had to be a rational explanation.

Dee's group parked near the river and waited. They would enter the cave through the tunnel Chris and his friends discovered. It seemed to be the shortest distance to the cave and the easiest to access with limited visibility by the townsfolk. The friends were scared. They had no knowledge of the creature's weaknesses and were hoping its body was fragile. Or at least had vulnerable places. There was no way to do research. The limited information they found were only myths or old stories poorly translated. They were also determined to save the children of the town and themselves.

If the adults were scared, the kids were terrified. It was a risk just to look out a window at night. They were in the night. They all assumed while they were driving, they would be safe, but once they parked and left the vehicle, they were targets. Delicious targets. As Steve described, sitting ducks. Abby was sure that she and Billy would know where the creature was. She was convinced they had a link to it. It had been in both of their heads. She could still feel the residue it left behind. They did not have a vantage point on the adults, but they had obtained a walkie from the deputies' vehicle. Steve had sticky fingers and had yet to be caught. Over the years, he had liberated candy and small toys from the Olde Time Ice Cream and Candy store. And more recently, cigarettes from the gas station. They all tried smoking. None of them took to it. If they made it through this, beer would most likely be his next target.

Nearby, Ray Dobbins was plotting his own mission. He knew that woman sheriff was on to him. He knew she was plotting against him. She did not understand that he was important. His money made him important. It made him matter in this shitty little town. She would respect him and his decisions. He had done a service to the community by removing Jane Russel. She was the menace. First, there was one more neighbor to be dealt with.

*****

After one Thursday morning, deputies Collins and Adams saw the unthinkable: movement at the opening of the tunnel. Adams saw it first and alerted Collins. The two watched in shock as the rock moved and a figure began to emerge. It was over a second before either made a move. Instincts kicked in, and they both shined their spotlights on the creature. Dee had a theory that this creature appeared to be nocturnal and therefore would not respond well to bright lights. She was right. What can only be described as a scream came from the creature as it covered its face with an arm and quickly scurried back into the tunnel.

Adams walkied Dee and explained what happened. "Good. Keep your lights on that tunnel. Hopefully, it will retreat." Then to her friends, "We're on." The group left Jack's truck and retrieved their bags from the truck bed. They jogged the short distance to the tunnel opening and hurried to the cave. They were not sure how much time they had, but they knew it was limited.

Once inside, they arranged themselves near as many openings as they could. They left the tunnel they presumed the creature would use open. Dee stood off to the side, prepared to block it after the creature entered. This was Jack's least favorite part of the plan. He did not like Dee blocking the escape of the creature. Its physical abilities were still unknown. Dee insisted and would not back down. Jack knew better than to argue. She was more stubborn than him.

As they waited in the dark, Dee remembered rules she had made as a child to protect herself from monsters. Rules like "As long as your feet are covered by a sheet or blanket, monsters can't get you" and "You have three seconds after turning off your bedroom light to make it onto your bed before the monsters can make a move. Then you just have to get your feet covered." It seemed so silly now, but the little girl inside was trying to make a new rule. Sadly, she no longer had the imagination of a child. She only had the logic and reason of an adult.

*****

While Dee was learning one of the many unfortunate things about becoming an adult, Ray Dobbins was slowly making his way to his neighbor's house. The best route was behind what remained of the Russel house. The streetlight in front of her house had yet to be replaced, but he did not want to risk walking down the sidewalk. This plan was far more basic than the last. He would kill the old bag and make it look like an accident. He had watched several movies over the years and paid close attention to the mistakes the killer made. He was sure he could get away with this. This and his other contributions—crimes.

He noticed only one light on in her house. He assumed it was her bedroom. As he picked the lock of her back door, Ray Dobbins did not notice the camera. He hadn't thought to look for them. Gladys Streigel had kept up on technology, including home surveillance. This was mostly due to her grandchildren, and when her ring doorbell offered security at the touch of her finger, she signed up. Her morning ritual consisted of coffee and reviewing her camera action from the previous night. Something Ray also did not know—could not know—was that the camera footage was automatically uploaded and saved to the cloud.

As Gladys slept to the comforting sound of her TV, she did not hear Ray Dobbins enter. She did not sense his presence in her home. She had wanted a pet but thought it irresponsible at her age. She did not want the pet to outlive her. Shelters were full of unwanted pets, and she would not contribute to that problem.

Ray Dobbins was able to navigate freely and quietly through the woman's home, comforted by the fact that he would be undetectable. He found his way to her bedroom and placed a pillow over her face. He wanted it to be a painful death, but he knew that was unwise. It was best to let people believe she died in her sleep.

Ray Dobbins held the pillow over her face, and at first, there was no movement. He thought to himself that this would be his easiest task to date. Then she began to move, thrash, and scratch his arms. The old woman had fight left in her. He increased the pressure and turned his head. It would be hard to explain scratches on his face, and he allowed her to kick and punch and thrash. He would win this. He won everything in his life.

He was right. He would win this battle. Gladys fought hard, but her frail body was no match. As she succumbed, she thought, *I wish I would have gotten that dog.* Ray Dobbins left her house as he had entered, undetected, or so he thought, and escaped into the blackness of early morning. There was a knowing smile on his face, a smile he had had many times before.

It would be hours later that he realized there were scratches on his arms, DNA under her fingernails. But Ray Dobbins had a solution to that. He had solutions to everything.

*****

Dee's group was in position, waiting, when she heard a noise from an adjacent tunnel. It was not the tunnel they expected the creature to use. Her brain calculated all the options—another creature, a tunnel they were not aware of, townsfolk who had figured out the creature existed, or something she could not imagine. What she didn't expect was five mostly grown shapes emerging from the opening. It was Dee's biggest fear. The kids had followed, and she had put them in danger.

Jack noticed the group of kids a fraction of a second after Dee. He was farther away. His immediate thought was to abort and get those kids home. He hated the idea of retreating but knew sometimes you had to retreat and come back stronger. Something he had learned on the job. One look at Jim and Jack knew they had to abort. Jim's face had gone pale, his eyes huge, his body tense. His kids and others he was responsible for were here. In the worst possible place. Jim had never felt fear like this before.

The two groups met near the center of the cave, and it seemed everyone spoke at once. Adults were asking why they were there. Kids were explaining, or trying to, why they were there. They were helping. Jim announced he was leaving and taking the kids. Dee agreed, and Jack suggested they all leave. Jim might need help getting the kids to safety, and they needed numbers to go against the creature.

"It's too late," Abby said, just above a whisper. "It's here." She had felt the string in her head pull, the link to the creature, moments before entering the cave. It was now tight, and words had crept in.

"Yeah, it's seconds away," Billy added. He, too, had felt the pull, the tightening, and whispers.

"Look away, kids!" Dee ordered as she aimed her shotgun toward the opening. "Jack." She did not need to say another word. He was aiming in the same direction. Their plan had changed. They needed to fire on it and possibly chase it through the tunnels. It could not get near the children. They would not allow it. Jim had placed himself in front of the children as they faced the wall. He had instructed them to cover their ears, which would help a little with the gunfire, but it would do nothing to keep the creature out of their heads.

Doubt entered Dee's mind—doubt of her abilities, doubt of her revised plan, doubt of herself. The barrel of her gun dropped slightly, and Jack put his hand on her arm. She snapped out of it. Those were not her thoughts. Those were planted. She looked at Jack, hoped it was not for the last time, took aim at the dark figure charging into the cave, and fired.

Charlie shined his spotlight on the opening, and the creature screamed. Dee swore she saw smoke or steam rising off its body. The creature stood around six feet tall. It was brownish gray and mostly hairless. It had ears like a bat, and its claws could only be described as talons. Dee was sure she saw a tale. In her nightmares, the tail had a claw as well. When it opened its mouth, Dee saw razor-sharp teeth. "The better to eat you with" came to mind.

The link between the creature and Dee had been restored, although it now seemed Dee was looking in. She saw images of a nest, of prepping, preparing.

"Shoot the belly!" Dee screamed as she began firing. "The fucking thing is pregnant!" Out of shells, Dee switched to her .45. She unloaded her entire magazine into its belly. She reloaded, and it turned, screaming and running away. Dee screamed, "I hope it hurts! I hope I fucking killed your baby! I hope you feel the pain of all the mothers in this town!" She ran into the tunnel after it.

Jack was on her heels because he always had her back, but mostly because he wanted to stop her. They could not go hunting this thing in tunnels it had most likely created. They had barely scratched the surface of mapping them. Dee had stopped running. She did not want to be ambushed. Jack tapped her shoulder. She knew he would follow. It was in his nature. He would never leave a man behind. Dee walkied her friends to get the kids out. She and Jack would handle this.

She was following a trail of blood that smelled rancid, like it had come from an animal that had died days before. She had a singular focus on tracking this thing. She still had the connection open. Normally, she would be surveying the area, planning escape routes, planning ambush points. She knew Jack was doing those things. She could follow the trail she felt in her mind.

The pair tracked the creature through the maze of tunnels. At the first fork. Dee knew to go left. At the next, she thought right. When they reached the third fork, Dee had lost the connection. The blood trail was gone, and she knew they had to back track their way out of here.

"It's gone," she said, defeated.

"We got it." And that was all Dee needed to hear. Affirmation. When they got back to the cave, Dee walkied her friends. They were still nearby next to Jim's car the kids had "borrowed" earlier. They wanted to make sure the pair made it out. Dee said they were fine. They'd meet back at Jim's.

Dee and Jack walked through the tunnel nearest his truck. Dee felt both failure and triumph. Maybe they had not killed the creature, but they saved the kids. And in her experience, the shots she landed were fatal. She had felt it's pain when she fired into its belly. She knew at least *that* creature was dead. And for now, that would have to be enough.

*****

Jim popped champagne in celebration. Dee did not know that Jim had champagne in the house, definitely not multiple bottles. And it was chilled. She gave him a sideways glance as she took her glass, and he winked at her. They toasted their win. Dee did so reluctantly. In her gut, she knew that thing was still out there. Yes, it was licking its wounds, but it would return. She saw Abby watching her, a knowing look in her eyes. She was sure she heard Abby's voice quietly in her head, saying it was over. Dee nodded at her, and Abby blushed.

It was nearly three in the morning as the group celebrated victory, new members included. Jack knew Dee was not satisfied. She, like him, needed to see the body, the evidence. He celebrated the victory of getting those kids out, getting his friends home, and having Dee's back. He had known since he was a young boy that he would be following this girl through his life, and he could not be happier.

Billy took Abby aside and apologized. He knew digging in people's heads, especially this group, was wrong, but he wanted to test his abilities. Abby understood. She was struggling with the gift as well. She called it a gift but thought of it as a curse. She did not want to be in the minds of people around her, however helpful it might be.

Jim was beaming, his kids were safe, his friends were safe, and he knew the creature was dead. He had given the kids a small glass of champagne each. They earned it, despite disobeying strict instructions. He forgave them the second he got them in his house, safe. He briefly thought to call his wife. Then he remembered who she was and dismissed the thought.

Adams and Collins enjoyed the champagne but enjoyed the beer more. They felt their small part was not worth honoring, were afraid of being accused of stolen valor. But Dee assured them that without their role, the night would have ended with no success. So they drank with people they hardly knew but now considered friends and enjoyed the victory, however small their part.

Charlie wished Jill was there, wished Jill knew what they had done, what they had been going through. He vowed to tell her. Obviously not tonight, but soon. He hoped his friends would help. He knew they would. He knew these were those lifelong friends you read about, people that would show up and deliver. He knew he was blessed. He hoped he could be half the friend that his friends had been—and would be—to him.

*****

Ray Dobbins woke in a panic. It was just after three in the morning. His arms were burning, the scratches. The DNA. He had to do something, so Ray Dobbins did what he always did. He solved the problem. He went to his garage and retrieved the two gas cans he kept for emergencies. He had a gas-operated generator and hated to be without power. He followed the same path he had traveled hours before and began pouring gas on the back of Gladys's house. He lit the small home then made his way back to his. He was still in his pajamas, which would lend to his cover when he emerged from his front door to see the commotion.

Gladys Striegel's home went up in flames. Moments later, neighbors woke. Some called for help. Others ran to her house to rescue her. They did not know that she had been dead for hours. They just wanted to help. Some even brought garden hoses. They aimed them at her home and prayed.

Dee got the call just before three thirty. There was a house fire. She looked at her deputies. They were enjoying the party. She told them and everyone else to stay put. She would be back. She approached the scene. Firefighters were already there, as well as paramedics, but all Dee saw was Ray Dobbins. Yes, he was dressed in pajamas, but it looked staged. She knew he was responsible. This was just another crime she had to pin on him. There was no reason to question him at this point. He would only lie. She had a deputy do it. Get his statement then prove he was lying. This was not a new strategy.

She met with the fire captain, and he confirmed one dead inside. The medical examiner would have to provide cause of death, and the fire department would determine the cause of the fire. He implied, heavily, that it was arson. Dee thanked him and called the sheriff of the neighboring county. Gladys had a grandson there. He needed to be notified. She wrapped up her duties at the now extinguished fire and left two deputies to finish questioning neighbors and onlookers. She had a full day, and she was tired. Exhausted.

After texting with Jack, she learned everyone had gone home. He was waiting for her at his. It was after five before she made it home. She collapsed into Jack's arms, Jack's bed. She needed this. She slept more soundly than she had since this started.

*****

Around ten thirty that morning, Dee was woken from a deep sleep. There was a huge break in the Striegel fire. Dee dressed, kissed both Jack and Ralph, and headed to the station. She was greeted by Adams. He was smiling and holding a cup of coffee for the sheriff.

"What?" Dee asked as she walked into the station. "And thanks," she said, sipping the coffee.

"There's video surveillance."

Dee's eyes were huge. "What? What's on it? It's Dobbins. I know it."

"It was. We have it all. Him breaking in, him smothering her, him coming back and setting the house on fire... We. Have. It. All!"

Dee had never heard more satisfying words in her life. She reviewed the footage, smiled brightly, and said, "Let's go get him."

"Just us? Or?" Adams asked.

"You, me, Collins." She looked around the station. "Is he here?"

"No, but I could call him."

Dee nodded. While they waited for Collins to arrive, Dee called Jack. "We got the son of a bitch," Dee said, almost giddy.

"Which son of a bitch?" Jack asked. There were several assholes they had been hunting.

"Dobbins. We're headed there soon," Dee informed. "He finally screwed up. There's video."

"That's outstanding! I can't wait to hear the details." He paused for a moment. "Shall I bring lunch for the crew?"

"That'd be great. See you in an hour or so."

Dee arrived at Ray Dobbins's house with two patrol cars in tow. She wanted to make a scene. She wanted her—the department's—presence known. As she approached the house, she saw neighbors watching. Dee beamed with pride. She did not need to knock on the door. Ray Dobbins saw them arrive and was walking out the front door of his house.

"Ray Dobbins, turn around." As he did so, Dee grabbed one of his arms and placed a cuff on his wrist, then the other. "You are under arrest for the murder of Gladys Striegel and the arson of her house." They were words Dee had been waiting to say for years. Maybe not the details, but the under-arrest part.

Ray Dobbins, in shock, did not know how to respond. He tried to argue, but nothing sensical came out. He could not fathom where he went wrong, what step he missed. Then it struck him as the cold metal handcuffs locked onto his wrists—cameras. That fucking bitch had cameras.

"Lawyer" was all Ray Dobbins said that day. Weeks later, he accepted a plea. The evidence was overwhelming, and his lawyer said they could not beat it.

One week into his sentence, a lifer took a shining to Ray Dobbins. Ray Dobbins would be his new bitch. He would do what he wanted. Ray Dobbins would live the rest of his days calling a very large man Big Daddy and pretending to enjoy it. He would do and experience things he never imagined. He would spend every day in pain, every day wishing he were dead.

*****

After Dee arrested Ray Dobbins, she took the rest of the day off. She felt like she had not had an hour to herself in weeks. She asked only to be disturbed in the case of emergency. Jack grilled steaks and asparagus. Dee mashed potatoes and opened wine. She threw the ball for Ralph and knew this was where she belonged.

Later, as they sipped wine by the fire, Ralph at their feet, Dee looked at Jack. "I love you, Jack. I think I always have."

"Took you long enough," Jack said as he kissed her.

Epilogue

In the days immediately following the group's victory, life in Eggers Cove returned to normal for most of its residents. Steve and Abby moved back into their parents' homes, and Billy took over the guest room in Jim's house. It was unclear whether his mother would ever be well enough to care for him. Alex stayed in Chris's room for several more nights, and Chris did not mind. Boards and foam and duct tape were removed, and the children slept soundly.

Dee moved fully into Jack's house, much to the delight of Ralph. The trio planned to take a few days away from town before winter set in, provided their respective workplaces could function without them. Dee was feeling more confident in her deputies, specifically Adams and Collins. She was confident enough to leave the station in their hands.

Jim had not heard from Mary in a week. He had planned to see a lawyer to start the divorce process now that things were normal again. Or at least normal adjacent. He would have the conversation with his boys. He assumed it would be a short one. The boys were not blind, nor were they stupid. Having Billy live with them was a blessing, and he hoped Billy would stay.

Jill accepted Dee's invitation to lunch after her husband pressed her. The two enjoyed light conversation but found—as Dee suspected—they had little in common. Jill no longer suspected her husband was having an affair with his friend. Mary's toxicity had left her. Jill had not seen Mary in days and found she did not miss her.

Mary spent her days in her dark motel room, drinking vodka and eating frozen dinners when it occurred to her to eat. She was plotting revenge—revenge on her husband, revenge on Dee, revenge on the town. Mary knew they were all responsible for her current state, and they all must pay. She supposed she would need to sober up to accomplish these tasks, but that could wait until tomorrow. Perhaps the next day.

Billy spent most of his time honing his new craft. He thought— feared—his gift would leave with the creature, but it had remained. He suspected Abby still had hers as well, but he did not ask her. She had made it clear that they should not be poking around in people's heads. He disagreed. For the first time in his life, he felt powerful. He found himself more self-assured and confident. He did not want to give this up. He would not give this up.

As Dee sat by the fire several nights later, she thought about the counter symbols to the creature's and wondered who or what had been warning or helping them. She hoped one day she would find out. But for now, she was content knowing that something or someone was watching and helping.

About the Author

Audra Ann lives with her husband in Central Texas. She has been writing stories from the time she was a small child, and most were of the horror or mystery variety. Primarily, she enjoys writing strong female leads who have supportive male counterparts.

CPSIA information can be obtained
at www.ICGtesting.com
Printed in the USA
BVHW041328060623
665472BV00002B/212